When So

Jeevani Charika writes women's fiction and contemporary romances with a hint of British cynicism. (In case you were wondering, it's pronounced Jeev-uh-nee.)

There's a whole lot of other stuff she could tell you – but mainly: she's a former scientist, an adult fan of Lego, an embarrassing mum, a part time geek (see 'embarrassing mum') and a Very Short Person.

She also writes romantic comedy under the pen name Rhoda Baxter. So why the two names? Well... Jeevani writes about British-Sri Lankan main characters. Rhoda, not so much.

Also by Jeevani Charika

When Soma met Sahan
A Convenient Marriage

JEEVANI CHARIKA

When Soma met Sahan

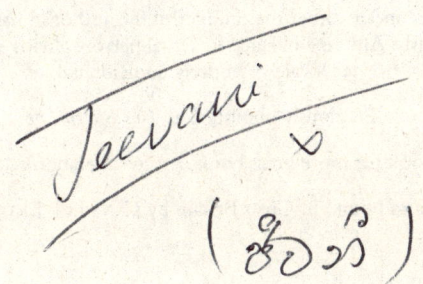

hera

First published in the United Kingdom in 2019 by Hera

This edition published in the United Kingdom in 2023 by

Hera Books
Unit 9 (Canelo), 5th Floor
Cargo Works, 1–2 Hatfields
London SE1 9PG
United Kingdom

A CIP catalogue record for this book is available from the British Library.

Print ISBN 978 1 80436 636 3
Ebook ISBN 978 1 80436 694 3

Previously published as *This Stolen Life*

Look for more great books at www.herabooks.com

Printed and bound in Great Britain by Clays Ltd, Elcograf S.p.A.

1

To my family. Thank you for encouraging me in this mad pursuit.

Chapter One

Escape was all Jaya wanted to think about. To be somewhere, anywhere else. She focused all of her mind on the idea. If she concentrated hard enough she could make herself believe she was the girl in the shampoo commercial. Walking free. Sunlight on her face, breeze in her long hair.

Her mother and stepfather would be home soon. She had to wait until the time was right to escape. A bag was stashed behind the woodpile. She'd hidden her slippers by the back door, so that even if her mother heard her leave, she'd assume she was going out to pee. Her stepfather wasn't likely to wake up, not when he came home drunk on arrak. She winced when she thought of her earlier encounter with him. There would be bruises.

There was no other preparation she could do, so she got back under her cotton sheet and pretended to be asleep.

Her stepfather and mother came home. She listened to them whispering as they got ready for bed. With her eyes shut and her breathing carefully deep, so that they wouldn't know she was awake, she listened. Her stepfather was snoring straightaway, thankfully. Her mother... it was hard to tell...

That morning she had tried, once again, to talk to her mother about her stepfather's drinking and the monster he

I

turned into, but her mother didn't want to hear it. There was a time when she would have fought lions for Jaya, but now... now she seemed care about nothing at all. Not even herself.

No. There was nothing left for her to stay for. She had to leave or turn into a hollow shell of a woman, like her mother had.

Jaya waited a short while and got up. Sticking to the shadows, she tiptoed out of the house she had been born in. Slippers on. Bag on her shoulder. Her stepfather left his bicycle leaning against the side of the house. Who was going to steal it in this place?

She wheeled it down the road, too slowly for the dynamo to light up the bulb in front. Once she was past the houses, she got on and pedalled as fast as she could for the main road. She had time. She would get to the bus stop on the main road well before the last bus, hiding in the shadows until she saw it approaching. The last bus always stopped there to let off people returning from late shifts. She wrapped a thin cloth around her long hair. Hopefully, no one would look at her closely enough to recognize her. Once she got to the bus depot, all she needed to do was wait until the early morning bus to Colombo and buy a ticket out to freedom.

—

Jaya shuddered. The village, and all its terrors, was three hours of darkness away and, as the bus rattled along at breakneck speed towards Colombo, she was getting further away by the minute. Outside the window, the sea was a menacing layer of black under the moonlit sky. Inside the bus it was humid and stifling. Crammed in between an old woman whose breath whistled as she slept, and an irritatingly chatty girl with a green plastic handbag, Jaya tried her best not to be frightened.

She hugged her own small bag on her lap. Her plan that had seemed so sensible before, now looked frighteningly flimsy. She didn't know where she was going, or what she was going to do when she got there. Her heart started pounding again. She struggled to breathe herself calm and imagine how this would work.

The money from selling her mother's necklace would pay for a room somewhere for a few weeks until she found a job. She was young and willing to work hard and she could handle an overlocker machine as well as anyone. She just had to find a sewing mill somewhere and she could pay her way. She wished she could have asked the supervisor in her old job for a letter of recommendation, but she couldn't have risked her telling someone about it. Running away had to be done in secret. Otherwise, the past followed you and dragged you back by your hair.

Beside her, the girl who said her name was Somavathi, started talking again. Jaya swallowed a sigh. So far she'd heard all about how Somavathi had got a job as a nanny somewhere; about how she had claimed to have looked after children before but it was only a 'tiny lie'; about how she was going to save enough money to move to Colombo when she came back. Jaya wasn't really interested, but Somavathi's chatter was comforting and distracted her from thinking about home, so she tried to pay attention. She let the other girl's voice wash over her and made listening noises until it lulled her to sleep.

—

The screaming woke her up. Shards of pain sliced her arm. She flew across a short space and slammed into something soft. And then again into something hard. Everything was battering and noise and pain. For a moment she was weightless, falling. A crash and suddenly everything was muted. Sleep and confusion disappeared to the realisation that she was under water. In the gloom she could make out the window next to her. She pulled herself through. There was faint light above her. She kicked out towards it.

Something tangled with her leg. She looked down. The girl Somavathi was floating, arms out, just below her. One arm had hooked around Jaya's foot. Somavathi's hair spread around her like a dark stain… and it seemed to be spreading. Blood. Without thinking, she reached down and grabbed a floating arm and dragged the unconscious girl towards the light with her.

A few moments of flailing in the salty water and her feet hit the sand. There was water and rocks and luggage and… oh, god, people… Still spluttering and coughing, she pulled the dead weight of Somavathi up to the beach. She was still trying to revive her, pressing her chest like they did on TV, when someone gently put a hand on her shoulder and said, 'I think you can stop now.'

The sun rose. Strangers gave her hot, sweet tea to drink and a cloth to wrap around herself. Someone brought her the hard green plastic handbag that had floated its way back to shore, thinking it was hers. Her own bag was nowhere to be found. She had lost her few clothes, her identity card and, most importantly, the necklace she was intending to sell. Her earrings were still on her ears, but they wouldn't fetch enough money for her to find a room.

A police jeep and a pickup truck arrived. Two policemen took the jeep down to the shore and ordered some of the local fisherfolk to help them pull the bus out of the water. Another two, a man and a woman, went to check the bodies that had been laid out at the top of the beach, where the coconut trees started.

They would come to her and the other survivors soon. With no money and nowhere to go, they would send her back. Panic burned the strength from her bones. He would not be pleased that she had tried to escape. Pain nipped at her from the tiny injuries on her breasts and inner thighs. Why did she think she could escape? He would always find her. He was big and strong and clever and she was just Jaya. A useless chit who asked for trouble. A stain. A piece of filth. He would find her and punish her and there was no escaping him. Jaya clutched the cotton sheet she was wrapped in and started to shake.

At the top of the beach, they covered Somavathi's body with a white cloth. Somavathi was gone. No one could hurt her. Jaya envied her. If Jaya had died, things would have been so much simpler. Death only happened once.

Somavathi had been so full of hope and now she was gone. Just like that. All Jaya had of her was the handbag. She would have to hand that over to the policewoman in a minute. Jaya looked down. Somavathi would have had money. Maybe even some jewellery. She was the sort of girl who would have kept all her valuables close to her. And Somavathi had no use for any of it now.

Suddenly, Jaya was no longer shivering. There was a thin sliver of hope. Hunching over, so that the sheet around her shielded the bag, she unzipped it. The first thing she saw was a bundle of papers with a passport on top, protected by the plastic bag they'd been wrapped in.

She removed the bundle and tucked it under her thigh so that she could return it later. A quick search revealed a purse. She removed most of the money and shoved it in her bra. It wasn't enough. It wouldn't take her far enough away.

Putting her hand back in the bag, she probed around inside searching for anything that felt like jewellery. *Anything* she could sell. *Anything.* Out of the corner of her eye, she saw someone approach. Fighting the urge to look up furtively, she dropped the purse back in and let the handbag fall. Pulling the sheet around her again, she started to rock.

A woman hunkered down in front of her. 'Child, do you want something to eat?'

Jaya shook her head. Her last hope was gone. She didn't feel hungry, she felt sick. Blood roared in her ears. She couldn't let them take her back. She couldn't. She wouldn't.

The woman clicked her tongue. 'Try and eat. You'll feel better.' She offered a cracked plate with two slices of buttered bread on it. 'It's hot bread,' she said, as though that made a difference. 'The bakery sent some loaves.'

Jaya reached out a shaking hand and accepted the plate. The woman watched her eat for a few minutes, then patted her shoulder and left.

The policewoman was coming round, taking statements. Jaya took Somavathi's documents from under her thigh. She would have to hand these over.

She cracked open the new passport and gazed at the photo that didn't really look like the girl she'd been sitting next to. The girl in the photo was solemn and still, while the girl in real life was a constantly moving flurry of words and gestures. Jaya glanced across to where Somavathi lay under a sheet, no longer moving. Sadness swept over her. She hadn't known her, but now she was gone. The only things left that could tell her about the girl she'd pulled out of the water were now sitting here on her lap.

She looked back at the documents and noted that Somavathi was older than her – twenty-five years to her own twenty. With the passport was a letter from an agency telling her where to meet the agency contact in Colombo who would give her the airline ticket to England, leaving the following day. There were other documents in English. She would have to decipher them later. Jaya put the papers back into the bag. This was the job that Somavathi mentioned. Looking after a baby, she'd said. Jaya had assumed it was near Colombo, but it must be in England. To think that Somavathi had all that future mapped out for her – a flight to England, a job looking after a little boy, all that adventure, lost in a bus that skidded into the rocky sea.

Tears sprang up in her eyes and Jaya wiped them away. 'Are you hurt?'

Jaya looked up to find a woman in uniform bending over her. She nodded and showed her arm. The woman set down her first aid kit and unwrapped the bloody, brine covered cloth that had been used to bind the wound. Soaking a pad with surgical spirit, she efficiently cleaned out the wound, ignoring Jaya wincing. When she'd finished, there was a neat, white bandage on it.

'Nothing serious,' she said. 'Some cuts from the glass only. You must have hit a window.' Briefly, her eyes flicked out to the wrecked bus, now being hauled out of the water. 'You were lucky.'

Looking down at the passport and tickets on her lap, Jaya nodded. 'Lucky.' Somavathi, with all her prospects, was dead. While she, Jaya, who had nothing but misery to look forward to, was alive. It was such a waste. Such a waste—

'What's your name?' said the woman.

The idea exploded into being sudden and fully formed. The photo in the passport didn't look much like either of them. They looked similar. If she feigned an overbite, she could pass for Somavathi. Without the paperwork, there would be nothing to identify whether the body was Somavathi's or Jaya's, so if only she was reported missing, they would think the body was hers. Even if her stepfather came to see the body, he wouldn't notice or care that it wasn't her... But if they caught her... if they caught her, she could be put in jail. Or worse, sent back to her stepfather. He would be very angry about that. But if she got away with it... if she got away...

The woman sighed and repeated her question, louder this time. 'What's your name, girl?'

Jaya looked up. 'Somavathi,' she said. 'My name is Somavathi.'

Chapter Two

She felt awful. The flight had been an ordeal. Her ears hurt from the descent. Her throat hurt from being sick on the plane. Her eyes hurt from tiredness. She was hungry. Everything hurt. Everything.

It was probably karma for taking Somavathi's papers. But Somavathi didn't need them any more and she wouldn't want to see them go to waste.

Utterly disorientated by the shadowless lighting and unfamiliar signs, she followed the crowd until everyone bunched up into a ramshackle queue. After what seemed like hours, she shuffled up to the high desk where a white man in uniform scrutinised her passport and the papers. Her heart pounded in her ears. She had made it so far without being caught. If she was found out at this final hurdle, she would be put in prison. Or shot. Or worst of all, sent home. She couldn't get caught. She swallowed hard and lifted her chin. *Somavathi*, she reminded herself. I am Somavathi. I am Soma.

The man looked up at her, comparing her to the passport. She pulled her lower lip in slightly to give the appearance of an overbite, so that she looked more like the picture. The man handed her papers back and waved her on. 'Welcome to Britain.'

Soma didn't have time to work out what he'd said, but she understood the gesture. She was through. She bowed her head, muttered, 'Thank you, sir,' and scurried in the direction that everyone else was taking.

It didn't take long to take her bags and follow everyone else out. Once she had explained about losing her bags in the bus crash, the agency rep had taken her to buy a few things. She had worried about the agency seeing through her, but they hadn't met the real Somavathi and they had no reason to doubt her. So she now had two bags, one containing jumpers and warm clothes and a cheap new handbag that held all her precious papers. Were those people in uniform watching her? Could they tell? Soma fought down the panic. All she had to do was walk through without drawing attention to herself. Look like she belonged there and everyone would believe she did. Nobody challenged her.

She'd got away with it so far, but she'd been one person in a stream of travellers. Once she left the airport, she had to stop moving and actually live a life. It was no good playing at being Soma. She had to *be* her. Truly. She bid a silent goodbye to Jaya and walked out of the gate.

English. It was everywhere, the signs, the conversations. She heard snippets of Sinhalese and Tamil from her fellow travellers, but there was so much English. She could understand it if it was slow and clear, but this babble was maddening.

And there were white people everywhere. It made sense. This was their country. But there were people of all other colours too, some in uniform. Perhaps it really was the land of opportunity here. She'd heard that, but never really believed it.

She looked around. She didn't know anything about the people she was coming to stay with. Although the agency paperwork gave a phone number to call, if she needed help, how would she find a phone?

Around her, people were being met by relatives, or were hurrying off towards the exits with phones held to their ears. As the crowd thinned, Soma spotted a woman in a big beige coat holding a piece of paper with 'Somavathi' written on it in big, curling Sinhalese. The woman was scanning the crowd, her lips pursed. Someone had come to meet her. Oh, thank goodness. Soma walked toward her.

The woman focussed on her. The frown deepened.

'Madam?' Soma said. 'I'm Somavathi. Soma.'

The woman looked her up and down, eyes narrowed. Soma thrust out her passport and pointed to her name. The woman read it, still frowning and nodded.

'I'm Yamuna Gamage,' she said. 'You can call me Madam.' She motioned her to duck under the barrier. 'Come.'

Mrs Gamage looked impossibly glamorous to Soma. She wore trousers, a long coat and shoes with heels that tapped as she walked. Soma, too cold in her dress, despite the jumper and leggings she had put on, hurried to keep up. She was glad she'd followed the example of other passengers and put on extra layers before getting off the plane because the first blast of fresh air was so cold it made her gasp.

Mrs Gamage stopped to see what was holding her up and smiled. The severe face softened. 'It's cold, isn't it? You'll get used to it, don't worry. This is nothing. It gets much colder.' She led the way across a road to a building packed with cars. Soma gawped. She had heard of these. Car park buildings. In the movies, people got shot in them. She clutched her bags a little closer and ran after her employer.

The car journey was unlike anything she'd imagined. Things she had only ever seen on TV unrolled past the window. Soma sat in the front seat, the fingers of one hand wrapped around the unfamiliar seat belt that tethered her to the car. Beside her, Mrs Gamage was concentrating on driving. Every so often she cast a sideways glance at Soma. It would have been a worry, if everything else hadn't been so completely fascinating.

—

Yamuna risked another glance at the girl. She seemed young and frightened, which wasn't surprising given that she'd travelled halfway around the world. From what the agent had said, this girl had never ventured more than a few miles from her home town. Yamuna frowned as she negotiated a roundabout. The girl didn't look like the black and white mugshot that she'd been sent. She looked, too young. Too rounded. Too... pretty.

She had chosen the girl with care. Even though she couldn't have specified a plain woman, preferably an old one, when she was looking for a nanny, she had done her best to choose one who had all the qualities she was looking for and was, frankly, not much to look at. This girl, who had appeared unremarkable in the photo, was quite gentle on the eye in real life. Not the sort of thing she wanted at all.

Yamuna sighed. She couldn't very well send her back because she was too attractive. What kind of a jealous, controlling harpy would that make her? Worse still, it made it look like she didn't trust her husband. Bim was a good man. She didn't really have a worry on that score. But why put temptation in his way?

The girl's mouth was hanging open while she stared at the street view outside. Yamuna felt a flash of empathy. She remembered all too well her own first sight of England, seen from the back of the taxi that she and her new husband had taken from Manchester airport. She had lived in India for a bit during her graduate studies, so she knew what it like to be in another country, but she too had looked out of the window and seen a strange world – familiar in sight and sound, but completely new in feel and smell. How long had it taken before the impossibly exotic became commonplace? A week? A year? Yamuna spotted the turnoff onto the motorway and effortlessly got into lane. Whatever the length of time had been, she felt at home in this country now. It was amazing how people adapted.

As the buildings and streets outside gave way to dull motorways verges, the girl... Soma, must remember to use her name and not call her 'girl' like some insufferable upper class doyenne... Soma seemed to shrink back into her seat.

'Your application said you speak English?' Yamuna said, in English.

Soma turned. There was a pause before she said, haltingly, 'Yes Madam.'

'How well?'

A blank look. She repeated the question in Sinhalese.

'A bit only, Madam. I will try and learn.'

'There's no need,' said Yamuna. 'I want you to speak to my son in Sinhalese, so that he learns the language. He'll get plenty of English language practice at school.' She paused. 'I want him to know about his heritage.' She and Bim would try, but they had been in England long enough that they spoke to each other in a mix of English and Sinhalese now. It actually took effort to remember to switch languages completely.

Soma nodded vigorously. She seemed eager to please. Yamuna sighed again. She was going to have to make the most of it. 'It's a long drive to Hull,' she said. 'Try and get some sleep.'

—

Madam led her through a door at the end of the garage. Soma followed. The door opened into a kitchen. It was bright and clean. So clean. Everything in this country seemed so muted and quiet and *clean*. No one beeped their horn when they drove. There were no loud pavement hawkers. No music spilling out from shops. There was no heat, no dust, no animals. It was as though all that was real had been locked down. It seemed that England was made for people in hiding.

The house was several storeys tall and smelled of cinnamon. When Mrs Gamage stopped to remove her shoes, Soma did the same. Even the shoes were put away immediately, rushed out of sight. She wriggled her toes into the soft carpet. It was very different from the hard floors at home. So soft.

'I'll show you where you'll sleep.' Mrs Gamage started up the stairs. 'You can put your bags down and then I'll show you the rest of the house.'

Soma followed up the stairs, torn between curiosity and fear. This was where she would be from now on. She could put up with most things, she reminded herself. She would be okay so long as no one found out that she wasn't really Soma.

There was so much to take in. Mrs Gamage showed her the room. It was small, a bed and a chest of drawers squeezed in between four white walls, but to Soma it was the most beautiful place in the world. There was a bed. A bouncy soft bed with a fat mattress. The window had pale yellow curtains that matched the duvet. A door that she could shut. Heaven. She dropped her bags on the floor. She turned to find that Mrs Gamage was still talking.

'I'm sorry, Madam,' she said. 'I didn't hear.'

'I said,' said Mrs Gamage. 'That maybe you'd like to have a wash before my son gets back from baby group.' She looked thoughtfully at Soma.

Soma wondered what Mrs Gamage saw. A tired woman? An unclean one? An untrustworthy one? Was this some sort of test that she had to pass?

'I will wash?' she said. It came out more as a question than a statement.

Mrs Gamage nodded. Soma went limp with relief that she'd said the right thing.

'Come. I'll show you where the bathroom is.'

Soma followed in a daze as she was shown a small bathroom with a shower in it and given a towel and some shampoo. Mrs Gamage left her, then quickly returned and, as an afterthought, showed her how the shower worked, which was just as well because Soma was too tired to see straight, let alone work it out. She nodded her understanding and scratched her head.

Mrs Gamage's eyes snapped to her head in an instant. 'Head lice?' she said. 'Sit down.'

Soma sat on the floor, too surprised to hesitate. Mrs Gamage bent over her and peered at her scalp. 'I thought this might happen,' she said, almost to herself. 'Stay there.'

Soma stayed and shivered. Was she supposed to have been checked for head lice before she left? Had something on her head given her away?

Mrs Gamage returned with a spray and a sheet, which she spread on the floor. She made Soma sit on the sheet and untie her plait, and sprayed some strange-smelling stuff on her head. After several sprays, Mrs Gamage clicked her tongue. 'This is not going to work.' She glowered at Soma. 'It'll have to come off.' She left the room, leaving Soma kneeling on the floor.

Mrs Gamage returned with a small machine, which she plugged into the wall. She hunkered down in front of Soma. 'Listen,' she said. 'Your hair is crawling with nits and it's so long, I can't use the special shampoo to get rid of them. So, we're going to have to cut your hair.'

What? She wanted to cut off her hair? But why? No one had said anything about having to cut off her hair for this job. Confused, Soma shook her head violently.

Mrs Gamage recoiled as a strand of hair flicked in her direction. 'Yes,' she insisted. 'I must. Look, I've set it to the longest setting.' She held out the device. Soma looked at it. There was a row of metal teeth behind a plastic guard. What was it?

'It will be very short, but it will grow back,' said Mrs Gamage, with exaggerated patience. A muscle in her jaw was twitching.

'My hair?' Finally, Soma understood. Mrs Gamage wanted to cut her hair. Short. Like they did with babies. To get rid of the nits and start again. Soma looked at the long black strands, tumbling over her shoulders, almost down to her waist. She loved her thick, long hair. She couldn't be the girl in the shampoo commercial without it. But with short hair she would look completely different. Starting again. That would be a good thing. It was only hair. She nodded, slowly. 'Yes, Madam.' She bowed her head.

Mrs Gamage gave a small sigh. 'Good.' She pressed a switch. The machine cricked and whirred.

Soma screamed and scrambled backwards on the floor.

Mrs Gamage said something in English and turned the machine off. 'Look. It's only a shaver. See. It will cut your hair. It will not hurt you.' There was a hard edge to her voice now. She was annoyed. That wasn't good.

Soma didn't want to annoy this person and be sent home. It was only her hair. That was all. She forced herself to breathe. 'I am sorry,' she said. She lowered her head and whispered, 'I am ready.'

It didn't take long to do. Mrs Gamage let the long strands fall onto the sheet. Soma watched them drop and cried. Tears dripped off her nose, but she didn't make a sound. When Mrs Gamage was finally satisfied, Soma could feel the air, cold against her scalp.

Mrs Gamage put her hands on Soma's shoulders and studied her. Her face softened a little. 'It was the best way,' she said, quietly. 'It will grow back soon.'

Soma, her throat tight, said, 'Yes Madam.'

Mrs Gamage sprayed Soma's head with the oily stuff again.

'Wait for ten minutes.' Mrs Gamage left her sitting on the floor, surrounded by her ruined hair. She guessed that the stuff on her head was some sort of foreign nit shampoo. It seemed that Mrs Gamage really objected to nits, but didn't have any other reason to be annoyed. Still, she didn't dare stand up.

There were knots either side of her shoulders, so tight she could feel them. Her mouth ached from trying to pretend she had an overbite. Her ears and throat still hurt from the flight. She was so tired. So tense. She drew up her knees, rested her arms on them and promptly fell asleep.

Mrs Gamage shook her awake, not roughly, but firmly. She reminded her how the shower worked, scooped up the sheet, hair, nits and all, and carried it off. Once she was gone, Soma finally looked at herself in the mirror. Her hair was only a fraction of an inch long. Without anything to frame it, her face looked thin and delicate. Her eyes looked too large. She barely recognized herself. She looked like a different person. Her lovely hair, the prettiest thing about her, was gone. Her eyes filled with tears.

She let herself cry for a minute, watching the tears meander down the face that looked like a stranger's. But that was good. Looking different was good. She didn't want to be Jaya any more. This was a new life. She would grow new hair to match it.

The shower was a wondrous thing. She knew what it was, of course, but she'd never actually been in one before. Warm water washed over her, washing away tension. She allowed herself a moment of triumph. She had made it this far. She was in England. She was in the house of her employer. No one had seen through her. No one had tried to stop her. She rubbed her limbs down vigorously, sloughing off all that was Jaya until it was only Soma who was left.

—

Yamuna checked the girl's head for lice eggs again. She would have to get her a small hair dryer of her own, when her hair grew back. It wasn't right to have to share one with the nanny. Another thing to add to the list. These were things no one ever told you about. Having a live-in nanny was all well and good, but getting one from rural Sri Lanka meant that you needed to look after them. She hadn't realised quite how helpless the girl would be. She had arrived with only a handful of warm things. They would have to go to Primark and get her more jumpers. Yamuna had a moment of amusement when she wondered if the girl had worked in one of the factories that made clothes for places like Primark. Would she end up buying something she herself had made?

She had got the room ready without thinking about the fact that everything would be strange to Soma. Until the girl was competent enough to go outside alone, she would need to be provided with everything. Toothpaste, soap and sanitary towels. Yamuna added things to a growing list on her phone. Again, she wondered what she'd let herself in for. Getting a maid from Sri Lanka had been her husband's eminently sensible solution to her worries about going back to work. That was the trouble with Bim. He was sensible. All the time. If you told him that something was wrong, he worked out how to fix it. He was rarely emotional, but eminently practical.

Their marriage had been one of those practical decisions. A sensible one for the time. Bimbisara Gamage was getting towards middle age. He felt he needed a wife in order to enter the next phase of his life. So he went out and found one.

Her family had seen his ad in the marriage proposals section of the paper and got in touch with him. Despite being of lower caste, he was rich enough and Yamuna was old enough for them not to be choosy. She still wasn't entirely sure why he'd picked her.

Bim wasn't a handsome man, but he had reasonably thick hair and good skin. On paper, the most attractive thing about him was his money. When Yamuna first met him, she was relieved to find that the 'slightly too old, but reasonably rich' potential groom was actually a softly spoken man who wasn't objectionable in any way. Okay, he was a little colourless, but then, who was she to complain about that? All the men she had been introduced to until then had been either odd, cowed by their mothers or dismissive of the value she placed on her work. Her parents thought she was fussy, but thankfully, didn't press her to accept any of them. Her first impression of Bim was that he seemed kind. The second was there was a quietness about him that reminded her of her own, slightly academic, father. He had asked her questions about her research topic and had seemed genuinely interested in her answers. The combination was enough to persuade her that life with him would be tolerable, maybe even enjoyable.

Yamuna knew she'd married up. A woman with her dark complexion and plain moon face wasn't likely to win a man who looked good and, as her mother had pointed out repeatedly, she was lucky Bim wasn't looking for much of a dowry because they'd spent everything on her education. Marriage was about solidity, her mother had said. Not lust. Love? That would come later. When there was a child to bind them together. Yamuna sighed. Yeah. Her mother probably really believed that.

The girl, Soma, emerged, looking cleaner and tidier and altogether different. Much better. She was less pretty too, with her shorn head; although the effect would only be temporary. Yamuna wondered once again what she was going to do with an attractive girl when she'd wanted a plain one. She had no reason to think that Bim had a roving eye, but she wanted this marriage to work, so why put temptation in his path? Yamuna sighed. They'd got the girl to come all this way, they may as well test her out and see what she was made of.

She was in the middle of explaining some house rules to Soma when angry wails announced that her son was back from baby and toddler group.

'Come and meet him,' she said, rushing downstairs.

Hilary, the cocky English girl from the babysitting service was still unwinding her scarf while the baby screamed himself purple in the pushchair. Yamuna leaned over and freed him from the straps that held him in. He didn't stop screaming.

'Has he had his milk?' she asked.

Hilary shook her head. 'He fell asleep before I could give it to him.' She pulled the bottle out of the changing bag. 'See.'

'Well, perhaps you could heat it up a bit and give it to him?' It took a lot not to snap. Yamuna jiggled her son on her shoulder and wished he would stop bawling. For once.

When Hilary returned, shaking a hastily microwaved bottle, Yamuna turned to Soma, who was cowering behind her like a terrified rabbit. 'Give the baby his bottle.'

She pointed to a chair that was placed in a corner of the kitchen. Soma took the bottle and reached for the baby. Yamuna handed him over. The girl's CV had said she had looked after babies before. Well, it was time to see if that was true.

Soma sat awkwardly in the chair at first, then settled little Louie against her and slotted the bottle into his mouth. As he drank, the baby relaxed and, little by little, so did Soma.

Hilary was fiddling with her phone. Yamuna watched her son finish his milk. Soma rubbed his back and gently burped him. The baby studied this new person, his face serious, making him look even more like Bim. Soma made a silly noise at him. Suddenly, Louie's face changed and one of his rare smiles appeared.

Soma responded with more cooing and ahhing. As Yamuna watched, her grumpy, weepy baby who didn't much like anything, sat giggling on the lap of a skinny bald girl who had travelled all the way around the world to be with him. Whatever doubts she might have had about Soma, there was really only one person who needed to like her. That was Louie. It was one test that Soma had passed with flying colours.

It looked like she was stuck with her.

Chapter Three

Sahan stood by the barbecue with his best friend Nate, baking in front and freezing at the back. Nate, as chief burger-watcher, was closest to the heat and wore a t-shirt and jeans. Sahan, who was threading pepper chunks onto skewers, was still in a woolly jumper. Inside, the girls were making salads. Music, turned up to deafening levels in the kitchen, trickled out of the open window. It was completely ridiculous to be cooking outside in the middle of winter, but two consecutive days of sunshine and Nate had declared he'd had enough of the gloom and decided they were having a barbecue.

'How about next weekend?' Nate said. 'I'm free, so is Cara. We could rent a cottage really cheap and go hang out in the Lakes.'

'It'll still be freezing cold.' Sahan pointed out. He passed a couple of skewers across and Nate arranged them on the spaces between the burgers. 'I really don't see the point of going on to a holiday cottage to freeze to death when I can do it right here for free.'

'Tsch, you're such a lightweight, man,' said Nate. 'Just 'cause you get to go back home to tropical sunshine.'

Sahan said nothing. This was his third year in England and going home to a bit of tropical sunshine would be welcome right now. He was tired of the low British sky. Tired of the interminable drizzle. It had been winter for so long he was starting to think that summer was a figment of his imagination. He looked at his hands. Underneath the vivid tomato and coriander marinade splashes, his skin was grey. Not brown, not even black, like Nate's. Grey. As though the drizzle had washed all of the colour out of them.

He looked up at the sky. The morning had been more or less clear, but now it looked like it was going to rain again. 'Might have to go get the umbrella,' he said, eyeing a dark cloud.

Nate glanced up. 'Hmm... yeah. We don't want the coals to go out.'

In the kitchen, he passed Nate's girlfriend Cara and a couple of her friends. They had finished chopping up bits for salad and were divvying up a bottle of red wine between them. Cara waved to him.

'Sahan. Come join us.' One of the other girls, Bex, waggled an empty glass at him.

He couldn't stand wine. 'Can't.' He grinned. 'I've got to get the umbrella over the barbecue. I told you it would rain,' he said pointedly to Cara.

'It always rains at barbecues,' Cara shouted after him. 'It's traditional.'

Sahan picked up his waterproof coat and the golfing umbrella that someone had 'liberated' from somewhere. He pulled his coat on as he went through the kitchen, grabbed two beers off the counter, flipped his hood up and dived back out into the drizzle.

The raindrops grew bigger and hissed onto the barbecue, releasing plumes of steam. He fumbled with the catch and got the umbrella up.

'Perfect timing.' Nate grabbed the tongs and flipped the burgers over with a flourish. The air smelled of rain, smoke and cooking meat. Sahan had to angle the umbrella away from himself in order to keep the barbecue dry.

The rain pattered against his face, despite the hood on his waterproof. He shook his head. 'This is ridiculous.' He looked down at the meat on the grill, which was blackened in places, still dull red in others. He knew that it would taste disgusting. The salad would taste of nothing. The meat would be mostly smoke and charring. The only way he was going to get through this was to get drunk. Which was fine for today, but would be hell on a plate tomorrow.

He wanted to go home. Where it rained properly in fat drops that submerged everything and made plants grow. Not this mean-spirited, spit-in-your-face rain. Where the sun made a proper effort. When you never, ever, EVER got so cold that you could feel your bones ache.

He must have made a noise because Nate looked up. 'You okay?'

'Just… thinking.'

'Sure?'

'I'm fine. Although I think that I could do with another beer,' he said.

A few minutes later the rain stopped. Sahan folded up the umbrella and leaned against the side of the house, drinking his beer.

'Hey,' Cara's friend Bex came out and leaned on the wall right next to him. Bex was, as far as he could tell, a nice person. She had brown hair, currently tied into childish plaits, and a freckled nose. Once upon a time, he might have found her cute. She was wearing an oversized cardigan, which had slipped off on one side to show a vest strap and a few inches of bare shoulder. Flesh exposed for effect. Sahan tried to shift away from her.

'So, how's the barbecue doing?' she said, making a show of craning her head to look, even though she could see Nate's handiwork at least as well as he could.

'I wouldn't trust anything that comes off that grill,' said Sahan.

'Yeah, well then you'd have to survive eating salad,' said Nate. 'And you know who made that.' He raised his eyebrows at Bex.

'Even I can't poison a salad, Nate,' she replied, laughing.

Sahan tried to laugh too, but couldn't. Nate threw a swift glance his way. Sahan ignored it.

'How's the play coming along?' Nate asked Bex.

Bex did lighting at the drama club. Sahan tried to listen to her chatting, but his jaws had clamped together and his pulse was in his ears. Bex somehow managed to edge even closer to him, so that her too-slippery-to-stay-on cardigan brushed his arm, making him jump. Acid rose in his throat.

'I… uh… just remembered I told my parents I'd call them before they go to bed. With the time difference and all… I don't want them to wait up.' Sahan peeled away from the wall. 'I'll be back in two seconds.' He managed to fake a smile before he dived back into the house.

He ran past the girls in the kitchen. In the safety of his room, he got the nausea under control. Not for the first time, he cursed Tamsin. He hadn't been like this before. He had been normal when he'd arrived in England to start his engineering degree. A little scared, a little naive, but mostly… normal.

The thought of Tamsin brought with it a combination of disgust and humiliation that made his stomach clench. If he didn't do something about it, release some of the pressure, it would carry on, building up in his chest until he couldn't breathe. There were things even beer couldn't shift. Everything around him felt tainted by Tamsin. The only place that was clean was home, but that was several thousand miles away. Another kick of homesickness to add to the mix. Well, at least that he could do something about. He pulled out his mobile phone, tapped into the cheap calls app and called home.

The phone rang for a while and went to answerphone. He left a short message to say he'd call back tomorrow and hung up. Were they out? He frowned and thought back to his conversation with them the previous week. Oh yes. There was that charity thing. His little sister, Priyanka, had been grousing about being made to go to it. While Sahan usually went along with what his father wanted, Priyanka seemed hell-bent on arguing about everything. He could picture them now, his father full of ebullient good will because he was in public, Priyanka sniping behind her smile about being forced to go to the event and his mother, always the peacemaker, trying to keep them both happy. He missed them so much it hurt.

The next best thing would be to call his cousin Yamuna.

On the other side of Hull, the phone rang in his cousin's hallway. 'Gamage residence.' Yamuna spoke English with a faint East Riding accent, as though she'd lived here all her life. It was one of the things Sahan admired about her. She'd figured out that the thing that stood in her way wasn't necessarily the colour of her skin, but her accent. She'd said to him 'learn to speak like you belong and people will forget you don't'. It was something he was trying his hardest to emulate.

'Yamuna Akki, it's me, Sahan.'

'Oh, hi Sahan. How're you? We haven't heard from you in a while. Are you okay?'

He felt a stab of guilt. He should have called to see her more often. He hadn't seen her or the baby in weeks. 'I'm okay. I was thinking it would be nice to see you guys again. I've been really bad at keeping in touch and I thought...'

'Sure. Sure. Why not.' She sounded distracted. 'Let me see.' He could hear her footsteps as she walked across the kitchen in her house. She would be looking at the big calendar where she blocked out dates when Bim was away on business. 'Why don't you come for dinner weekend after next?'

'That would be brilliant. Thanks, Akki.' He drew breath to ask her how everyone was. Little Louie must be nearly four months old now.

'Listen, Sahan. I have to go,' she said. 'Can I call you back tomorrow? Maybe in the afternoon?'

'Uh... sure. Of course. If not, I'll see you in a few days anyway.'

'Yes. Lovely. I'll see you soon. Have a good rest of the weekend.'

'I will. We're having a barbecue—' But she was gone. Odd. She wasn't normally that brusque. Still, he had his dinner invitation. That was all he needed right now. He leaned his head back against the wall and concentrated on taking deep breaths. A few more minutes to get himself under control and he could go back downstairs. He'd have to stay well away from Bex, though. This was the second time she'd tried to flirt with him.

–

Yamuna waited up for Bim that evening. It was later than usual, but he had dutifully called Yamuna to say he would be late. She had, just as dutifully, thanked him for letting her know. She had mentioned, briefly, that the girl from Sri Lanka had arrived. It was quiet in the house and, since the girl had sat with Louie until he fell asleep, Yamuna had finished her chores and even had time to drag out some paperwork to look at.

When Bim arrived, she sat back and rubbed her eyes. Bim shut the door quietly and, leaving his shoes and briefcase neatly by the door, he padded into the kitchen, stretching his neck from side to side as he went. He walked past, not looking in her direction, so he didn't notice her.

Yamuna watched him put the kettle on. She had left a mug out for him, like she always did. She smiled to see his hand stray to the wrong cupboard before he remembered where they kept the tea bags. They'd been in the new house for well over six months now, but he still automatically reached to where he used to keep things in his bachelor days. He had kept everything out on the work surface, ready for when he got home. Yamuna liked things put away. He had never objected. In fact, he rarely objected to anything she wanted. She was quite lucky, really. She sighed.

Bim startled and turned around. 'Oh, hello,' he said. 'What are you doing up?'

She went over and took another mug out. 'Let me.' She took down the teapot and put in couple of tea bags. 'How was work?'

'It was fine. Busy.' He leaned against the sink and watched her. 'You didn't have to wait up for me, you know.'

'I know.' She didn't look up. Before Louie, she had always waited up for him, or tried to. When she was pregnant, he'd come home many an evening to find her asleep at the kitchen table, her notes from work spread out in front of her.

'So, the new servant girl arrived,' he said.

Yamuna looked up sharply, frowning. 'You can't call her that,' she said.

'Why not?' He looked genuinely baffled. It astounded Yamuna how he had managed to live in England for so long and yet remain so clueless about social norms. On the other hand, he would never have had to consider domestic details like servants before.

'That sounds all wrong. People don't have servants here. She's a nanny.' She had considered 'au pair' but that didn't quite fit.

Bim stared at her, in that thoughtful way of his, for a few seconds. 'You've really thought about this. I'm glad I have you to stop me blundering into things.'

She didn't know what to say to this.

He smiled. 'The nanny, then. Anyway, she arrived okay, clearly.'

Yamuna nodded and took the teapot over to the table. He followed her, carrying the two mugs.

'She's asleep now,' said Yamuna. 'She looked exhausted after the flight, poor thing.' Should she mention that the girl looked different to the photograph the agency had sent? Probably best not. Bim would only ask her how that was relevant to her ability to look after Louie – which, of course, it wasn't. Instead, she said, 'She and Louie got on well, which is a relief. She seems good with him. I'll stay with them for the next couple of days – teach her how we want things done – but I think she'll be fine. He likes her.'

They sat together in a silence broken only by the sound of Yamuna pouring tea. She pushed the mug over to him.

'Oh, and Sahan invited himself over for dinner,' she said. 'I was going to order some food in from that place in Leeds. They'll deliver if we pay extra.'

He nodded. Before Yamuna had arrived, Bim had had no idea that there were Sri Lankan restaurants outside of London. Within a few weeks of starting work, a foodie colleague had mentioned one in Leeds and one in Scarborough to Yamuna. She assumed people must have told Bim about it too, but he simply hadn't registered it. He seemed to have lived his life in a peculiar bubble – where business was all that mattered and everything else was irrelevant. She and Louie came into the bubble, just, but how long for? What happened when they drifted out of it? She pushed the thoughts back. Not helpful. She had to focus on the here and now, not worry about things that might not even happen.

'How is Sahan?' Bim seemed to get on with Sahan, which was lucky for Yamuna. Although by no means stupid, Bim himself had never gone to university. He had come over to work as an accounts clerk, but a lucky investment had made him wealthy. He had soon discovered that he had an eye for investment, which had led him to where he was today.

Sahan, on the other hand, was academically gifted and had been pampered by his parents. She wouldn't have been surprised if the two men had hated each other on sight, but they hadn't. They seemed to regard each other with respect and perhaps even affection. All of which meant that keeping an eye on her little cousin was a pretty painless experience for her.

'He's okay, I think,' said Yamuna. 'I hadn't heard from him in a while. It's his final year, he must be busy.' She smiled. 'He only calls me when he's homesick and wants some proper food.'

Bim laughed softly. 'He's young. Why would he want to come and spend time with two middle-aged people like us?' He added, quickly, 'Well, me, anyway. You're not so old.'

She resisted the urge to roll her eyes. 'Thanks.' Having Louie had aged her, she knew, but she was still seven years younger than Bim was.

'You look tired,' he said. He may as well have told her she looked old. Of course she looked tired. Louie didn't let her sleep. She didn't expect him to understand; Louie's cries never seemed to penetrate his sleep.

'I *am* tired,' she said. What else was there to say?

He picked up his mug and stood up. 'Then let's go to bed.'

She nodded and stood up too. He waited while she rinsed out the teapot and they tiptoed upstairs. Yamuna whispered that she would go and check on Louie and went up the next flight of steps. The door to Louie's room was ajar, even though she'd given Soma a baby monitor, so that she could shut her door and Louie's.

Having the door slightly open meant that Yamuna could pop her head in and check on her sleeping son. He lay flat on his back, arms spread out like he'd been knocked out. Totally relaxed in sleep. Yamuna watched him breathing. This was her boy. She had hoped that she and he would become a unit, a powerful team of two. Bim's interest could wane now that he had an heir, but it wouldn't have mattered because she and her baby would have a bond so powerful that it would sustain them both. She had expected to feel an intense connection to this little creature she had grown from her own tissue and bone. Instead, she felt… nothing. Tired, grumpy, sleep deprived, yes. But emotionally, nothing.

To make things worse, friends and family kept telling her how she must be feeling overwhelmed with love. Too ashamed to tell them the truth, she forced a smile and agreed with them.

Everyone had a dream of their future buried in their hearts and hers had included marriage and family, a Disney-like fable of true love and motherhood that would make her complete. When her previous relationships had ended, she'd told herself there was plenty of time to meet the right man. Yet she'd got older, passed the full bloom of her youth, and true love had never showed up. She'd had a career she liked, but it wasn't enough, not really. In the end, when all the men she knew were married, she'd asked her parents to find her a husband. She didn't mind that Bim was ambivalent towards her, because she was ambivalent towards him. But her baby… surely it was impossible for a normal woman to be ambivalent towards her child. Clearly there was something wrong with her, some deficit of personality that made her unfeeling. She had never been like that before, so maybe it was something that had come on later in life.

Yamuna sighed and drew back from Louie's room. As she tiptoed back downstairs to the bed she shared with her husband, she couldn't help feeling cheated.

Chapter Four

Look what you made me do, little bitch.

Soma woke up with a cry. In her nightmare, she was pinned to the floor by a dark shape. She lay still, rigid with fear, too afraid to open her eyes in case he was still there. The waking day filtered into her mind. Something was pressing down on her face. Something big, but not heavy and stale as she'd feared. She couldn't smell *him*. In fact, it smelled nice in this dark place she didn't recognize. Holding her breath, she listened. There were noises, clinks and gurgles. Somewhere she could hear voices. Recognition of where she was came all at once. In England. The thing on top of her was the duvet. She had somehow got it over her head. Excitement and fear tussled it out, making her feel ill. She opened her eyes and cautiously pushed her head out from under the bedcovers. The light, which she had left on when she went to sleep, illuminated her tidy little room. It was still cosy and bright and safe. She sat up and hugged her knees.

My name is Soma. She had to remember she was called Soma now. If she failed to respond to her name, Madam would suspect something. It was important that Madam didn't suspect anything. The best way to achieve that was to be as quiet and inoffensive as possible. That went with being Soma. She had to do whatever Madam said and do it well.

Hard work wasn't a problem. She had been working at the garment factory since she was fifteen. A sudden pang of sorrow for what could have been surprised her. It could have all been so different. Teenaged Jaya had had a plan. She was going to save up her wages from working at the factory. Maybe she could have met someone. Maybe that young security guard who always smiled at her when she clocked in at work?

She shook her head and the strange lack of weight made her reach up. Her scalp was covered in a thick layer of bristles. Her hair. Her beautiful hair that made her look like the woman in the shampoo commercial. Suddenly, her eyes were full of tears. She could never go back. That man had taken it all away. There had to be a new plan now. And that involved being Soma. Jaya and her ruined life had to be shut away and forgotten. It was the only way.

She brushed the tears off her face and once again her fingertips touched the places where her hair used to be. No. She would never be the same person again. Maybe, if she tried, she could be someone luckier.

Sliding out of bed, she looked for another layer to put on. Footsteps came up the stairs. She froze.

Someone knocked on the door, a smart, impatient rap. Soma hurried to the door, removed the chair from where she'd wedged it, and opened the door. Madam was outside the door, fully dressed. Soma felt a stab of alarm. Was she supposed to have been up and ready?

'I'm going to take Louie out for a few hours,' said Madam. 'I wanted to say, you can relax and get to know the place, if you want.'

Relieved, Soma opened the door a bit more until it caught on the chair. Madam peered in and frowned. 'Did you put the chair against the door?'

'Sorry Madam. I…'

Madam held up her hand. 'Don't apologize. It's okay.' She examined the door frame. 'We'll get a latch put on this door for you. You should feel safe in this room.' She glanced back at Soma. 'I'll ask my cousin to come and put the latch in. Until then, you can wedge the chair under the door if that makes you feel safer.'

A small knot unravelled in Soma's chest. A room she could lock. What a kind lady this Madam was. 'Thank you, Madam.'

'Now, the rooms on the floor below are out of bounds,' Madam carried on. 'But you are free to go anywhere else in the house. There will be no one here for the next few hours. Have a look around.'

A wail rang up the stairwell.

Madam clicked her tongue. 'Coming, Louie,' she called, over her shoulder. 'I'll be back in a few hours. After lunch, I'll take you to the shops. You'll need to buy some warm clothes.' With that, she turned and disappeared down the stairs.

Soma listened as mother and baby left the house, slamming the door shut behind them. After that, she stood still, her cheek resting against the side of the door, and listened to the house gurgle and creak. She had heard of houses that made noises like that. Her own home had no plumbing. There were no pipes to hum, no wood to creak. How did people sleep when the house itself made so much noise?

After a while, she got dressed. She was so cold, she put on all the clothes she had, then, as she warmed up, took a couple of layers off. Finally, dressed in leggings, t-shirt, a dress, a jumper and a cardigan, she went in search of breakfast.

There were all manner of things in the kitchen. The only foods she actually recognized were bread and bananas. So she had a few slices of bread with butter. She bit into a banana and almost spat it out with disgust. Those weren't bananas. Funny looking plantains, maybe, but they weren't any sort of banana she recognized. Because she knew better than to waste food, she ate the horrible, pasty thing anyway.

She walked through the house. Everything looked and smelled impossibly exotic, from the soft carpet underfoot to the funny contraptions that plugged into the wall and made the place smell of cinnamon. In the sitting room downstairs, she found a TV and DVDs. She wondered if she was allowed to watch TV. The thing the Gamages owned was enormous and flat, completely unlike the small TV at the shop that she and her mother went to watch the tele dramas on. Soma looked behind it. It was a screen without the back bit. Incredible.

–

Yamuna took Louie to meet his NCT contemporaries. These mid-morning meet ups usually took place in coffee shops on Princes Avenue, and were the only mother and baby things she could bear. She had tried all the others – bounce and rhyme, messy play, whatever, but Louie was such a grumpy baby that she'd stopped. This group, well this was different. At least they'd met her before she'd had a baby. They might see her as something more than the shadow that pushed the pram.

A couple of the others were already there, their happy, chuckling babies on their laps. Bugger. It was the two yummy mummies. They'd both found time to do their hair and make-up and they looked positively glamorous. Ugh. Yamuna, took a deep breath and strode towards them.

It had been fine when they were all hugely pregnant and sharing their fears. Most of the women were younger than Yamuna by nearly a decade, but that hadn't mattered so much when they all had huge bumps, interrupted careers and impending motherhood in common. Then the first babies showed up and there was all the talk about the amazing experience and the trials of breastfeeding. Not all babies took to it. Louie, for example, refused to latch on properly, making the whole process agonising. In the end, Yamuna had given up and put Louie on the bottle. While it worked well for Louie, it was another mark of her failure as a mother.

She greeted the others and made the obligatory admiring noises at the babies. 'Louie's asleep,' she said apologetically. 'I might go grab a cup of coffee before he wakes up.'

'Oh sure. We'll watch him for you,' said one of the mums, looking up from waving a toy at her daughter.

Yamuna hurried to the queue and ordered herself a strong coffee and a slice of cake. If Louie stayed asleep, she might even get to drink her coffee this time. She didn't really have to concentrate on the conversation, just 'ooh' and 'aah' and let the other two talk about homeopathy and baby yoga or whatever else the superbabies were doing this month. The moment she sat down, Louie let out a teeth-jarring screech.

'I guess he's awake,' she said.

The others rolled their eyes and laughed in sympathy. As though their perfect babies did that sort of thing too.

In the few seconds it took for Yamuna to get Louie out of the pram, he had got everyone's attention. She liberated him from the blankets and joggled him on her hip. He wasn't due for a feed, so she checked his nappy. Nope. His wailing paused for a moment while he had a look around.

'Let's go meet your little friends,' she said. 'Won't that be nice?'

Louie's improved mood lasted all of three minutes before he started up again. People looked up from their coffees. Even the other two babies gave them funny looks. In the end, Yamuna fumbled around in the changing bag and got out a bottle of milk to shut him up.

'Ah, he was hungry,' said one of the other mothers. She was under thirty years old and had managed to shrink back to more or less her original size within a couple of weeks. Yamuna still wore maternity tops with jeans.

'He's always hungry these days,' said Yamuna. 'I'm wondering about weaning him.'

'Oh, you can't wean him until he's six months. Anyway, I thought bottle-fed babies got fuller than breastfed ones.'

Was that a dig about the bottle-feeding? Yamuna gave the woman a quick glance, but couldn't tell.

'Are we the only ones coming today?' said the other one.

'I think so. There are fewer and fewer of us, these days,' said the first, raising her eyes heavenwards.

'I won't be able to come from next week,' said Yamuna. She shifted Louie a little, so that she could catch a dribble of milk that escaped from the corner of his mouth. 'I'm going back to work.'

The news was met by a studied silence. Then, 'Wow. That's soon. Is the maternity provision at your work really bad?'

'Not really, I...' Her employer actually had an excellent maternity policy, but Yamuna couldn't wait to get back to being a functioning human being. She was a rubbish mother, she knew that. At least at work, she was a competent scientist. It would be a relief to be good at something for a short while each day. 'I thought it was best to go back. You know... professionally.'

The other women nodded. 'It's a fair point,' said one. 'I'd go back to work, but by the time I've paid for childcare, I'd be making a loss.'

'What are you doing for childcare? Did you find him a nice nursery?'

'We're hiring a nanny.' Au pair, nanny, all good descriptions, but none really covered the frightened girl that she'd picked up from the airport the day before. 'She seems good with Louie, so far.' At least that was something.

'Oh, lucky you! I wish we could hire a nanny!'

Yamuna said nothing. She'd left Soma sleeping off her jet lag. The girl was young, she would recover from her flight in a day or so and then she and Louie could get to know each other better.

Louie had finished his bottle and was lying with a thoughtful expression on his face. Which probably meant he was planning to fill his nappy. Yamuna reached over to take a sip of her coffee. It had cooled down to tepid. She picked up the cake and lifted it to her mouth.

Louie's bottom made a series of popping noises. The smell rose from him almost instantly. Yamuna put her cake back down uneaten and reached for the changing bag. As she stood up, Louie began to howl again, and people turned to look at them. Yamuna wished she was somewhere, anywhere, else.

Chapter Five

Soma was freezing. It was warm enough in the house, but the minute you stepped out, it was awful. Out on the street the cold was brutal. Madam had lent her a hat, which at least covered her head and ears, but her neck, which felt cold anyway now her hair was gone, felt raw and painful. Even inside the warm shop, she couldn't shake the chill that had sunk into her bones. She checked the blanket that was tucked around Louie. He was looking at the bright lights of the shopping mall ceiling from his nice, warm cocoon of a pram. His eyes were huge and dark brown. He really was the most beautiful baby.

Madam was marching them through a large clothes shop. She was dragging a plastic basket on wheels behind her, picking up clothes and tossing them in. Every so often, she would turn and hold something up against Soma, and decide for or against it. It was like shopping with a machine gun.

'Let me see if this would fit.' Madam held up a chunky woolly top. 'Turn around.'

Obediently, Soma turned and felt the top being placed against her shoulders. She held a long sleeve against Soma's arm. 'Hmm. It's a bit big.'

'I can hem it.' The words came out before she had time to consider them. She could sew by hand, if necessary, but give her an overlocker and she could speed through dozens of garments in an hour. The 'Juki machine' job at the factory had paid well. She had always held a small amount back before she handed her weekly pay over to her mother. Without that, she would never have managed to find the bus fare to leave.

She wondered how many of the garments in this shop had been pressed to a sewing machine with tired fingers like hers.

'That's useful,' Madam said. 'In that case, we'll take it. Remind me to get some thread that matches.'

'Yes Madam.'

Louie fidgeted and made a face. Soma leaned over him. 'Baby?'

He made another face, his expression one of extreme concentration. Then the smell wafted up. Soma looked around. What did she do? She needed to change his nappy, but she couldn't do it here. Outside was too cold. She looked around and could see nothing but racks of clothes. 'Madam?' she said, tentatively.

Madam looked up from where she was rifling through a rail of jumpers. 'What is it?'

'Baby needs changing…'

Madam looked at her blankly.

'I don't know where is best…'

'Ah,' said Madam. 'Of course. You don't know about baby changing facilities. Come. Follow me. I'll show you what we do.'

The toilet with the baby on the door was huge, but it was still a squash with two adults and the pram in it. Louie's wailing, bounced around the small space, making it feel even more cramped. Madam pulled down a plastic ledge. Soma stared. Was the baby supposed to go on that? Madam then pulled a padded mat and some plastic packs from the bag that hung over the back of the pram. She looked expectantly at Soma, who had no idea what she was meant to do next.

Madam let out a controlled sigh. 'Lie Louie on the mat.'

Soma took the baby out and laid him gently on the mat, her hand cradling his head. She had hoped that the first time she changed a nappy, she could do it by herself. She had watched cousins change their babies before, but they all wore cloth nappies. What was she supposed to do with all those plastic packets? Where did used nappies go? Madam was expecting her to change Louie now. Hesitantly, she worked the poppers on his little trousers, all the while shushing him.

Clearly, she was taking too long, because Madam clicked her tongue. 'Let me do it. Watch.'

Soma watched carefully and noted the ritual of wiping down the mat, the cream that went on the baby's bottom, the special bin for the used nappy. Madam seemed to sense her observation and looked up. 'You'll have to do it the next time,' she said. 'When I'm away at work, you will be in charge of looking after the baby.' She frowned. 'I don't want you two to sit at home all day. It's not good for either of you. I will show you the park. You have to take him there. He likes to look at the trees and the fresh air is good for him.'

Madam had a long list of things that she thought were good for Louie. All well and good, Soma thought, but she didn't seem to include time with his mother on that list. Her own mother had always been around when she was a child, a reassuring, smiling presence. That had been before, of course. When her father was still alive and life was still good.

She shook her head. She couldn't think about that life now. This was real life now. This tiny family, with their tall, tall house that separated them from everyone else.

Louie was adorable. His mother's views on childcare were probably how they did things in this country. She couldn't have any confrontation anyway. She had to watch and learn and keep her head down so that no one gave her too much attention.

—

By the afternoon Soma was exhausted. The constant cold was helped by the new puffy coat, scarf, gloves and hat, but it still bit at her face, ears and eyelids. Signs she couldn't read clamoured for her attention and she struggled to understand what people said. When Madam finally loaded them onto a bus, she sank down next to the pram, wanting nothing more than to close her eyes.

In the pram, Louie was asleep after having a full bottle of milk, warmed up in a microwave that was tucked away in a special 'baby feeding corner' in a big department store. How strange this country was. They provided special rooms for changing and feeding babies as though they were a guilty secret that no one wanted to acknowledge.

'We get off here,' Madam said to her in Sinhalese.

Soma nodded, thankful that Madam hadn't insisted on testing her English. When she was in Sri Lanka, it had seemed that she could follow a conversation in English, even if she couldn't speak it, but she hadn't taken into account the accents and how much concentration it required. The bus drew to a halt and Soma kicked the brake off the pram. The bus floor lowered to let them off. Another unexpected concession towards the pram.

She trudged behind her employer, almost leaning on the pram for support. How much more was there to learn? How on earth would she remember it all? They walked a short way and turned in at a set of black iron gates. A few steps down the tree-lined path, the sound of the traffic seemed to quieten. Mind you, the streets were quieter here anyway. People didn't shout. Horns didn't blare. And nothing seemed to smell much. It was as though everything was muted by the cold.

This must be the park. The path of packed earth was edged by tall hedges that were miraculously green, which was in contrast to the bare trees. She knew about the seasons, but had never experienced them before. It couldn't be winter because there was no snow. Winter was the one with snow. This must be another one. Autumn? But there were no yellow and brown leaves which always signified autumn in the books she'd seen. Soma shivered. If it was this cold now, how much worse would it be when it was actually cold enough to snow?

The hedge on one side ended and suddenly they were in a big green park. Soma stopped walking and stared. There was a playground and grass and bare trees and patches of brown earth that might be flowerbeds, even though there were no flowers. Dotted around there were wooden benches. It was one of the most beautiful spaces she had ever seen.

A small sound from the pram made her look down. Louie moved his fist up to his face and went back to sleep. When Soma looked back up again, Madam was watching her. Her expression was softer than it had been all afternoon.

They sat down, with the pram parked in front of them.

Madam was staring at her son. 'Do you have everything you need?' she said, without looking at Soma.

She wasn't sure. She now had warm clothes. A safe place to stay. Food. So yes, she did. But Madam meant something more than that. 'I think… yes, Madam.'

'You know what you need to do for Louie's routine?'

The list of activities in Louie's day was long and the timings for them were very specific. Madam had written it all down for her. 'Yes Madam.'

'Good,' said Madam, still looking at Louie. 'That's good.'

In the silence that followed, Soma said nothing. She let herself relax enough to enjoy the wide open park. A couple of women jogged past. A group of young women pushing prams walked by, chatting in a language that didn't sound like English. A figure in a thick coat threw a ball for a big Alsatian.

'You will look after Louie.'

Soma looked around to see Madam was staring at her intently now. It wasn't a question. She was stating a fact. You *will* look after Louie properly or I *will* send you back.

'Yes, Madam.'

–

Soma shut the door to her room. She pushed the chair against it too, for good measure. She had been there nearly two weeks now and no one had entered her room apart from herself and Madam. And Madam knocked. But she still felt safer with the chair against the door. When she woke up in the middle of the night, panic clawing in her chest, being able to sit up and see the chair still wedged against the door helped calm her in a way nothing else could. This was a safe place.

47

The baby monitor sat next to her alarm clock on the bedside cabinet and emitted a soft glow, so that her room was never completely dark. It crackled as Louie stirred in his sleep. When he was still, she could hear all his little noises. She smiled. He was a lovely baby. Cranky when he was tired, but then, who wasn't?

Soma threw herself down on the bed and folded her arms behind her head. She still found it hard to believe that she was here. She had her own room. With a carpet and everything. What would her old friends say if they could see her now?

Of course, she couldn't tell them. As far as they were aware, she had disappeared. Gone. So her good fortune had to stay her own secret.

She was lucky with Mrs Gamage too. Madam was cold and distant, always giving the impression that Soma was somehow under suspicion, but she wasn't unkind. She had taken Soma shopping, although some of the money was to come out of Soma's first wage. Without that, Soma would have frozen to death. The clothes she had brought with her were hopelessly inadequate. She hadn't really understood the meaning of being cold when she'd bought them.

Then there were the little things. This room. The baby monitor, so that Soma could hear Louie without having to keep her door open. The selection of soap and toothpaste. These small kindnesses meant a lot to her.

Soma's duties mostly related to Louie's needs, but she also helped cook and clean at the weekends. She and Madam made pots of mush – for the baby to try. Soma had to keep a diary of what Louie ate and drank, and when he pooped. Soma was given a plate of whatever Madam and Sir were having. She ate by herself in the kitchen once Louie was asleep. The food during the week was strange; pasta and noodles and lumps of meat and vegetables cooked together. At the weekend Madam and Soma cooked what Soma considered to be proper food – curry, rice, coconut sambal. Again, this was done either early morning or late at night, when Louie was asleep. She got her share of those meals too, which was the highlight of her week.

Considering she was a servant, she felt she was treated well. Carefully, she got changed and got into bed. She'd put a hot water bottle at the top of the bed, which she now pushed down with her feet, so that her toes were warm. This bed. The first bed she'd ever had with a proper mattress. Her bed at home had a mat on it. A sudden memory assailed her. She turned onto her side, pulling herself into a ball. She didn't have to fear *him* any more. He belonged in Jaya's life, not in this one. That life was over. She must not think about it. Ever.

Chapter Six

The walk from the bus stop to his cousin's house in the Avenues wasn't long, but it was very pleasant. Sahan looked up at the houses as he passed. It was quiet around here, probably because people who lived in this part of town didn't like noise. The avenue was wide and tree-lined. It was bright right now in the brittle winter light, but once the trees had leaves again, it would be pleasant and leafy. Strains of something classical floated down from an open window. Very refined. It was a world away from the grubby student house he lived in.

He'd grown up in Colombo, a noisy city, in a house full of people. Although there were only four people in his family, the house was home to a variety of staff – the home helps, the cook, the gardener, the drivers who turned up every morning to take the family members to their various destinations. His father's political ambitions meant that there were often guests for dinner and his mother had ladies from her societies and other political wives round for tea. The house was large and airy, with open spaces and even an indoor water feature. While this helped keep the air moving and kept the house cool in the baking heat, it also made the distances in the house bigger and people would raise their voices to call to each other. His sister, Priyanka, for example, could holler clean across the house. When their mother objected, Priyanka had taken to phoning her or Sahan, even if they were in the next room. The house was never quiet.

The thought of his family made him smile. He missed them, especially his mother and sister, so much so that it sometimes felt like he couldn't breathe. They missed him too. They waited up until midnight if he said he would Skype them in the evening. His sister sent him postcards, which stood out like jewels among the bills and rejection letters that made up the regular post. His mother sent him long emails with news about all the people he knew, and even about some he didn't know. Sometimes, when he read them, all he wanted to do was pack up his things and go back to where he was safe. Like most middle class kids, Sahan had had a carefully controlled life – school, a few sports clubs, extra tuition classes – all under scrutiny. He was always dropped off and picked up by someone. His peers, as they got older, had a bit more independence, but because of their father's fear of anything that would hurt his future political career, Sahan and Priyanka never saw the slackening of the reins. Unlike his sister, Sahan didn't feel the need to fight against it. His parents had given him everything he'd ever needed and all they asked back was for him to finish his engineering degree, get a steady job, settle down and be happy. Why would he want to fight that?

He moved the bag containing a box of chocolates from one hand to the other. He liked it in England, most of the time. Someone had once told him that Hull was like a big village and he could see what they meant. It was quirky, with its white phone boxes and friendly people. Being at the university meant that he met people from all over the world. There was a place here for everyone, but sometimes he felt as though he would never fit in.

It wasn't that he wasn't malleable. He had adapted well enough, but there were some things that still caught him out. Once his exams were over, he would have to find a job either here or at home. These were the last few months of his freedom. He should enjoy it. Should. It was just another thing to add to the long list of things he had to do. Anyway, he didn't really want to kick back or socialise. The reliance on the pub and nightclubs for all social activity didn't help. He knew better than to drink too much now. He had learned about hangovers the hard way.

He stepped to the side to let a man in a motorized wheelchair go past. The old boy gave him a cheery wave. Sahan nodded back and plodded on. Maybe things would have been different if he was able to go out without feeling hunted. He would have had so much fun if he hadn't ever met Tamsin. But then again, if he hadn't had such a sheltered life, maybe he could have handled the Tamsin episode better.

His throat clenched. This always happened when he thought of Tamsin. He shook his head. That was two years ago. Nate had a point. It wasn't such a big deal. Most guys would have laughed it off. He had to get over it and start going out again. Maybe even date someone. Sahan shuddered. He knew not all girls were like Tamsin, but somewhere deep in his hindbrain, he knew he couldn't take the same thing happening again.

He arrived at his cousin's house and paused to admire it. Bim did something that involved investing in things. Yamuna had told him, but he'd forgotten the details. Whatever it was, it paid for a nice tall house with white walls and window boxes. The evening sunlight cast the whole place in a pale yellow glow. His parents had originally wanted him to live with Yamuna. Thankfully, Yamuna had listened to Sahan's suggestion that he should have the full university experience and argued on his behalf, emphasizing the importance of his learning to live independently. His sister had helpfully pointed out that Yamuna was newly married at the time and probably didn't want a smelly boy cousin getting in the way. After all that, he hadn't exactly been able to come to Yamuna for help when the Tamsin incident happened.

Sahan sniffed. He could smell food. Proper food. Frying rampe and garlic. Cinnamon. The smell transported him from the chilly spring evening to hot afternoons on a veranda at home. The feeling was immediate and overwhelming. His breath caught in his throat. Home.

He turned aside and took a struggling breath, inhaling the dry air, to replace the smell of spices. This happened from time to time too, this longing to be back where everything was familiar, but he knew that he wasn't going to go back without a fight. His parents were well-to-do, but sending him to university in England had not been cheap. They had made sure he hadn't been denied any opportunity. He couldn't exactly turn around and quit. Besides, he wanted to get a good job. He had to finish his degree for that.

Sahan reached the white front door. He raised his hand to the doorbell. Suddenly, from somewhere above, there came a song. A voice, sweet and clear, sang a lullaby. The song was so familiar it bypassed all filters and hit him straight in the chest. He knew it by heart, even though he'd never consciously learned it. His mother had sung that song to him. His aunts sang it to his cousins. Yamuna was probably singing it to her son. It was the song of home.

The voice wasn't Yamuna's. It was too high, too young, too clear. It tugged at something deep inside him, taking him back to tropical Sundays. Sahan closed his eyes and leaned his forehead against the doorframe, listening. The lullaby filled him up and stilled the thoughts that kept him awake. For the first time in months, years even, he felt at peace. He couldn't have moved away if he'd tried. After a few minutes, the singing became softer, then softer still, until the baby she was singing to fell asleep, then finally, it stopped altogether.

Released from the spell, Sahan looked up at the house. The song was in Sinhalese, so it had to have come from Yamuna's house. The owner of that voice was in there, somewhere. When he rang the doorbell, Yamuna answered. 'Sahan, come in.'

He entered the hallway and looked around, half expecting a girl with a clear voice to materialize there and then. He exchanged pleasantries and followed his cousin into the dining room, where Bim was setting the table. It surprised Sahan to see Bim and Yamuna doing anything remotely domestic together. They were such a stiff couple; he imagined that they inhabited independent circles, pulling into each other's orbit only rarely, when they had a social engagement to attend. He privately considered it a miracle that Louie could ever have been conceived.

He accepted a beer. There was still no sign of anyone who could have been singing. There was also not as much evidence of Louie as usual.

Curiosity got the better of him. 'I heard someone singing a lullaby when I came to the door,' he said. 'Have you got someone staying?'

'Oh, that'll be the new nanny,' said Yamuna.

54

Sahan felt a stab of disappointment. A nanny. He had half expected to hear that a semi famous actress or singer had somehow come to visit.

Yamuna checked a pan of devilled potatoes on the hob and, pulling on oven gloves, started to remove dishes from the oven. 'We got a girl from Sri Lanka, so that Louie could learn to speak a bit of Sinhalese. He'll pick up English from playgroup, but we wanted him to have some exposure to Sinhalese as well. Even if he can't speak it, he should at least be able to understand what people say to him when he goes to visit the grandparents.'

'Won't he get that from you?' Maybe Yamuna didn't talk to her son. The poor kid was going to grow up thinking it was normal to live in a household where everyone kept their distance.

Yamuna gave him a funny look. 'Well, yes, I suppose, but we don't get that much time with him during the week. It made so much more sense to get someone to come and help out with him.'

'And this girl... she was the one I heard singing?' He tried not to sound too interested. Really, he was only curious about this new person that had come to live in his cousin's house. Nothing more. He needn't tell Yamuna the effect the singing had had on him.

'Probably,' said Yamuna. 'She seems to have settled in okay. Louie likes her.'

Bim's phone buzzed. He stopped what he was doing to check it. To Sahan's surprise, Bim didn't put the phone back in his pocket, but started typing away on it. Yamuna didn't seem to find this at all odd and carried on putting dishes on the table.

Sahan rushed over to help. He carried the large bowl full of pilau rice across to the table. 'Wow, you must have been cooking for hours.'

Yamuna laughed. 'I was going to order in, but now that there's someone around to take care of Louie, I have a bit more time. So I cooked.' She put the last dish on the table and motioned him to sit down. 'So, tell me what's going on with you.'

Throughout the meal, Sahan kept an eye out for the mysterious nanny. He wondered if she was as beautiful as her voice. But the woman never came downstairs. He wondered whether she had a small kitchen upstairs. Did she always eat separately from the family? He looked across at Yamuna and Bim, who were discussing something politely. No, a nanny would hardly be invited to eat with the family. That wouldn't do.

He wondered how he could engineer a way to see her, just to assuage his curiosity. Perhaps she lived in a room next to the baby, like Victorian nannies in films. He couldn't ask without his interest being noted. Yamuna would want to know why he was so interested in a servant. Even he didn't know why he was so interested. Hearing that voice singing such a familiar song had reminded him of home and lifted him from his sadness, just for a moment. It had been a wonderful thing. He wasn't sure it meant anything more than that, but he still felt compelled to see the singer.

The evening wore on. The dinner was fantastic. It felt so good to eat proper food. He ate bacon sandwiches and kebabs and chips, just like everyone else, but sometimes he craved flavour. He often had Indian food from the curry house he worked at, but that tasted nothing like home. He relied on his visits to Yamuna, or his rare excursions out to one of the Sri Lankan restaurants to fill the gap. Yamuna always packed up some leftovers for him to take back, so he would have at least one more meal that tasted real.

It got late and there was still no sign of the nanny coming downstairs. It was nearly time to leave.

'Can I pop up and have a look at Louie?' Sahan said. 'I haven't seen him in months and he must be getting so big now.' Of course, the baby would be asleep. 'Would it disturb him if I had a peep?'

If Yamuna thought this was a strange request, she didn't show it. 'I don't think that will be a problem,' she said. She pushed her chair back. 'Come. I'll take you.'

The child's room was at the top of the house. Sahan followed his cousin up the many flights of stairs and wondered at the houses stacked so tall and thin, jammed in against each other. They had both grown up in airy middle class homes where big windows let in light and a welcome breeze. Here everything was tightly sealed. Keeping the occupants in and nature firmly out.

'Shh.' Yamuna said, unnecessarily, as they reached the top.

They crept quietly to the door which had Louie's name made out on it in colourful wooden letters. Sahan glanced around. There were two other doors. One, left ajar, clearly led to a small toilet. The other was shut. Perhaps the owner of that voice lived in there.

As Yamuna creaked open Louie's door and peered in, Sahan had a moment of clarity. What was he doing? Sneaking around, trying to catch a glimpse of a servant. So, the woman had a beautiful voice. So what? She was still a servant in his cousin's house. She was probably ugly too, despite the voice. What would his sister say if he told her? She would tease him mercilessly, of course. His parents… well, he'd never talk to his parents about something so stupid.

Yamuna gestured him forward. He went to the door and peered in at the baby. Louie was fast asleep, his chubby features bathed in the glow from the nightlight. In repose, the boy looked like his father. Sahan smiled. His own mother would have loved to see this. She loved babies.

There was a sound behind them.

'Madam?' That voice. Soft now. No longer crooning but whispering and puzzled. He turned slowly.

The girl was wearing a thick green dressing gown that was too big for her. It made her appear shapeless. She had no hair to speak of. He had been expecting that because Yamuna had mentioned the whole head lice scenario, but it was still a shock to see. And her face… Her face. Sahan stared. The lack of hair gave her an ethereal quality, like she was part fairy, part real. Her eyes were huge and wary. Her features were big for her oval face, but that only added to her look of wide-eyed innocence. Her skin was flawless. There wasn't a hint of make-up on it and it was still perfect.

Her gaze flicked from Yamuna to Sahan. Catching him looking at her, she flinched away, wrapping her arms around herself and stepping backwards towards her own room. Was she scared? Of *him*?

'It's okay,' Yamuna said. 'My cousin and I were looking in on Louie. Go back to bed.'

The girl nodded, but didn't raise her eyes from the floor. She seemed to have shrunk into herself. Her vulnerability hooked into something in his chest. He wanted to step forward and tell her that there was no need to be frightened of him. He would never hurt her. He wouldn't hurt anyone.

'Come Sahan,' said Yamuna. 'We should let Soma and Louie get their rest.' With that, she started back down the stairs.

Soma. So that was her name. At the top of the stairs he looked back over his shoulder. The door to Soma's room was open, just a crack. He saw her face, watching him. When he looked at her, she pulled backwards like a startled bird. He followed Yamuna downstairs. At the landing, he risked another glance. Her door was still closing, as though she'd spent a few extra seconds watching him leave.

Yamuna was talking, but Sahan didn't hear any of it. Soma, with her shaved head and enormous eyes, had triggered a maelstrom inside him. The fear in her eyes resonated with him. It was similar to what he felt about going out and being sociable, but amplified many fold. For the first time since he'd come to this country, he had met someone who was clearly more scared than he was. To his surprise, he wanted to help her.

He couldn't focus on anything Yamuna said. He claimed tiredness and Bim offered to drive him home. 'Thank you, but I'll be okay on the bus,' Sahan said, because all he really wanted was time to think.

'I'll see you in a few weeks, then?' said Yamuna, as she saw him to the door.

'A few weeks?' Had they agreed something? He must have missed it completely.

She rolled her eyes. 'You were going to fix a bolt on the nanny's bedroom door.'

His heart gave an unexpected little skip. 'Oh. Yeah. That's fine. I'll come on Saturday.'

'Can you buy the bolt too? I'll pay you back, of course.'

She opened the door for him. 'The poor girl wedges a chair against the door when she sleeps. It didn't occur to me before, but this must be a frightening change for her. She seems a bit naive for her age.'

He had been frightened when he first came over to England, but he had known where he was going. He spoke good English. And look how that had turned out. He thought back to his first few weeks in halls. 'I think, if my door at uni didn't have a lock, I'd probably jam a chair against it too,' he said.

'Yes well, you're at uni. She sleeps at the top of this house. It's not likely she's going to encounter passing vandals here,' said Yamuna. 'If she needs a lock on the door to feel safe, then it's not a big deal. She should be able to relax. This is her home too now.' Yamuna sighed. 'Besides, if Louie needs her, I don't want her to have to remove a blockade before she can see to him.'

As he walked briskly back to the bus stop, Sahan's thoughts drifted back to the nanny. She had looked so vulnerable. Completely unlike anyone he'd met before. It must have been that, combined with the sound of her singing that had made such an impact on him. He wanted to protect her. There must be something kind he could do for her.

For the first time in a long time, he felt in a position to help someone. That made him feel strong. After all this time feeling powerless, it was nice to remember what strong felt like.

Chapter Seven

When it came to the end of the first month, Madam said, 'I need to talk to you.'

Soma immediately felt a stab of alarm. Had she done anything in the past few weeks to annoy Madam? She had done her best, following instructions to the letter, keeping her head down, being as inconspicuous as possible once the baby was in bed. What had gone wrong?

'Don't look worried,' said Madam, kindly. She motioned for Soma to sit across the kitchen table from her and said, 'Soma, are you happy here?'

Soma hesitated. Was she happy? She wasn't unhappy. She missed Sri Lanka with a kind of visceral tug, but she was also glad to be away. Here, she lived in more comfort than she had ever done before. There was always enough food, even at the end of the week. She didn't have to creep around avoiding her stepfather. And she could sleep, safe in her own room. *Her own room!* 'Yes, Madam. I am happy here.'

Madam nodded, as though it was no more than what she was expecting. 'That's good. Now, I've decided not to deduct the money for your clothes from your salary. So I will pay the full monthly amount into your account. You know how to use a bank account?'

Bank account? People like her didn't have bank accounts. She shook her head. Rich people never understood. They had so much money they could pay a bank to look after it for them. Everyone knew the best way to save for an emergency was to buy jewellery. She thought of her mother's necklace, lost somewhere in the Indian Ocean, and felt a wrench of guilt. That necklace was the total of her mother's savings.

Yamuna sighed and made a note on the piece of paper in front of her. 'The agency would have sorted it out for you. Fine. I'll take you to the bank to see someone about it.'

Soma's mind flicked back to the meagre set of ID papers she had. Someone at the bank was bound to scrutinise them carefully. She had put on a bit of weight since arriving. Would she still be able to pass herself off as the girl on the passport?

'Please Madam. Do I need to go to the bank? Can't I just…'

'What? Keep your money under your mattress? No. You can't. It's not safe.' Madam frowned. 'Ah. You think you'll have to pay. Don't worry, the agency already charged us for setting it up and banks don't charge for everything here like they do at home.' She made another note on her list. 'You'll be wanting to send most of your money home to your family, I suppose. I'll show you where the Western Union place is. They will take cash.'

Soma kept her mouth shut and nodded. If she said she wasn't sending money home, that would sound odd. She didn't want Madam asking questions about home. The more she told Madam, the more she was likely to let something slip. If suspicions were aroused, Madam might say something to the agency, who would make enquiries… and who knows what that would unearth?

'I expect you to do your personal jobs like banking and taking money to Western Union on Saturday when you're not looking after Louie,' Madam continued. She frowned, as though something had occurred to her. 'I will show you everything this week. If you want someone to come with you in future, let me know.'

'Yes Madam. Thank you.'

'Now,' Madam pulled out the notebook where she wrote down Louie's meals. 'This is what we'll be making for this week.'

–

Yamuna sat on the sofa, with Louie on her lap. They were reading *The Very Hungry Caterpillar* together. Louie was all smiles and giggles now. She dropped a kiss on his head and helped him poke a finger through the holes in the book.

He was so much nicer now than he had been a few weeks ago. Common sense told her it was just that he was older now, but sometimes she wondered if it was Soma's influence. The girl and Louie seemed to have bonded. He clearly adored her and she seemed to have infinite patience with him.

She tried to turn the page, but Louie kept pulling it around. 'Darling, how am I supposed to read this to you, if you keep moving it about?' she said to him, in English. She always spoke to Louie in English now that Soma was around to speak Sinhalese to him. When he started to speak, she would see about sending him to playgroup a couple of times a week to make sure he spoke unaccented English. She straightened the book.

Louie burst into wails. Yamuna noticed Soma, who was folding baby clothes on the other side of the room, tense. Louie hardly ever cried when he was with her.

'Oh, hey, okay. Here. Have the book,' said Yamuna. But Louie no longer wanted the book. She picked him up and cuddled him, nestling him against her shoulder. It didn't make any difference.

She stood up, joggling Louie, shushing him, as she walked around. Soma continued to fold the clothes, but Yamuna could feel her attention. Listening. It was like a challenge to see if she could soothe her own son. Well she had given birth to this baby. No slip of a girl was going to make her feel inferior.

Shhhh, baby. shhhh.

'Has he been fed?' Yamuna asked Soma, even though she knew full well that he had.

The girl nodded.

Yamuna paced and joggled.

Motherhood hadn't come easily to Yamuna. It had been swift on the heels of her marriage. Bim was fastidious in that as he was with everything. But she hadn't been prepared. All those things that people didn't tell you. She'd spent days at NCT classes going over birth plans which the midwives all but ignored. Everything had been focused on the actual event. She wished people had told her more about the real, day-to-day, stuff. Or, even better, if they hadn't romanticized the whole thing.

By the time they handed Louie to her, she was too exhausted after hours of labour to feel anything. She'd him taken against her, skin to skin, as she had been taught. The midwife rammed him onto a breast. She watched him suckle and felt... nothing. She had expected a rush of hormones; an endocrine reaction that automatically changed her from Yamuna, driven scientist, all round planner and organized person, into Yamuna the mother. Something that turned on a tap of emotion, letting her love pour in. But there was nothing. She'd thought at first that it might have been exhaustion, but hours, days, weeks went by and she felt only the huge burden of responsibility.

She fed him, changed him, burped him and cuddled him. All the things that the book said you had to do, she did. She worked out a routine, then adapted it, adapted it some more. But nothing shifted the block inside her that stopped her from finding that bond. Finally, exhausted, she'd asked Bim if they could hire a nanny. She told him she wanted to go back to work.

It was Bim's suggestion to employ a girl from Sri Lanka, to give the boy a cultural touchstone. Make sure he understood basic Sinhalese, even if he couldn't speak it. At the time it had made perfect sense. Someone who knew what they were doing could look after Louie, freeing Yamuna to go back to work and do something she was actually competent at.

But the girl had arrived and formed a bond with Louie instantly. Just like that. It wasn't fair. Yamuna realised she was pacing fast now. She forced herself to slow down. She shifted Louie's position against her. He wailed in her ear.

'Madam?' Soma appeared next to her. 'Shall I take him?' She held out her hands.

Yamuna's first reaction was to tighten her hold on him. He was her son. She could calm him. She looked at Soma's face, which had no hint of gloating in it. She looked at the girl's hands, which were still held out to receive the baby. 'Fine,' she muttered and gently handed the boy to Soma. Louie stopped yowling immediately and subsided to a whimper. He buried his face in the girl's neck.

Soma spoke to him, in that wheedling, high-pitched voice that people used with babies. 'Shall we go and look at the cars outside the window?' she said in Sinhalese. She carried him to the window and started to point out different cars.

Yamuna watched as her son, who had been inconsolable thirty seconds ago, peered out of the window, still pouting, but calm. He clearly loved Soma far more than he loved her, his mother. Anger rose, making her face feel hot and her jaws ache. She marched out of the room before she said anything she'd regret.

Storming into the room that she shared with Bim, she sank onto the bed and told herself it wasn't Soma's fault. Soma wouldn't have had a chance if Louie had loved his mother even a little bit to start with. Tears rose, making her eyes ache. Louie was only a baby. What did he know? It wasn't his fault he had a crap mother.

–

Madam took her to the bank on Saturday. Yamuna followed her into the building, a big, open place where people were queuing neatly. Soma had been to a bank before, with the father, when she was very young. It had been a hot, intimidating place with sweaty, uncomfortable people pressing against the counters on one side and neatly dressed people with ledgers and typewriters under lazy ceiling fans on the other. The whole bank would have fit in the entrance of this one.

Somehow the impersonal quiet was terrifying. She gripped the handle of Louie's pushchair more tightly. Madam explained what they were there to do and that she would have to sign a few documents. Thankfully, she had practised Somavathi's signature often enough before she left Sri Lanka, that she could replicate it, even under Madam's watchful eye.

The bank forms were with Madam. In her own handbag, which was slung against her body, under her coat, so that pickpockets wouldn't get it, she had the passport.

A lady in a smart uniform took them into a small office and got them to sit down. Soma parked Louie's pram facing the glass partition, so that he could be distracted by the people in the bank outside. He seemed happy enough, chewing on his toy and staring at the bright lights.

Madam explained what they wanted and the lady took the forms and looked them over. 'Have you got any ID and proof of address?'

Madam handed over some papers. 'This is the employment paperwork,' she said. 'She lives with us.'

The lady flipped through the documents. 'This should be okay. We have a special account for people who are new to the UK.' She smiled at Madam, and then, as an afterthought, at Soma. 'Do you have ID?'

'Passport?' said Madam, pointedly.

Soma dropped her bag in her hurry to extract her passport. What if this bank lady saw her for the fraud she was? The man in the airport had been waving people through so fast, he might not have looked at her properly, but this lady had been right in front of her, looking at her face for minutes now.

She found her passport, passed it over and bent down to shove the things that had fallen out of her bag – a hairbrush and her small wallet – back in.

When she sat back up, the lady looked at the passport in her hand and back at Soma's face. She frowned. The hairs on the back of Soma's neck stood up on end. This lady could see that it wasn't the same person.

Finally, the lady smiled again. 'I'll just photocopy these. I'll be right back.'

Soma went limp with relief. Louie dropped his toy and started to grizzle. Soma leapt up to see to him. She must not look guilty or Madam would suspect something was wrong. Thank goodness Louie had distracted her. She gave him his toy back and tickled him to say thank you.

The rest of the process took some time and Madam had to translate things for her so that she understood what she was signing. The woman said they had a translated version in Urdu, which seemed like an odd thing to say. Louie had to be taken out of the pram and given a bottle, it took so long. Finally, they stood up to leave, with a promise that a card would be sent in the post.

As they left, Madam said, 'Do you know how to use a machine?'

Soma shook her head. She knew that the card went into the machine, from seeing the Ceylan bank advert. Madam showed her how to use the machine, using her own card. The words on the screen were in English. Soma could read them, if she had the time to work it out, but Madam was impatient and quick.

'See?' Madam said. 'If you press this, it tells you how much is in there. You press here and you can put in how much you want to take out. Do you understand?'

Soma nodded. 'Please Madam, can you write down the words on the screen, so that I can learn them?'

Madam gave her a surprised glance, then a nod. 'I will do that,' she said. For the first time there was hint of approval in her expression. 'You can read English?'

'Only very slowly,' said Soma. She knew the letters and their sounds. She could sound the words out, but had no idea what some of them meant.

'Good,' said Madam. 'Now, how about I get you a bit of money to buy your essentials?'

She had no idea what Madam was talking about. She didn't need money to spend. There was food, and heat, and safety at Madam's house. She had enough to wear. What more did she need money for? Also, she had no idea what this funny money was worth.

Madam sighed. 'We'll get twenty pounds,' she said. 'You type it in.'

Soma followed her instructions and was soon holding a purple note. She put it carefully away in her purse.

'Now,' said Madam. 'I'll show you where you can buy toothpaste and soap and things like that.'

So that's what she meant by 'essentials'. She could buy some cream, maybe. Her skin was all dry and grey because of the cold. She thought of the note in her bag. She could buy some cream that smelled nice.

Shopping in England was exhausting. There was so much of everything. At home, she could go into the shop and ask the mudhalali for what she needed. He had only one brand of anything.

When her father died, the shopkeeper and his wife had done her and her mother a hundred little kindnesses – passing on the bananas that were too bruised to sell, the bottle of shampoo that was leaking, packets of soup that were past their sell-by date. All that had stopped when her stepfather moved in.

There was no human connection here. Soma stared at the vast array of soap, paralysed by choice. In the end, Madam suggested she buy the cheapest for now. Grateful to have a solution, Soma grabbed a bar of soap and toothpaste and a tube of cream by Yardley, because she recognized the logo, and followed Madam to the ordeal of the till.

With Madam standing a short distance away, watching, she stood in the queue. Her heart thundered in her chest and her face felt hot. She had to talk to someone in English. She knew how to say, 'how much is it please?' In her mind, she'd added up how much her purchases came to. She had to say 'thank you' at the end. She took deep breaths.

She noticed the person ahead of her didn't ask how much, the girl at the till just said hello and scanned everything through the machine. Maybe that's what she should do. Hand things over and then pay. So long as there wasn't anything else to say.

By the time it was her turn, she was breaking into a sweat. She pushed the items across. The girl smiled. She said something, which Soma didn't get. Soma looked around at Madam. The girl repeated it, slowly. Bag. Something about a bag. Soma shook her head. The girl serving her smiled kindly and gestured to the total on the display. Soma handed her the money and took the change. She didn't actually have to speak. Then, just as she was turning to leave, she remembered and stammered, 'Thank you.'

The girl at the till gave her a cheerful smile in return.

Soma reached Madam and Louie and felt like she'd conquered a mountain. Madam, looking amused, said 'Well done. You'll get used to it.'

Soma was happy to be praised, but she really didn't think she'd be able to do that again.

Yamuna heard the connecting door from the garage open and knew Bim was home. She was sitting in the study upstairs, trying to get her head around the paperwork she had to take back for her return to work. Now that Soma was settled in, there was no reason for her to hang around the house all day. She was increasingly starting to feel like a spare part that was getting in the way of the Louie and Soma show.

Going back to work would be strange, but she was looking forward to it. At least in the lab, she knew what she was doing. It would be difficult getting back into her stride after a break of so many months, but other people seemed to manage it easily enough. She was looking forward to being somewhere where there were other adults to talk to during the day. Immediately, she felt guilty for thinking that.

She hauled herself out of the chair and went downstairs. Bim was standing at the kitchen table, looking through the post she'd left stacked there for him.

'Have you eaten?' she said. It was an automatic question. Her mother had always asked her father that if he ever came home late. Unlike her, her mother had always waited for her husband before eating, but Bim's days were unpredictable. He and Yamuna had discussed this. It was safer to assume he was not coming home for dinner. If he was, he would always call ahead and tell her.

'Yes. I ate at the meeting,' he said. 'Shall I put the kettle on?'

This late evening cup of tea was the only thing that felt normal in their lives. Yamuna had imagined married life to be… more interesting. Her friends had all got married and had children a decade before. They talked about their lives with their husbands and there was so much animation there. When she finally got married herself, she hadn't expected hearts and flowers, but she'd expected a little romance, at least a nod towards love. But Yamuna's marriage to Bim… it was different. They lived together, they talked, politely. Everything, even sex, was polite and dutiful. Materially, he gave her everything she needed, but emotionally, he seemed incapable of giving anything of himself. There was comfort and respect, but that was it. They had been married for over two years and he still felt like a stranger to her. Unlike her friends, she had a marriage based on practicality. She might have asked for advice, if she'd had anyone close by, but since she was now living in England and far away, she didn't have anyone she could really talk to. When talking to her friends in rare Skype conversations, she ended up pretending everything was 'normal'.

He was nice enough. He didn't make her *unhappy*. Perhaps that was the best she could hope for.

She stood next to him and made cups of tea. She asked him how his day was and normally listened carefully to his quick summary of who he'd dealt with. Bim wasn't precious about his work like some men could be. If she asked questions, he would answer them. But that evening, she couldn't concentrate.

'I'm going back to work tomorrow, remember,' she said.

He had clearly forgotten. He put his head to one side and watched her for a moment.

'Are you sure you are ready? You still look tired.'

'I'm always tired.' She forced a laugh. 'It's part of being a mum, I think.' She handed him his tea and turned to lean back against the work surface. 'Soma is able to manage

Louie without me now. I can go to work with a clear conscience.'

'Conscience?' said Bim.

'You know what I mean.'

'Louie is happy and well cared for. He gets to play with us in the evenings and weekends. It's no different to hundreds of other children. There's no need to feel guilty.' He gave her a funny look when he said it. 'But don't feel you have to go back to work if you're not ready. If you feel it would be better to spend a few more weeks relaxing and getting things straight, you can do that. We don't need the money.'

'I know that.' They were lucky. He earned enough that she didn't have to go to work to make ends meet. Some of her friends had chosen to give up careers to bring up children. She had wondered, dreamed even, about staying home with her baby, basking in their bond, being one of those calm homemakers that she'd read about in all the parenting books. She now knew she could never do that. Quite apart from that fact that she was a rubbish mother, her baby didn't seem to like her much. She gripped the mug tightly and took a deep breath. 'I think I need to go back, though. I need to remember what it was like to be me.'

'If that's what you want.'

He never told her what to do. Originally, she'd liked that. She'd thought it was because he respected her independence, but since Louie, who had changed her dull, stable life into a shifting maelstrom of uncertainty, she wondered if it was merely that he wasn't interested.

'I think it is... I'm not sure...'

He frowned and sipped some tea, eyes focussed somewhere across the kitchen.

'Perhaps, the only thing to do is to try it and see. If you find it doesn't feel right for you, you can stop. You don't have to send the nanny home, just because you're at home too. You can share the job between you.'

Hah. There was no chance of that. Louie would object most strenuously. Yamuna said nothing. She had to remember how lucky she was to have a man like Bim take her on at her age. Once you got into your late thirties, there were so few eligible men left. She was lucky to have been able to have Louie too. There was no reason to let her insecurities ruin everything.

'I'm going in for three days this week, to start with,' she informed him. She had told him before, but he was bound to have forgotten. 'Then four days the next week and then full time. I had a chat with Richard about what work I'd be taking on when I get back and, well, I'm looking forward to getting back into it, to be honest.'

'I can understand that,' said Bim. 'I would miss my work if it were me, but I thought…' He turned, his eyes finally focusing on her face. 'I don't want you to feel pressured into going back. Or staying at home. I don't mind either way. I want you to be happy, that's all.'

'Thank you,' she said, quietly. How easy it was to make 'I don't care what you do' sound like 'I'm supporting your decisions, whatever you decide'.

–

The front door slammed, telling Soma that Madam and Mr Gamage had left for the day. Now it was just her and Louie… and she could relax. Loving Louie was the one thing that cost her no effort at all. It was as though the love had been there, waiting for him to tap into it with the first gurgle. Maybe he was the reincarnation of the baby brother she never knew.

Soma deftly caught a gobbet of porridge before it slid off Louie's chin and popped it back in his mouth. He gummed it, dribbling some back out again.

'Eat up, bubba.' She smiled at him and was rewarded with a sticky smile back. 'After we've had this, I'll have something to eat. Then we can do what's on the list amma left us.'

Madam had a strict routine for Louie. She wrote it out, with timings and instructions on the order in which things had to be done. When it was playtime, Louie had to play, whether he wanted to or not. He was to eat at mealtimes only. If he didn't eat it, she wasn't to keep trying to get the food into him. 'If he's hungry, he'll eat,' Madam said. 'No need to play silly games to force him to eat.' Soma, who was used to babies being fussed over, found this idea startling and wrong, but Madam was the boss and Soma couldn't afford to mess this up.

She scraped the last of the porridge off the bowl and fed it to Louie. Giving him an empty bowl and a spoon to play with, she grabbed herself some bread. The bread here came ready bagged and didn't have a crust. She liked that it was already sliced, although sometimes she wondered if they baked the bread in little squares, they were so uniform. It tasted strange too. And it was brown. She spread a good layer of butter and jam on the bread. She took down the activity list for the day to read it while she ate.

'So, today, we've got some play time with... the toys in the blue box... and then a nap.'

Back upstairs, she got out the prescribed toys and sat cross-legged on the floor, with Louie in the hollow of her lap. Playing with him required focus, Madam had said, and eye contact and a constant commentary of what was going on, so that he could learn more words. Soma did all that when Madam was around, but when it was just her and Louie, she gave him a little freedom. Leaning against her for support, he patted the doll she was holding and made the bell on its hat tinkle. He let out a self-satisfied gurgle and did it again. She congratulated him and kissed the top of his head.

As he tried his newfound trick again, she leaned back against the wall. Freed from worrying about the baby, her mind immediately filled up with an image of the man on the landing a few weeks before. Reliving her only meeting with him was her current favourite hobby. It made her smile and prevented her from thinking about other things, so she clung to it like it was a life raft. The memory spooled through her mind like a film clip. She had heard a sound on the baby monitor and gone out to investigate, expecting to see Madam doing a spot check on Louie. Instead she'd opened the door to see a man who was definitely not Mr Gamage, standing on the landing. He was looking over Madam's shoulder into Louie's room, so he hadn't noticed Soma until she'd shifted position. Hearing her, he'd turned. He was the most handsome man she'd ever seen outside of a cinema screen. He was tall and broad in all the right ways and had curly hair that was a bit too long. His eyes were light enough to be brown, rather than black. The minute they turned to look at her, she'd felt as though her heart was going to fly out of her body.

Louie took too energetic a swat at the doll and toppled forward. Soma gently righted him. Noticing that he had dribbled, she wiped his chin with a muslin cloth and found him a different toy to play with. She put a hand around his middle to keep him stable.

Madam had described the man as her cousin, so he was one of Them. He would never look twice at a servant like her. And even if he did, it wouldn't be with love. That only happened in films. It was silly of her to think of him like that. Daydreaming was all very well, but she shouldn't give that single meeting any more significance. When she stopped to think about it, she wasn't even sure she wanted it to have more significance. Falling in love meant touching and holding and... she didn't want to be touched. She sighed and wiped another trail of drool off Louie. No. She didn't want it be anything more than a pleasant sighting.

Except, there was no harm in daydreaming, was there? She could pretend she was like the girl in the shampoo commercial. The one who men fell in love with, but never touched.

She daydreamed about film stars all the time and that was fine because they weren't real and couldn't hurt you. This man may as well not be real. People like him didn't talk to people like her. He was from a rich family, well-educated and smooth. People like him *employed* people like her to clean their houses and look after their children. They didn't make friends with them. She didn't really even want him to. The man in her imagination was good and kind and would keep her safe. Getting to know the real man would only ruin it.

In her lap, Louie stopped playing. She felt his little body clench. There was a soft pop in his nappy. Soma smiled. 'It's okay, little one,' she said. 'I know my place. You don't have to remind me of it.'

She picked him up and went off to deal with baby shit.

Sahan hummed to himself as he made a sandwich for lunch. His last revision paper had gone really well and he was on track with his plans for revising the next module. He might even entertain the thought that he was doing okay.

'What is that tune?' Cara opened a cupboard next to him and pulled out a packet of value custard creams.

'What tune?' Sahan surveyed his sandwich for a second and decided it needed some black pepper.

'The one you've been humming all the time,' said Cara. She picked up the kettle and moved towards him, stopping short of pushing him out of the way. Despite being a very touchy-feely person, she rarely touched him, because she knew about Tamsin. He appreciated that.

Sahan moved up so that she could reach the sink. Had he been humming? It was the lullaby that he'd heard Soma singing to baby Louie. The tune, and Soma, had drifted into his mind from time to time. He hadn't realised he'd been humming it aloud.

Cara put the kettle on and leaned against the work surface opposite him. 'It's some sort of ballad?' she said.

'It's a Sri Lankan lullaby.' He avoided her gaze and concentrated of cutting his sandwich in half.

'Uhuh. And you're humming it because...?'

He took his plate over to the table. 'Earworm.'

Cara said nothing, but he could feel her gaze boring into his back. After a while, she came and sat next to him, bringing her custard creams with her. 'Sahan,' she said. 'Are you okay? You've been a bit distracted lately. Are you starting to stress out about exams?'

Sahan finished his mouthful and shook his head. 'No. I'm okay, Cara. Honestly.' He paused to examine her face.

She looked pale and tired, but then they all did these days. The impending threat of exams put a strain on everyone. 'How about you?'

She rubbed her eyes. 'I'm okay.' She pulled a face. 'Well maybe a bit stressed, but otherwise okay. I mean, we're all a bit stressed this year, right?'

'Nate?'

Cara smiled. 'Everyone except Nate. That guy, honestly. He doesn't seem to worry about anything and then boom! Straight A's. So irritating.'

'Tell me about it,' said Sahan.

Cara dunked a custard cream in her tea. 'But that's why we love him, right?'

Sahan took another bite of his sandwich. Cara loved Nate, he knew. They were, to him, the template of an ideal relationship. They were friends. They respected each other and teased one another. He would love to have that with someone, one day. But then again, he saw the way they reached for each other sometimes and he could never do that. Not without thinking of Tamsin. He put down his lunch.

'What are you guys going to do after exams finish?' he said.

Cara smiled. 'I'm going to look for a job. Nate's got to get through the rest of medical school.'

'Are you going to get married?'

'Might do,' she said. 'I'm not sure.'

'But you love Nate, right? And he loves you.' They would go off and start a grown-up life together. While he, Sahan, had no idea what he wanted from life.

'Doesn't mean we have to get married,' said Cara. She put her head to one side and scrutinized him. 'What's that face for? What are you thinking?'

Sahan pulled his thoughts back in. Things had to change. That was life. He should be happy for his friends. 'I was just thinking that you guys have been so kind to me. You know, after the whole Tamsin thing. I know it was weird.'

Cara shrugged. 'We're your friends. That's what friends do.'

'I know, but well, you still look after me a bit. I don't know how I can thank you.'

She laughed. 'You don't have to, you know. Like I said, it's what friends do. Tell you what though, if you want to keep the karma balance going, just pay it forward. Be a good friend to someone else.'

He smiled at her and shook his head. 'I will do that.' He stood up and took what was left of his sandwich to eat in his room. Thinking about Tamsin had ruined his appetite, but it would return in time.

'Er... Sahan,' said Cara. 'Are you likely to come out for a quiet drink at the weekend?'

He paused and turned. 'Why?'

'I happen to know that one of my friends likes you and—'

'No.' He knew she meant Bex. He couldn't handle girls flirting with him. Not yet.

'Oh come on, Sahan. She's really nice and really non-threatening. It's been ages. You can't let Tamsin ruin everything for you for ever.'

'No,' said Sahan. 'I... can't. I've got too much revision to do.'

'Sahan...' Cara stood up and came over to stand in front of him. 'You have to let it go.'

'You don't understand, I can't! Every time a woman tries to flirt with me, to touch me, all I can think about is what happened with Tamsin. I don't ever want to be in that position again. Ever.'

'But Sahan, most girls aren't like that. You can't let it stop you from leading a normal life. That means she's won.'

When he said nothing, she sighed and said, 'Besides, you can't study all the time. You'll go crazy.'

Which was a good point. He grabbed a glass of water and headed back to his room.

'I'll think about it,' he told Cara as he went out. 'But I'm not promising anything.'

Several hours of study later, he realised he was humming again. An image of Soma drifted across his mind. It must be lonely for her, being stuck in the house with Louie all day. Yamuna and Bim were great, but not exactly keen conversationalists. He thought about Cara's comment on paying it forward. He smiled. He knew just how to do that and take a break from his studies at the same time.

–

Yamuna rubbed her eyes and reached for her tea. Her inbox was more or less clear now. She'd achieved this by deleting anything older than a week and ruthlessly going through what was left. It was like coming back to a new job again. She had hoped that this would be the one place where she was still the bright and competent person she had been before she got pregnant. Instead, she felt ill-informed and at sea. It seemed so unfair that Louie had ruined this for her as well.

She glanced at the pile of reading that was on one side of her desk. The folders that leaned against the windowsill were all familiar, but she couldn't remember a single thing that was in them. But in the lab, where she was easing herself back into it by helping one of the PhD students with a DNA prep, the pipette had fitted back into her palm as though there was a groove ready for it. There must be a separate muscle memory that childbearing couldn't touch.

A colleague had said, 'Don't worry, it'll come back... well, most of it will anyway. For the rest there's Post-its.'

Yamuna had laughed at the time, but the words were horrifyingly true. It was as though someone had found her short term memory files and deleted them all. She had suddenly become incapable of retaining any information. When had this happened? Why?

Her tea was cold. She grimaced and put the mug back down. Would things ever get back to the way they had been before Louie? Louie. She felt a twinge of guilt. She hadn't thought about Louie all afternoon. What kind of a mother was she that she could forget to think about him? She wondered if anyone else had noticed that she hadn't mentioned him unless someone asked. Did they think she was a cold bitch?

Perhaps she should call home and check how things were going. She pulled her phone out of her pocket. But Soma wouldn't answer the phone. She had been told to call if anything went wrong, but no one had instructed her to answer the phone and the girl wouldn't use her initiative like that. Even if she did answer the phone to someone, she wouldn't have been able to understand what was said anyway.

For a moment, Yamuna distracted herself by wondering how much English her nanny spoke.

She must understand something, surely? How could she not? She seemed fairly bright, if unusually subservient.

She had never heard Soma speak English though, apart from 'yes' and 'no' when they were at the bank. As far as she was concerned, it didn't matter. Louie would learn Sinhalese from his nanny and they already seemed to understand each other well enough. Louie was happy with Soma. She didn't need to check on him. He would be happier with her than he'd ever been with his mother. Yamuna scowled and put the phone back in her pocket.

Chapter Eight

That Saturday, Sahan rang the doorbell, armed with a small bolt and screws. He knew from experience that Bim owned all manner of power tools, but had no idea how to use any of them. Louie's cot, with its pastel coloured bits of wood had baffled Bim. In the end, Sahan had built the cot. And the changing table. Bim had, however, installed the mobile above the cot. The pride on his face on achieving that had amused Sahan no end.

Yamuna answered the door, wearing an apron. 'Oh hi. You're early,' she said, gesturing him to come in. 'I'm in the middle of making Louie's food. Come on through.'

He slipped off his shoes and followed her into the kitchen. It was relatively quiet downstairs. No singing today. 'Where's... Louie?' he said.

'He's upstairs, having his nappy changed.' She lifted the lid on one of the pots. The cloud of steam that rose up smelled of carrots.

'I'll go up and say hello.' Had that come out too eager? Would Yamuna notice? Soma had drifted into his thoughts a lot in the past few days. It puzzled him. He was often bothered by his feelings towards women he didn't know. The revulsion that arose was nothing to do with them and everything to do with Tamsin. The only women he could deal with were the ones he'd known for a long time or in a completely platonic context – Yamuna, Cara, Deepthi from work, all were fine. But strangers always made him want to run and hide. Yet Soma crept into his thoughts quietly, when he was least expecting it. The need to see her again was like a persistent hum – he wasn't aware of it most of the time, but when he noticed it, it felt like it had always been there.

Yamuna switched the hob off with a deft flick. 'I'll come up with you,' she said. 'I can show you where the bolt needs to go.'

As they mounted the stairs, the sound of Louie's giggles floated down. Such an infectious sound. It made Sahan smile. He reached the landing and through the open door to the nursery, he saw Soma lean over and blow a raspberry on Louie's tummy, making him giggle again. Neither Soma nor the baby had noticed them.

'Soma. We're going into your room a minute,' said Yamuna. 'Sahan is going to install a lock for you.'

Soma looked round. Her gaze met Sahan's for a moment. Her eyes grew bigger. She flushed and looked away. Sahan felt a tug of… something. How odd. Perhaps it was some sort of residual affection from how he felt about Louie.

'I think it should go into the frame, shouldn't it?' Yamuna said.

Sahan focused. The bolt. That was why he was here. He checked the door frame, which was a plain, solid affair. 'Oh yes. That should be pretty easy to do. I'll need the power screwdriver, if you can find it.' He went into the room, pulled the bits out of his pocket and laid them on the bed. He took a quick look around. The room was small and, even to him, not very homely. There were no pictures on the walls, although there were a couple of hooks. The bed was made and the curtains tied back. Apart from a hot water bottle on top of the small chest of drawers, there was nothing to show that the room belonged to someone. It was as though Soma was expecting merely to pass through. Or perhaps, it occurred to him suddenly, she simply didn't have anything to put out.

He turned just as she came out of Louie's room, carrying Louie on her hip. Now that she was no longer swamped in a huge shapeless thing, he could see that she was slim and angular, almost boyish in her lack of a chest. She wore no jewellery. With her hair that was no more than a thin fuzz of black on her scalp, she should look like a boy, but she didn't. She looked beautiful. Her neck, he noticed, was slender and smooth. Yamuna had mentioned that Soma was around twenty-five, but she looked younger. She blushed again when she spotted him looking at her.

'I'm... er... putting a bolt on the door,' he said, unnecessarily.

'That's very kind, sir.' She didn't look at him. 'I... should take baby downstairs.' She lifted her gaze for a second to meet his and dropped it again as though she'd been scalded.

'Right. Okay.' His conversation skills seemed to have deserted him.

At the top of the stairs, she paused. Looking over her shoulder, she said, 'I have never had a room that I can lock before.' She smiled and Sahan's world tilted. A momentary elation flooded through him and he felt suddenly weak, as though the sight of her had sapped him.

He watched her go down the stairs. What was that all about? He'd met girls before. Why did he feel so strongly about this one?

There was a murmur of conversation on the landing below and Yamuna arrived with the power screwdriver. It took Sahan less than five minutes to install the little bolt. Remembering what Soma had said, he wished he'd gone for something bigger now. Maybe one of those that had a chain. Something that said 'I'll keep you safe' more clearly.

'Thank you so much, Sahan. I don't know what we'd do without you,' said Yamuna, when she came to inspect his handiwork. 'Bim and I are both so rubbish with practical things.'

He grinned at her. 'Any time,' he said. 'Besides, you look after me so much. It's the least I can do.'

She gave him a smile that made her look old. It occurred to him that she looked really tired. The Yamuna he had known before had been quick to laugh. This woman had bags under her eyes so deep that they looked like black rings. Her mouth pinched down at the corners. 'Yamuna,' he said. 'Are you okay? You look... tired.'

Yamuna stared at him. Her mouth trembled. For a moment he thought she was going to cry. Or pass out. He took a step towards her. She sighed. 'I'm fine. Tired, yes. But that's only to be expected, right?'

He put a hand on her arm. Yamuna had been around during his childhood, a grown-up cousin who drifted into his view at holidays, weddings and funerals and then drifted away again. She'd found out she was to marry Bim roughly around the same time as Sahan had decided he was going to university in England. It was knowing that they would be in the same neighbourhood that had brought them together. They had no other relatives in the UK and his father's friends only knew people in London, which was two hundred and fifty miles away.

When they got to know each other, they surprised themselves by getting along rather well. She had kept him from going insane with homesickness when he first arrived. He suspected he might have fulfilled a similar role for her. 'How's being back at work?'

'It's okay. Not bad. It's nice to be using my brain again.' She lifted her chin, as though daring him to argue.

'Yes, it must be,' he said, taken aback.

'Anyway, enough about me. How are you getting on with your studies?' Yamuna asked as she took the screwdriver off him and headed downstairs. 'It's your final year. You need to work hard. It's the key to your whole future.'

'I know that.' Sahan followed her down the stairs. Something was bothering Yamuna. He didn't consider himself to be particularly observant, but if even he'd noticed, it must be something big. 'Akki, are you sure you're okay? You sound...'

'What, Sahan? Tired? Well, are you surprised? I told you, I've gone back to work.'

'I didn't mean—' He held up his hands. 'I'm sorry. I didn't mean to upset you.'

Yamuna gave him a hard stare. 'No. I suppose not. I'm sorry I snapped. I'm just tired. There's nothing else. Come on. Let me get you a tea.'

When they got to the kitchen, Soma was already down there feeding Louie something mushy and orange with a plastic spoon. She looked up, saw Sahan and hurriedly looked away, her focus apparently wholly on Louie.

Standing next to Yamuna, Sahan watched Soma's back as she fed the baby. Her movements were fluid and graceful. Her head was framed by soft black fuzz from where Yamuna had shaved it. He had a sudden urge to touch it. He told himself to get a grip. This was a servant.

He had barely noticed the servants at home, and if he had, it was certainly not with any sense of attraction. They weren't part of his world in that way.

Yamuna started talking to him again, this time about job prospects. He should listen to her. But all he could do was watch Soma's slender fingers as she wiped Louie's face. Her back was stiff and radiated wariness. He hoped it wasn't him she was scared of.

'Oh, I forgot. I saw some job adverts that might be of interest to you,' said Yamuna. 'Let's go to the study and I'll show you.'

He reluctantly followed her out. Soma didn't turn around to see him go, but he could see her shoulders drop a fraction.

In the study, Yamuna pulled up some bookmarked pages on the computer. He read over her shoulder, ready to politely point out that this wasn't the sort of job he was looking for, but to his surprise, they were actually relevant.

'That's quite far north,' he pointed out. 'Although the work looks really interesting.'

'Not everything needs to be in the south-east,' said Yamuna. 'Besides, the competition will be less and you'll be able to afford more for the salary. Don't discount places that are out of the way.'

Which was a fair point. He skimmed through it again. 'Can you email that to me?'

Yamuna did so, all the while chatting about what he wanted to do with his degree. In reality, he had no idea. He had enjoyed his project work on process engineering, maybe he could go into that. He was fairly sure he didn't want to do a higher degree, which his parents were hinting they would like. To his surprise, Yamuna agreed with his view that he was better off getting a job.

'Having a PhD is nice, but you're better off getting some work experience first,' she said. 'Work out what you're really interested in and then get a masters or a PhD that takes you closer to where you want to be.'

They discussed possible careers. It was easier to focus when Soma was not around, but Sahan could still feel her presence, as though he had a homing dish in his gut that kept pulling him towards her wherever she was in the house. It was puzzling and frightening and exciting at the same time.

Later on, as he walked home, he tried to work out what it was that pulled at him. There was something about the way she made herself as small as possible, as though she didn't want people to notice her. It must be bringing out the big brother in him. He had always felt protective towards his sister and even towards Deepthi at work. Yes. That must be it. Of course, she was a servant at his cousin's house, so he couldn't exactly hang out with her, but maybe he could help her in some way. What had Cara said about paying it forward? He could do that. Help Soma in some way. That would be paying it forward. Nothing more.

Chapter Nine

Even in the few weeks that she'd been there, Soma had grown to love the park. There was precious little of nature to be found in front of the house. Even the back garden was mostly paved and host to a collection of plant pots with nothing growing in them. On the street, the trees dotted along the pavement were bare. The trees in the park had buds that hadn't become leaves yet, but there were bushes and shrubs that were green. Shoots were starting to poke through the soil in the flowerbeds. None of it looked anything like the aggressive fertility of home, but somehow it felt soothing, as though it proved that nature was still there, struggling to be noticed against all the things that had been built by people.

Louie was awake. She pushed the hood of the pram down so that he could look at the sky and poor, bare trees. People in the street all seemed to nod and say hello to each other. This terrified her, so she kept her eyes down. When she was with Louie, people paid more attention to the pram than to the person behind it. She liked that. Being noticed was bad.

They passed the playground, busy with bundled up children. 'When you're bigger,' she told Louie softly, 'I'll teach you to climb and I'll push you on that swing.'

Louie's big brown eyes focused onto her face. He was getting that glazed stare that meant he was probably going to nod off soon. If he did, she would walk over to one of the quieter benches, away from the playground and the young women who stared at their phones whilst the children fell over each other in the sand pit. Soma wondered if those women were the mothers, or whether, like her, they were watching someone else's baby grow up.

She pushed the pram round the route she always took, chatting to Louie quietly, so that people didn't notice that she wasn't speaking their language. As Louie's eyes started to drift closed, she talked to him about his mother's cousin. His uncle. Louie was the only person she could confide in without fear. Louie couldn't tell anyone if he tried. 'He has really thick hair,' she told him. 'Like Sanath Gunathilake when he was young. Or Shah Rukh Khan. And these amazing eyes. When you grow up, I hope you're as handsome as he is.'

Louie's eyes finally stayed shut. His head lolled to the side, his little mouth turned up into an adorable pout. Soma smiled. 'You're very handsome already,' she said.

Sahan had replaced the constant worries as her favourite thing to think about. Their brief meetings had been replayed in her mind, over and over, to the point where she was no longer sure whether she'd imagined it. Just thinking of him made her stomach flutter in a way she'd never experienced before. It was a good way to distract herself from the worries that gnawed at her. This helped. She even had the odd night where she wasn't plagued by the relentless nightmares. There was precious little else to make her happy, so she clung to her daydream.

There was an empty bench ahead. It was a nice thing to have benches dotted along in this place. It was even nicer that there weren't beggars stretched out on them, like there would have been at home. Soma parked Louie's pram by the bench, carefully putting on the brake, as she'd been shown, and sat down. Not for the first time, she wished she had a magazine to read, but where would she find a Sinhalese magazine here? Instead, she took out a children's book and tried to read it, in halting English, to herself. She had seen Yamuna read this to Louie and the baby seemed to like it. He would be able to ask for it soon, so being able to read it would be a useful thing. If she was going to live in England, she should really get better at the language. If only she could watch some children's television with Louie, she was sure it would help them both. But Louie wasn't allowed television.

Maybe she could get a television herself. Madam had shown her some shops that sold second-hand things. She was sure she had seen a small TV in one of them. Now that she had money, she might be able to afford it. Was she allowed one, though? She'd ask Madam the next time she had the opportunity.

She was busy frowning over the unfamiliar words when someone approached and stopped next to her. Her heart sped up. Hairs rose on her back of her neck. A stranger? What if they tried to talk to her? She kept her eyes down and hoped the person would carry on walking. She hooked her foot around the wheel of Louie's pram, in case this stranger was a baby thief.

'Are you Soma? Who works for Mrs Gamage?' A male voice said, in Sinhalese.

Soma jumped and looked up. The face that she'd been imagining over the past few days looked down at her. Her heart leapt to her throat and hammered at it. He was real. He was standing next to her, as though she'd conjured him up. She didn't know where to look. She didn't know if she was happy or scared.

'Do you mind if I join you?' He sat down next to her, not too close.

She couldn't look at him, in case her face betrayed that she'd been thinking about him. People like her had no place thinking about people like him. It was all very well him being a way of distracting herself from the things that frightened her, but she didn't need him distracting her in real life as well. She looked straight ahead and said 'Sir.'

'Your name is Soma. Am I correct?'

'Yes sir.' She glanced at Louie and fussed with the edge of his blanket. Anything to avoid looking at him. Her heart galloped. She wasn't sure whether it was from fear or excitement.

'I'm Sahan,' he said. 'And you don't have to call me sir.'

She didn't reply. Her mind whirred. Should she be talking to him? What were the rules? Madam hadn't mentioned this sort of thing. What should she do? What should she do? She knew nothing about this man. Without thinking about it, she shrank back, huddling into her coat to make herself small.

'Don't worry,' said Sahan. 'I won't hurt you.'

At this, she risked a glance. He had a kind face. There was none of the hardness about the eyes that she'd come to recognize. He wasn't looking at her as though appraising her for value. He didn't mean her any harm, she could tell. 'I know,' she said.

'You can talk to me,' he told her. 'If you want to. It would be nice to speak Sinhala to someone my age. I... don't get to meet many people my own age who can. But I realise you're at work, so if you'd rather I went away, just say.'

Soma felt pinned to her seat. His being there was nerve shredding. It made her skin tingle and her pulse flutter in

94

panic. But the idea of his going away was suddenly too terrible.

'No,' she said, a little too quickly. 'No. Don't go.' She finally turned her face to look at him properly. In daylight, she could see the cheekbones, the long eyelashes, the eyes that were more brown than black. He was so beautiful. She could stare at him all day. 'Don't go.'

He smiled then, and the world brightened. He leaned forward, still facing the path. 'So, Soma, tell me about yourself. Where are you from?'

She was so enchanted, she nearly told him where she was really from. Luckily, she caught herself in time. 'Matara,' she said. Thankfully, the real Somavathi's home wasn't too far away from her own. She had been to Matara town a few times as a child and could talk about the place plausibly. So long as she didn't have to talk about the actual area Somavathi came from, she could get away with it.

'I'm from Colombo,' he said. Of course, he would be. Colombo was the big city. From what she'd gleaned from listening to Madam talking, she guessed that Sahan came from the more exclusive area of Colombo too.

She looked away. They sat in silence for a moment. Even under all the layers of clothing, her skin seemed to be extra aware on the side nearest him. It was all she could do not to shift away from him. She wished he would go away so she could stop feeling so awkward. At the same time, she didn't want him to leave her. She stole a sideways glance at him. He had his hands pressed between his knees and looked almost as tense as she was. Catching her looking at him, he smiled again. One of his teeth was slightly crooked. It was wonderful.

'So, how long have you been working for Yamuna and Bim?' he said.

'Six weeks.' Which was an age and not long all at the same time.

'Are you enjoying it? Are they kind to you?'

Madam was a little frightening at times, but she wasn't actually unkind. Sir was… she didn't really see him much. He was rarely home in the daytime and even if he was, he seemed to barely notice she existed. It was easy to avoid Sir. 'They are kind.'

Was she enjoying it? She looked at Louie, peacefully asleep. She loved him, she knew that already. Even if Mr and Mrs Gamage had not been nice people, she would have put up with it to be with Louie. 'I am happy.'

'I'm glad.'

Another silence.

'I saw you were reading,' said Sahan. 'Can you read English well?'

This made Soma giggle. 'I can read a little. Not enough to read a big book. But I will try to read to Louie. We can learn together.'

'I can teach you,' he said. He leaned towards her.

She looked at him properly then and her stomach flipped, making her catch her breath. He had kind eyes. He wouldn't hurt her. If he was teaching her to read… she would have to see him again. But what if someone saw them? Even though she knew there was nothing going on, Madam might think there was. That wouldn't be good.

'But, Madam—'

'Madam need not know,' said Sahan. 'You only come to the park when she's at work. I doubt Yamuna knows anyone here.' He looked around. 'We can meet there.' He pointed to a bench in a more secluded area. It would be less obvious, but still not exactly hidden. When he looked back to her, she felt her stomach flutter again.

It would just be him teaching her to read. He need never know that being near him made her feel this churn of panic and excitement. They could meet in the open, where nothing untoward could happen. Besides, if she wanted to stop meeting him, all she had to do was not leave the house. If he touched her, or tried to touch her, she would know to stop coming. She glanced sideways at him. He didn't look like a bad man.

Learning to read English would be so useful.

'Then I'd like that. Very much.' Feeling a rush of boldness, she added, 'Sahan.'

His smile widened when she said his name. They looked at each other and he seemed as lost in the moment as she was. Finally, he cleared his throat. 'So, let's have a look at your book, then.'

He moved a little closer, but thankfully, not close enough to touch her. With all her senses screaming, she tried to concentrate and slowly, began to read.

–

In order to supplement his income, Sahan worked a couple of nights a week as a waiter in Mr Ghosh's Indian restaurant. As he recovered from his encounter with Tamsin, he'd come to the conclusion that the strict confines within which he had been brought up meant that the real world was unnecessarily shocking when he met it. He needed to meet it on his terms, which meant breaking some of his father's norms, like getting a casual job.

When he was trying to find excuses to not go out on a Friday or Saturday, Nate had suggested he got a casual job, which would give him a handy excuse as well as providing extra income. Sahan had never even considered a part-time job before. His parents usually provided anything he needed. Besides, people who were waiters and shop assistants were poor and uneducated, weren't they? They were in Colombo. No middle class kid would ever do a job like that. Nate and Cara had soon disabused him of this notion. It turned out that a lot of his fellow students were waiters, shop assistants and factory workers in the summer holidays.

Applying for a job had been a learning curve. Not only did he have to get his head around the fact that there was nothing disreputable about having a low skilled job, he also found that he was being turned down for them. This shook his belief in himself even more. He has assumed that these sorts of jobs were there for him to take, if he'd ever wanted to. After all, he was smart and almost had a degree. The fact that he would need experience to be a waiter seemed preposterous. It wasn't exactly rocket science. When, finally, he had got this job at Mr Ghosh's restaurant, he had been pleased and dejected in equal measure.

He'd finished setting up the tables and leaned against the counter, flicking through the photos his sister Priyanka had sent him through WhatsApp. Neither he nor his sister were allowed on social media, lest they posted something that embarrassed their father or his political party. WhatsApp was the best they got. Priyanka had been to a birthday party of a mutual friend and the familiar faces smiling out of the photos made him ache for home.

'Who's that? The girlfriend?' said a girl's voice.

Sahan looked up to find Deepthi, Mr Ghosh's daughter, leaning on the other side of the counter, craning her neck to see his screen. Deepthi came by every so often to do the accounts for her father. She was seventeen, sharp and pretty, in a homely kind of way. She had looked at

Sahan coyly from under her eyelashes in the beginning, until he'd made a pointed comment about how much she reminded him of his baby sister. After that she'd given up flirting with him. Which was just as well because old man Ghosh would have sacked him on the spot if he thought Sahan had any designs on his daughter.

Sahan straightened up, putting some distance between them. 'No, my sister.'

'Oh, the famous baby sister. Let's see.'

He slid the phone across to her.

'She's cute,' Deepthi said. 'I thought she'd be younger.'

'She's the same age as you,' Sahan responded. He took the phone back and slipped it into his pocket. 'How's it going deciding which unis you want to apply to?'

'Oh you know. The olds want me to go to the local one. I want to go as far away as possible. The usual.' Deepthi waved away the discussion.

Mr Ghosh appeared from the kitchen. 'I don't pay you to stand around talking,' he said to Sahan.

Sahan looked across at the empty restaurant.

'Tha,' said Deepthi. 'You don't pay *me* at all.' She went over to stand next to her father.

His manner softened at once. 'Ah, but someday, all this will be yours.'

The phone on the bar rang and Sahan sprang to answer it. By the time he'd written down the takeaway order, father and daughter were sitting at one of the tables, looking over the receipts that Deepthi had logged.

Sahan took the order to the back. Deepthi was a nice kid, but if he wanted to keep this job, he had to make sure he kept out of her way.

It was only once she'd pulled into the garage that the exhaustion hit Yamuna. She looked out towards the door and felt the weight of her bones holding her down. Her hands slid off the steering wheel and she let them fall to the seat either side of her thighs. A few weeks of work and she was already exhausted; this wasn't a good sign. It was strange that she didn't feel so bad when she was at work. The skills were coming back to her, even if her ability to retain information wasn't. Conversations with colleagues had moved past questions about Louie and tended towards discussions about work, or even what was on telly, these days. She would have to start keeping an eye on what was on, just to keep up with it. It seemed years since she'd been able to laugh and joke like that. And she relished the feeling of competence, something she hadn't felt in a very long time. It was so nice to be *good* at something again. She looked back at the house. Louie would be waiting. She should go in.

It took counting to three and muttering 'go' to herself to get moving again. She hauled herself out of the car, rescued her bag from the back and trudged towards the house. When she opened the door, she heard Soma's voice, drifting down the stairs, chatting in baby Sinhalese with Louie.

What was wrong with her? She should be raring to go up to her son, not feeling a vague sense of dread. Perhaps it was because she was so tired. It was a shock to the system to have to go back to work. It would wear off. She hung up her coat, kicked off her shoes and made her way upstairs, picking up the pile of post on the way. She paused at a letter from the nanny agency. What now? Ripping the white envelope open, she found another cheap envelope inside. Stuck to it was a Post-it explaining that the letter was for Soma and had been sent to the agency via their Sri Lankan office. The girl had apparently not sent her new address to her people. Odd.

In the playroom, Louie was sitting on Soma's lap. He looked happy. He would have been fed and freshly changed.

'Look baby, Amma's here,' said Soma, pointing to Yamuna. 'Say hello.' She held his chubby little fist in her hand and waved it gently. Louie blew a spit bubble.

Yamuna smiled and wished she'd put a fleece over her work clothes before she'd come to see Louie. Still, baby drool was easy enough to wipe off. At least it wasn't milk or snot. Soma stood up, holding Louie to her, and carried him over to his mother.

'You have a letter.' Yamuna took Louie and handed Soma the envelope in exchange. 'Has he been okay?' She gave the boy a quick kiss on the cheek. He got spit on her. 'You know you can ask your family to write to you directly. We don't mind you getting letters.' She looked at Soma for the first time.

The girl was staring at the envelope and didn't reply.

'Soma?'

Soma stuffed the letter into a pocket and looked up. 'Yes, Madam. Let me tell you about Louie's day.' She launched into her report of the day, speaking fast as though afraid Yamuna would interrupt. 'I wrote it down in the book,' she said and darted towards the exercise book that Yamuna had bought for the purpose.

The idea was that Yamuna could look back over the week and see that everything was okay. Weirdly, even though she could barely remember what she'd said two minutes ago, Yamuna had perfect recall of every bite, nap and poop that Louie had taken in the last week.

'He slept a long time,' she said, when Soma had finished. With her, he never napped for more than forty minutes. She wondered what Soma did to him to drive him to somnolence.

'I took him for a walk in the park.'

A slight quirk in Soma's voice made Yamuna look up. 'You must have walked a long time.' She watched the girl carefully and noticed that she seemed a little flustered. She was probably wanting to go off and read her letter.

'No. Well, a bit,' Soma said. 'Whenever he looked like he was going to wake up, I walked more.' She moved away and started to pick up toys. 'He should be able to stay up for another hour now. If you want to play with him.'

'I'll be the judge of that.' Yamuna hitched Louie to her hip and marched down the stairs. He was her son. Who was Soma to tell her what he was ready for? She stormed into the kitchen and stopped. Louie blew another spit bubble and neatly dropped dribble down her collar. 'Ugh. Louie. Stop that.'

She found a sheet of kitchen towel and wiped his face and her neck. 'Don't do that, silly boy.' She looked around. What now? She had the baby. What did she do with him? She strapped him into his high chair. He grizzled at her.

'All right, all right.' She found him a toy and plonked it on the tray in front of him. This seemed to calm him down. Yamuna put the kettle on. She stood by the work surface and stared at the kettle. Her shoulders ached. It felt like a weight was pushing down on her. She bowed her head and tried not to cry.

Hesitant footsteps approached. Yamuna blinked hard to beat the tears back. In front of her the kettle started to boil.

Soma scuttled into her line of vision. 'Madam, let me get you your tea.'

Yamuna left the girl to make the cup of tea and went back to sit next to Louie. 'Thank you,' she said, without looking up. Perhaps she was being unkind in her dislike of Soma. After all, the girl had done nothing wrong. She watched Louie happily batting his toy and sighed.

Louie looked up, spotted Soma and gave her a gummy smile. A proper, spontaneous smile. She had never seen him look so pleased. How come he never did that with her? Clearly, her being back at work suited Louie too. So she'd made the right choice to leave the child-rearing to someone who was good at it and go back to work. That was a good thing. So why didn't it feel like it was?

–

For the rest of the evening, the letter in her pocket burned in Soma's consciousness as she tried to carry on as normal. Who was writing to her? Was someone coming to find Somavathi? Her resemblance to the real Somavathi was only passing. Now that her hair was gone, she looked even less like her. Anyone who knew the real Somavathi would never be fooled for a minute.

When, finally, Louie was asleep, she bolted the door to her room and sat on the bed. The letter had been sent via the agency. The familiar rough brown paper envelope and the stamps showing national monuments from Sri Lanka made her want to cry.

She stared at it for a long time, not wanting to tear apart this fragile new life she was building for herself. Finally, because it had to be done, she ripped the envelope open and pulled out a carefully folded piece of foolscap paper.

The letter was written in carefully rounded Sinhalese. It was from the dead girl's mother. It spoke of concern. Was she alright? The agency had said she was safe in her employer's house, but she hadn't written and the family were worried. Why did she not write? Why did she not wire money home, as she'd promised? What had happened to the girl they knew?

The words swam in front of her eyes, forcing her to stop reading. She put it down and wiped her eyes with the back of her hand.

Here was a girl who was loved. Someone who was being missed. While she herself would not be missed at all. Her mother might have grieved her disappearance once, but since the baby died... her mother barely noticed her. What little affection there was left had been poisoned by her stepfather. Slowly, she had lost her friends. By the time she ran away, she'd had very little to leave behind.

For one yearning moment, she wished she could see her mother. Not the dead eyed woman she was now, but how she had been... before. But all that was gone now. With one snap decision that morning on the beach, Soma had stolen a future; a whole life that was better than her own could ever have been. The real owner of that life was dead. But she hadn't stopped to think that there would be others who would be affected. Of course Somavathi's family would search for her. How stupid not to realise that.

She tried to read the letter again, but couldn't. Somewhere far away, a mother was searching for her daughter. At some point, they were going to find her. What happened then? How could she tell them that their daughter was dead? That she had stolen her identity? This poor woman thought her daughter was still alive. Someone else was living her daughter's life. For the first time Soma saw herself and what she had done as other people would. She was a monster.

She couldn't tell them the truth. Because once the secret was out... What then? They would surely tell the police and she would be sent to prison. Prison was preferable to home. All this – the life she'd built for herself, little Louie, the secret and much dreamed about visits to park to see Sahan – would be lost. Fear cut deeper than the cold outside. Her head pounded, making her ears buzz. The scars on her ribs throbbed. Soma curled herself into a ball and wept.

Later, much later, when she'd run out of tears, she sat up. Tears were Jaya's territory. She was Soma now. She had to think clearly. She read the letter again. In the words she read desperate worry. Fear. What could she do? Could she write to them, pretending to be Somavathi? She recoiled at the thought. Pretending to be Somavathi in front of people who knew nothing about her, like Madam and Sir, that was one thing. But to pretend to a dead girl's parents...to make them think she was still alive. That was wrong on a whole other level. No, she couldn't do that.

Could she send them money, like Somavathi would have done? She could. That might help assuage the guilt. But any contact was dangerous. It would give them more clues to follow, more chances to realise something was wrong. She was bound to slip up and raise suspicion.

The only way she could get away with what she'd done was to shut herself off from Somavathi's past.

Somavathi's mother didn't know she was dead and was clearly trying to reach her. When she didn't get a response, she would try harder. She might try to send someone out to look for her. It was a matter of time.

Soma folded the letter over and over, smaller and smaller until it didn't bend any more. Something was coming, but there was nothing she could do to stop it. If she had to run away again, she would do it. Until then, she just had to keep her head down and hope that they gave up. In the meantime, she would keep a bag packed, with some of her money safely tucked in it, so that she could get away at short notice. The idea of being alone in this strange country was terrifying, but it was better than what was waiting for her at home.

–

Yamuna woke up to the sound of a muffled scream. She leapt out of bed. Beside her, Bim sat up. 'What's going on?'

Yamuna's first thought was that something had happened to Louie. She flew up the stairs and into the baby's room. She flicked the light on. Louie lay in his cot, seemingly asleep. She leaned over and checked that Louie was breathing. He was. A wave of relief ran through her. Her heart slowed down a fraction.

Another shout came from the next room. There was a sharp knocking from the landing outside and Bim's voice said, 'Girl. What is wrong? Open this door.'

Yamuna rolled her eyes. Bim had forgotten Soma's name. She turned the light out in Louie's room and pulled the door to behind her.

There were no more screams, only the sound of sobbing. Bim stood on the landing, looking baffled. Yamuna put her hand on his arm and moved him out of the way so that she could tap on the door.

'Soma? What's the matter? Soma, open this door.'

Nothing happened. Yamuna frowned. Either something was wrong, or the girl was refusing to answer the door. Either way, she needed to know what was happening. She knocked louder. 'Soma. Open this door at once,' she commanded.

Footsteps shuffled to the door. The bolt slid back and Soma's tearful face appeared round the door.

'Are you alright?' said Yamuna, pushing the door back gently. She peered into the little room. The bedside lamp was on. There didn't seem to be anyone or anything unusual there. She looked back at the girl. Soma was standing at the foot of the bed. She was pale and her eyes were red. She was twisting the fabric of her nightie in her fists and her hands were shaking.

'I'm sorry Madam,' Soma said. 'I... had a bad dream.'

Yamuna remembered the letter. Perhaps it was that which had caused all this. She drew back and gestured to Bim that things were okay. Turning back to Soma, she said, as kindly as she could, 'Is everything okay at home? You had a letter.'

'Y... yes, Madam. That... I... it was just a bad dream, Madam. I didn't mean to wake you.' Soma bowed her head. Not for the first time, Yamuna was amazed at how young she looked. She suddenly felt sorry for her. Soma was capable and good with Louie, so Yamuna had assumed that she was dealing with everything with equal calm. But moving to another country was a big deal. Soma never talked about her family, but she must be missing home.

'But you're okay?' said Yamuna. When the girl nodded, she said, 'Would you like to get a cup of milk or something? I can come downstairs with you.'

'No Madam. I'm fine, Madam. I'll just go back to bed…'

Yamuna sighed. 'Okay.' She stepped backwards out of the room. 'You know you're safe here.'

'Yes Madam.'

Yamuna stood at the top of the landing and listened as Soma shut the door and slid the small bolt across. She yawned. At least Louie had slept through it. Yamuna shrugged and went back to bed.

Soma pulled the covers up to her chin and lay there with the light on. She heard Madam go downstairs and back into her bedroom. She kept still, listening to the sounds of the house, for hours afterwards. Too frightened of her dreams to close her eyes.

Chapter Ten

Yamuna checked her hair again and fluffed it up with her fingertips. It framed her face nicely, but it didn't make her look any less tired. That sense of release she'd felt when she first started back at work had fizzled away now and the tiredness had settled deep into her bones. Entertaining Bim's friends was the last thing she felt like doing. This dinner party was important to Bim. She hoped the food was up to standard. She hauled herself to her feet. She should check on things.

Bim wasn't home yet. Upstairs, she could hear Soma singing an old lullaby to Louie, getting him ready for bed. Ordinarily, she would have gone up at bath time. Louie was always at his most amenable when he was in the bath. Yamuna liked to sit next to the bath and talk to him. He mostly ignored her, but she didn't mind. It gave her a chance to feel as though she was being a proper mother, like she was pretending to be. Plus, there was a chance to check that he had no funny rashes or bruises on him. She lived in fear of him catching some scary illness and her not noticing.

This evening, she had so much to do that she'd asked Soma to handle bath time. If the girl was surprised at the request, she didn't show it, merely said 'yes, Madam' and took wriggling Louie from his mother. She never seemed to mind being asked to do extra work. Yamuna knew she should be grateful, but really, it niggled at her. Was it normal to be so subservient? Or did Soma take Louie so readily because she thought he had a rubbish mother?

She rubbed her temples. Before Louis, she had been strong and capable. Now, she kept second-guessing herself all the time, feeling like a fraud. It was as though Louie, growing inside her, had drained her bones of confidence as well as calcium. She knew she wasn't made for motherhood, but it was unacceptable to say that. She had to keep pretending she was capable, even if she knew she wasn't.

At least Soma was capable of looking after Louis. More than capable, she was actually good at childcare in a way that Yamuna could never be. She could trust the girl to do what was best for him.

Yamuna got herself a glass of water and considered the servants they'd had at home. She had grown up with them around and was close to them. Close enough to remember to take them individual presents and go and catch up with their news whenever she went back home. Had they been so subservient towards her mother as Soma was to her? She couldn't remember. Perhaps they were. Perhaps she was comparing Soma's attitude to that of the agency nannies she'd hired from time to time. To them it was just a job. Soma at least cared. She finished her water and turned on the oven.

The kitchen smelled reassuringly spicy. One of the things that Bim had often commented on when they'd first got married was her cooking. She had been quite adventurous with it in the early days, but since Louie had come along, she'd let things slide a bit. The same meals appeared every other week. Bim liked to have proper Sri Lankan food at least once a week, which meant that Sunday mornings were a frenzy of cooking. Sometimes, if they had a busy weekend, she would order the food from the takeaway. Bim never criticised as such, but his quiet 'oh, has it been a very bad week? Is there anything I can do to help?' always made her feel bad enough to make the effort the week after.

The guests they were having that evening were Sri Lankan, but Bim had warned her that the wife didn't particularly like hot food, so Yamuna had cooked things herself, so that the curries were mild. It had taken up most of her Sunday to cook and freeze it all. Luckily, Soma had helped with some of the preparation, while Louie had cheerfully messed around with potato peel.

Yamuna dipped a spoon into the chicken curry and tested it. It really didn't taste right without any chillies in it. Both she and Bim liked their food fiery. She frowned. She couldn't make the dishes any hotter, but there had to be something she could put on the table to help alleviate the problem... She stood at the work surface, tapping her fingernail on the edge, mentally scanning through her cupboards. Chilli sauce. She had some chilli sauce somewhere. And chutney. The proper stuff from home, not the sweet pale thing from Tesco. She sped around the kitchen, taking down jars. There was some coconut in the freezer. Scraping fresh coconut was such a faff that Yamuna only did it a couple of times a year. She'd done a load in the weeks running up to Louie's birth. Did she have enough time to defrost it and mix it up into a sambal?

She was standing in front of the microwave, anxiously watching the coconut defrosting, when Bim arrived.

'Hello, hello,' he said. 'I got your text. I have picked up wine.'

She listened for any tone of disapproval in his voice and found none. She felt she shouldn't disturb him with domestic things. Her mother had always dealt with the running of the house, while her father brought in the money. Things were simpler in those days. As a woman who also held down a job, which bits was she supposed to let go of? What did Bim expect her to do?

He had never found fault with things, apart from once suggesting that he would really like to have curry and rice at the weekends because his meals were so inconsistent during the week. It was hard to tell with Bim if he was displeased. He was always so impassive. There must be things that knocked his equilibrium, but she was yet to find out what they were. Maybe she never would.

Bim stood next to her and pulled bottles out of a Waitrose bag. 'He's quite interested in wines, I think,' he said. 'I didn't want to put him off with any cheap stuff.'

Yamuna knew nothing about wine, but she assumed that expensive was good. She paused the microwave to run a fork through the coconut. There were still ice crystals in the middle. She mixed it up and put it back in.

'Hopefully,' Bim continued, 'he will want to go into partnership with me and invest. It's a high-risk venture, but I think the guys who run the company are onto something. I'm almost tempted to put the full amount in myself.' He made a balancing motion with his hands. 'It is a lot, though.'

Yamuna nodded, not taking her eyes off the microwave. She didn't really understand how Bim chose which companies he invested in. He seemed to rely on a magic mix of reading a lot of paperwork, interviewing people and taking a wild guess. Clearly, Bim was good at it and that was all that mattered.

Ah. That looked done now. She opened the microwave again and took out the warm coconut.

'I mentioned about the chillies?' said Bim, glancing at the bowl.

'Yes. The food is all mild. I thought I'd make something hot for everyone else.'

'Good thinking.' He smiled. He had a kind face when he smiled. For an instant, she had his full attention. She didn't often see him like that. He was usually only half there, as though the major part of his mind was hiding away, reading stock market analyses. 'You look very nice,' he said.

She felt a flush of warmth in her face. A burst of shyness. How ridiculous to feel shy around a man she'd had sex with. They had a child together. But all that was… it was what you did when you were married and wanted to start a family. He didn't often look at her. Really look at her, as though he noticed. When he did, she wondered if he liked what he saw.

'I like the new hair.' He raised his hand half way, as though to touch it, then lowered it. 'Very nice.' He looked down at the wine bottles. With that, he was off again. 'I think I'll put these on the side table, ready to open when they come. Unless you want a glass now? Would you like one?'

'No. I'm fine, thank you.' While he went into the dining room with the wine, she threw the coconut in a bowl and pushed in the onions that she'd diced a few minutes earlier. Adding chilli powder, she squeezed in half a lime. Rather than have to get the food processor out, she quickly washed her hands and started to mix it with her fingers.

The doorbell rang. Yamuna cursed under her breath. They were early and she was up to her wrist in coconut sambal.

Bim popped his head into the kitchen. Seeing her holding the mixing bowl, he said, 'I'll let them in.' He withdrew, then reappeared. 'Don't worry. It'll be proof positive that you made all the food yourself.' He gave her another rare smile and disappeared again.

Yamuna stopped mixing and allowed herself a moment to accept her husband's approval. Good. At least she was good for something. She had borne him a son that she couldn't look after, but at least she could still cook a meal good enough to impress potential business partners.

Not for the first time, she wondered if Bim had ever really wanted to get married. He hadn't pretended that he could give her hearts and flowers, but then she hadn't been bothered. Since she had failed to find a love marriage for herself, an arranged marriage was a sensible option. Getting married was a chance to get away from home and get on. A practical arrangement to avoid being left alone in her old age. She thought about her single colleagues at work who desperately haunted dating websites, and smiled grimly. The dream of a happy ever after was the same all over the world. She had a man who respected her, a comfortable home and a child. She wasn't going to be alone. Perhaps she should be content with that.

Yamuna sighed and returned to her mixing, rubbing the ingredients together until they meshed into one.

—

The smell of curry wafted up the stairwell. Soma picked up the portable unit from the baby monitor and went to the top of the stairs. There was the sound of muted conversation from the dining room. She wondered if she should go downstairs. Madam had said that she would leave something in the pans for her. The idea of real food was appealing. Madam was a good cook and the food she made during the week was nice, but it wasn't the same as proper food from home. On weekends, when Soma and Louie spent time in the kitchen with Madam, Soma helped with the chopping and peeling. She watched and she learned. She had thought she knew how to cook, but now she realised that there was a world of food she knew nothing about. Even the curries – there were more types of curry than the three she could make.

Heading downstairs, she paused again before stepping out into the ground floor landing. The door to the dining room was shut. People were talking. It seemed they were still eating. Soma tiptoed past the door and into the kitchen. She lifted the lids and looked into the pots on the stove. Her stomach growled. She got a plate out of the cupboard and dished herself up a decent portion. When she heated it up and tasted it, it seemed to be totally bland. She checked for the chilli sauce, but couldn't find it. With a sigh, she sat at the table to eat a meal that smelled like heaven, but fell short.

She had only just started eating when the doorbell rang. Someone answered it. Soma carried on eating. The door to the kitchen opened and Madam came in, with a thin, rat faced man. She handed him a plate. 'Help yourself to the food,' she said. 'You'll need this.' She put the bottle of chilli sauce on the table.

Soma tensed. Was this man going to come and eat his meal in here now? As always, strange men, especially Sri Lankan ones, made her chest constrict in fear. Sahan didn't, but then he wasn't exactly a stranger any more. She started to eat faster. She could go and sit in her room after she'd eaten.

Madam paused on her way out. 'Is Louie okay?'

Soma nodded towards the baby monitor, which was sitting on the side. 'He went to sleep without a fuss.'

Madam nodded and turned back to the man. 'When you've finished, you can stay here in the kitchen until we're done, or go back to the car. Up to you.' Her eyes flicked to Soma and back. 'We are in the next room.'

It sounded like warning. To whom? Was she warning the man not to hassle Soma? Or was she warning Soma?

'Thank you, Madam.' The man's smile made Soma want to run and hide. There was something about him that tripped alarm bells in the animal part of her brain. She focused on her plate.

'I'm Kemasiri,' said the man. He came over to stand near the table, next to her; too close. The smell of fresh cigarette smoke came with him. 'I'm Mr Perera's driver.'

Soma did not reply. She had a sudden image of a glowing cigarette tip, held between rough fingers, inches from her face. Her throat clenched, making it hard to swallow.

'What's your name?'

She could *feel* him looking at her. Her skin prickled. She knew that feeling. She reminded herself that she wasn't trapped here. She could go upstairs and lock her door. If he touched her, she could call out and Madam would come. She wasn't poor, frightened Jaya now. She was Soma. She could handle this.

Kemasiri picked up a plate, moved over to the pans and served himself some food. Now that he wasn't leaning over her, she felt better. She had to get a grip. Her stepfather couldn't follow her here. She couldn't carry on being frightened of strangers or cigarettes for the rest of her life. She had to let it go.

'You are Somavathi, aren't you?'

Soma jumped. What? How did he know? The letters sprang into her mind. What did he know?

Kemasiri was watching her. She said nothing.

'Where are you from Somavathi?'

'Galaga—' she started to give her real home town without thinking, then remembered that Somavathi wasn't from there. 'Matara.' She glanced up to see if he'd noticed her slip.

His eyes narrowed. He'd noticed. 'Which is it then?' he said. 'Matara or somewhere else?'

'Matara,' she said, quickly. Too quickly. She saw the quirk in his eyebrows and realised immediately that she'd made the wrong choice. He had spotted something was amiss.

'Oh really? I know it well. Where did you live exactly?'

No! She hadn't considered the possibility of him knowing the place. She would have been safer talking about a place she actually knew.

'I have family there, you know,' he continued.

Fear ripped down her spine. Had he met the real Somavathi? She sneaked a glance at him. He was watching her from across the room, his lips pressed together in a strange half smile.

'Really?' she managed. Her plate was still half full, but her appetite had gone.

'You might know my brother,' he said, slowly. 'He runs the furniture shop next to the Cooperative. Big, fat man. Bald.'

He was watching her. Oh god, she should answer. It sounded like the sort of person everyone knew. 'Uh… yes. I remember him.'

There was a flare of something sharp in his expression. 'Yes. He is very… memorable.' Kemasiri nodded.

She couldn't stay here. If she continued to talk to this man, it was only a matter of time before he asked her a question she couldn't bluff her way out of. She walked over to the bin and started to scrape the remainder of her meal into it.

'Ah, you haven't finished already?' said Kemasiri. He put his own plate in the microwave. 'You'll waste away if you don't eat properly.'

'I… I'm not that hungry. And I have to go and check on baby.' She washed her hands, rinsed her plate and put it next to the dishwasher. Madam didn't like her to stack the dishwasher.

She turned to find Kemasiri standing next to her. She gasped.

'I'm sorry,' he said. He smelled of cigarettes and curry. 'Did I frighten you? I didn't mean to. Please, stay and chat.' He took a step back. 'It's not often I meet someone from near home. It would be nice to… talk.'

Soma backed away. 'I'm very sorry.' She snatched up the baby monitor. 'I have to go and check on baby. Enjoy the meal. It's very nice.' With that, she fled the room.

When she got into her own bedroom, she pulled the bolt across and, for the first time in weeks, jammed the chair against the door handle. Had she given herself away? How had he known who she was? Had Soma's friends been in touch with him, hoping he could find her? She sat on her bed, arms wrapped around her knees and tried to stop shaking.

Chapter Eleven

Sahan leaned his elbows against the counter, thinking about Soma. Her English was coming along nicely. She was still hesitant to speak, but she could understand quite well. When she got it wrong, she would lower her eyes and bite her lip. The thought of it made him smile. A lot of things about her made him smile. Even the way she said his name. Especially the way she said his name. *Sahan*, like it was meant to be said. He realised that very few people pronounced his name properly in England. Most people called him Sahaaan, with extra vowels at the end. The only person who said it properly, who wasn't family, was Soma.

He felt a flare of guilt at the thought of his family. They wouldn't like his hanging around with Soma – they would worry about him falling in love and wanting to marry her. Soma was completely unsuitable for him. There were rules about that sort of thing. He had to marry someone from the right sort of background – upper middle class, same caste, ideally Buddhist too. These 'rules' went deeper than edicts about social media. They were so fundamental that Sahan had never bothered to question them. They were within the bedrock of his parents' world view. To break them would be to say he didn't care about them – which was something he would never do.

He wasn't actually doing anything wrong, was he? All he was doing was teaching her to read and helping her with her English. That was a kind and altruistic thing to do. Paying it forward, like Cara had said. He was helping Soma better herself. That was all. 'Hey, Sahan, take over the takeaway orders, will you.' His colleague's voice snapped him back into the real world.

There was a new takeaway driver leaning against the back door, waiting for the next order. A quick glance told Sahan that the man wasn't Indian, or Pakistani, but Sri Lankan. He couldn't tell how he knew. He just knew. The driver looked him up and down and grinned.

'I'm Kemasiri,' he said, nodding to Sahan.

'Sahan.'

'Sri Lanka?'

'Yes.'

They looked at each other. Sahan took in the cheap trousers, the hair smoothed back with oil, the discoloured teeth and immediately assigned Kemasiri to a social class below his own. This was not the sort of man he would talk to back at home. A driver or a gardener or something.

He caught his train of thought just in time. He was doing it again. At some point in their friendship, Cara had told him that he was a snob. It was something he'd absorbed from the people around him at home and it had been there for so long, it was an innate part of him. He was trying to change, but it was hard work. He had to remember that things were different here. Here, sons of doctors and lawyers mingled with children of cooks and shopkeepers and cleaners. Being poor didn't automatically make someone stupid. Nate's dad worked in a canning factory and Nate was going to be a doctor. Here, Sahan was a student who worked as a waiter. Who was he to dismiss this guy as 'just a driver'? He gave the man a polite smile.

'Good to meet you,' he said. 'I'll catch up with you later, yeah?'

Kemasiri moved his head to acknowledge him – something partway between a nod and a shake of the head. It was a particularly Sri Lankan gesture that Sahan hadn't seen since he'd left home. Seeing it now, against the backdrop of his workplace unnerved him, as though the balance of the world was slightly off. He ignored the feeling and went back out to work.

They didn't meet again until Sahan took his break. He sat on a stool at the back of the kitchen and tucked into his thali, plate balanced on the edge of a counter. Indian restaurant food wasn't what he considered to be real curry, but it would do. He'd got used to the heavier flavours now. Besides, it was free.

Kemasiri came in, bringing the smoke from his last cigarette with him. He leaned his elbows on the surface next to Sahan and started talking. Sahan, still eating, made listening noises and nodded.

He learned that when Kemasiri wasn't working at the restaurant, he was a personal driver for a businessman of some description. 'I only work here once a week,' he said. 'When my boss doesn't need me.'

Sahan nodded, glad that his meal relieved him of having to think of a response. He got the distinct impression that Kemasiri didn't have many people to talk to.

'Heh,' said Kemasiri. 'His wife thinks he's away on business, visiting one of his companies down south. Really, he's got a mistress out in Goole. I drop him off and then get the night off. So I work here.'

'Aren't you tempted to actually have a night off?'

'What would I do all evening? I have a room above the boss's garage. I can't go there. There's nothing else for me to do, so I earn some money.' He made a sign for cash with his fingers. 'How about you, son? What do you do when you're not working in this place?' Kemasiri looked around him with apparent disdain. He was small man, with a ferret like intensity to his eyes. Sahan felt a twist of dislike. He told himself it was merely his class snobbery getting the better of him again.

Sahan shifted in his seat. 'I'm a student,' he said. 'At the university.'

Kemasiri sniffed. 'Oh. One of those. Very fancy.'

Yes. One of those. Sahan didn't bother to respond. Snobbery, it seemed, could cut both ways. The chip on Kemasiri's shoulder was nothing to do with him. He wasn't going to apologize for being middle class. He looked down at his plate and wondered if he really wanted any more. The quicker he finished, the sooner he could get away.

'So what are you doing working in this place?'

'Earning some extra money. Same as you.'

Kemasiri laughed. 'Underneath the polish, we're all the same, eh, son?'

The use of 'son' annoyed Sahan. It was as though the man was trying to establish superiority over him. Which was ridiculous. Okay, the man was older than him, but not by a whole generation. This guy was a driver. He probably worked for someone like Yamuna or Bim. Sahan's parents had drivers. He had spent most of his childhood being driven around by them. It wasn't snobbery on his own part, this guy was just rude. He made no response.

Kemasiri didn't seem to notice anything amiss. 'There aren't many Sri Lankans around this way,' he said, wistfully. 'Not like in London. Or even in Leeds. There's never anyone to talk to.' He nodded, as though agreeing with himself. 'There's the boss and a couple of guys he does business with.' A small smile. 'One of them has a new girl working for them.'

Sahan tensed. Was this guy talking about Soma? He had to be careful not to respond or let slip that he knew her. She was his cousin's maid. He couldn't mention her at all. To anyone.

'Pretty little thing,' Kemasiri continued, staring thoughtfully into space. 'Her haircut is a bit strange, but I suppose it's not a big thing. It's not like we have much choice of Sri Lankan women around here.' He gave Sahan a nudge, as though making him a co-conspirator.

When Sahan didn't reply, Kemasiri said, 'but servant girls aren't for the likes of you, eh?'

Sahan picked up his plate with the remainder of his meal. 'I have to go,' he said. 'I've finished my break.'

He escaped to front of house, leaving Kemasiri leaning against the counter.

As he prepared a drinks order, he wondered at how strongly he felt about what Kemasiri had said. What if he was talking about Soma? Sahan really didn't like the way Kemasiri talked about her as though she was a target for his romantic aspirations. Kemasiri didn't like her, clearly. He didn't even know her. He had met her once and was interested because there was no one else. Soma wouldn't be interested anyway. Would she?

He picked up the nozzle to dispense the soft drinks. Kemasiri was the same social class as Soma... maybe she would be interested. The idea made Sahan's dinner churn inside him. Cola overflowed from the glass. 'Oh. Shoot.' He put the nozzle back in its place and found a cloth to mop up the tray. Mr Ghosh gave him a stern glance as he went past.

Sahan tried to focus on his job. What Soma did in her spare time was no business of his. But the thought of her, biting her lip and looking up at Kemasiri made him feel a harsh churn of emotion. He tried to ignore it.

He would take care to avoid Kemasiri in future.

—

Louie stirred in his cot. Soma, who had come to check on him, stood and watched him by the blue glow of the nightlight. He was so adorable when he was asleep. He was adorable when he was awake too. Hard work, but adorable. Louie's mouth sucked at an imaginary dummy for a few moments before he relaxed back into deep sleep, his mouth falling into an open pout.

She was suddenly reminded of another baby, blue tinged and still. Her half brother who died before he was born. When he died, something of her mother had died with him. Nothing had been the same since. If he had lived, would he have been adorable like Louie? Would her mother be like she'd been before? Would her stepfather have stayed sober enough to keep himself in check? Would Jaya's life have turned out differently?

Soma shook her head. She mustn't think of such things around Louie. She shouldn't think of that old life at all. It was gone. Left behind. She need never go back there again.

She tiptoed quietly out of the room, leaving the door ajar so that it didn't make a noise when Madam came up to check on Louie before she went bed.

In her own room, she closed the door and locked it. The bolt reminded her of Sahan. She liked that she could associate him with something that kept her safe. With a fingertip, she moved the bolt head so that it lay flat. There wasn't any need for it, really. No one had ever tried to come up here. This room was a safe place. So was this house. *That* man would never find her here. She thought of the letters. If he did find her, she would run away again. It was time she let go of her fear of him.

She sat on her bed and admired the television that Madam had helped her choose from the charity shop. It was small and chunky and the picture wasn't as clear as on the one downstairs, but it was the first television she'd ever owned. She watched it for a bit, flicking through the channels, trying to find something that could hold her attention. After a while, she gave up and turned it off. From under her pillow, she pulled out a book about some children called *The Famous Five* that Sahan had given her. It was slow going, but she was getting faster at reading now. The more she read and watched TV, the easier it was to understand people. What had originally sounded like babble with the odd word of sense, was now more intelligible. She still couldn't understand exactly what people were saying sometimes, but at least she knew what they were talking about.

Sahan tried to make her speak English when he was with her. Soma smiled. The mere thought of Sahan made her heart beat pick up. It was hard to believe that someone so clever and handsome chose to spend time with her. She didn't flatter herself that he thought of her as anything more than a little distraction. People like him didn't fall in love with people like her. Maybe he felt good about taking a poor girl under his wing and teaching her to read and speak English. Whatever the reason, she was grateful for it.

Madam would disapprove, of course. She would say that Soma was getting ideas above her station. No one would blame Sahan, obviously. He would just step away and get on with his life. In fact, he would move on in a few months' time anyway, when he finished his exams. Over time, their conversations had moved on from focusing on the reading. He'd told her about the jobs he was applying for. It all sounded impossibly exotic to her, London, Scotland, Sheffield, Teesside, places she'd heard of, but had trouble believing were real. When he got his job, he would leave and his project of teaching her to read would end. Every time he said he had an interview, she was torn between hope and despair.

He only told her these things because he had no one else to talk to, but sometimes they felt like intimacies. Little snippets of information that tied her ever closer to him bond by fragile bond. He sometimes asked about her life, but she tried not to tell him anything significant. The more he knew about her, the bigger the risk that he'd realise something wasn't right. Besides which, she would much rather hear about him.

Climbing into bed, she stretched her legs out under the duvet. She was getting used to this life now, even if she still slept with the light on. She would never get used to the cold and the cruel wind that cut through whatever she was wearing, but even that was getting better now that her hair was growing back. She touched her head and let the soft new hair tickle her fingers. It was unbelievable how lucky she had been: finding the handbag, the fact that Madam was a kind woman, her passing similarity to the real Soma… it was lucky that rich people never really looked at the people they employed. So, so, lucky.

Hopefully, her own family would believe she was dead. Even if her mother tried to look for her, her stepfather would sabotage any real search. She had nothing to link her to her old life any more. With every day, she became more and more used to being Soma. With her bank card and passport, it was now easier than ever for her to be Soma. Soon no one would ever remember that she had once had another name. Not even her.

Since Madam paid her wages into her bank account, Soma carefully saved most of it, apart from the odd wodge that she took out whenever she tagged along with Madam to the shops. This she stashed under her mattress, just in case. The numbers weren't huge, until you converted them into their worth in rupees. She was collecting up a nice little nest egg. The letter from the agency had said the job was for two years. When she had to go back, she would have enough money to rent a room in Colombo for some time. She could find a job there. She need not go back home ever again.

Through helping Madam to cook, she was learning how to make dishes she'd never heard of before. Her favourite was lasagne. She loved the way it went from a gloopy red mess and sheets of pasta to a bubbling, golden treat. If she observed and learned enough, she could prob-ably get work as a cook.

She'd gone from having nothing, to suddenly having prospects. She liked that. The big weakness in her plan was Sahan.

It was a risk, meeting him. An extra danger that might ruin everything. She couldn't get complacent. If he found out the truth about her, he would be furious. He would tell Madam and that would be the end of everything. She really should stop meeting him. It wouldn't take much –

changing the times she took Louie to the park would do. When she failed to turn up a few times, he was bound to give up and go away. She could end it, quietly, just as it had begun. He would probably end it soon enough anyway. But while it lasted… she smiled and wrapped her arms around across her chest… oh, while it lasted it was pure happiness.

Thinking about a life without her chats with him made the world lose colour. Even if it meant nothing to him, to her their meetings were a bright spot in the greyness. To be with him was to risk losing her hard-won happiness. But to destroy their relationship before it had even begun was to guarantee unhappiness. She thought of his voice and smiled. Yes, she would have to be extra careful when she was with him, but he was worth the risk.

–

Sahan ambled downstairs, rubbing his eyes. The essay he was working on was nearly done. He rolled his shoulders to get rid of the tension. In the kitchen, Nate, Cara and Cara's best friend Bex were finishing off a couple of bottles of wine. Bex gave him a tipsy grin and waved. 'Hi Sahan.'

He smiled politely back and put the kettle on.

'We're thinking of going to the pub for last orders. Fancy it?' said Nate.

Sahan looked down at his bare feet. 'I dunno. I've got a bit left to do on my essay.'

'I'm sure you'll need a break after all the time you've put into it,' said Cara.

He could take a break. There wasn't that much left to do… he looked up to find Nate had stood up and was pulling Cara to her feet. 'Come on, mate. It's just a swift pint.'

His eyes felt sore and his brain felt like it had been pummelled. A break from his books suddenly felt very attractive. 'What the heck,' he said. 'Just give me a minute to grab some shoes.'

They set off in the crisp night. Nate and Cara strode on ahead, leaving Sahan to walk with Bex. He kept a good gap between them and tried to relax. Bex was nice enough, and not all that scary, really. Glancing sideways at her, he acknowledged she was pretty too. Tall and slim with shoulder-length hair. She was the sort of girl who threw herself into everything she did. They might have been friends, if she didn't keep trying to flirt with him.

They chatted about what a pain exams were and how they really interfered with enjoying the nicer weather. She started telling him about a play she'd been to see. He let her talk and let his mind drift, comparing Bex to Soma.

Next to Soma's neat features, Bex seemed like an ungainly giantess. Too tall, too gangly, too... fake. Soma wore so many layers of clothing it was sometimes difficult to tell what shape she was, but her face was a study in emotion. It was as though every thought she had was there on display. The naked joy when she saw him, still undiminished after weeks of meeting in the park and talking. The love she showed when she looked at Louie. Even though she was twenty-five, she had an almost childish naivety about her sometimes.

The only way he could help her was to teach her English. She was a surprisingly fast learner. He wondered if, given the chances he'd had, she would have proven herself far cleverer than he was. For a moment, he indulged in his fantasy where he could train her, Henry Higgins style, into being a middle class girl. Someone he could introduce to his parents.

He dug his hands into his jacket pockets. Oh, it was madness. He knew it was. She was a servant. Not someone he should be talking to. He never mentioned her when he spoke to his family. He just made it sound like he was studying too hard to have a social life. His parents didn't even know about his job at the restaurant. They would be horrified if they did.

'Helloo. Earth to Sahan?' Bex's voice brought him back to reality.

'What? Sorry, I was miles away. Thinking about… work.'

Bex gave him a mischievous smile. 'See, you did need a break. Good job you came out.'

'I guess it was.'

'We need to get your mind off work for a little while.'

He laughed, he hoped convincingly. Bex slipped her arm through his. He tensed and wondered how he could shake her off without being rude. He walked with his elbow held stiffly out from his body. They neared the pub and Bex moved closer. 'We're here,' she said, redundantly.

Sahan hesitated.

'You coming in?' said Bex. 'Or have you come up with a better idea?' She leaned closer. He could smell the wine on her breath and it repulsed him. Her eyes were fixed on his face. If he didn't do something she would try to kiss him. The very thought made him flinch.

He gently removed her arm from his. 'I'm sorry, Bex,' he said. 'I don't think this is such a good idea.' He patted her hand before letting it go. 'I'm… really sorry.'

Bex's smiled dropped. 'I see,' she said. She crossed her arms over her chest. 'I see.' There was the slightest tremor in her voice. He felt like an ogre.

'Bex, I'm really sorry. It's just my head isn't in the right place for—'

'I'll let the others know you've gone back. Hope you get your essay done.' She stalked off before he could say anything else. She disappeared into the pub, without pausing or looking back.

Sahan stared after her, aware that he'd just hurt a girl who didn't deserve it. But it was better than stringing her along. It was the right thing to do. He turned and started walking back. After a few minutes, he broke into a run, because he didn't want all that time to think. Bloody Tamsin. Bloody, bloody Tamsin. What had she done to him?

His first week at uni had been a scary, exhilarating experience. It was the first time he'd been away from home and he was unleashed into a strange country. Back home, he had barely a moment where someone wasn't with him. Under the guise of keeping him safe, his father kept him tightly reined in. His parents had warned him, repeatedly, not to lose sight of his goal. *Don't get distracted, son. Remember to study.* But studying was the last thing on his mind, that first week. The fearsome responsibility of having to do everything for himself was matched only by the elation of being able to do whatever he wanted, whenever he wanted.

University life in his imagination had been a mix of imagery gleaned from American TV shows. He now knew that Britain was a very different place to TV America. It was less clean, less wholesome. Still, a whole lot of fun. The first person he met was Nate, who was also the first black person he had ever spoken to. A few hours in the bar later, they had become firm friends.

If his friends from home could see him now, they'd see a guy who'd embraced freedom; who was standing in a bar with no set time to go home, drinking a beer he didn't have to hide, hanging out with his black best friend. They wouldn't recognize him. His father would probably have a coronary in horror.

Well, his father wasn't here now. He could do whatever he liked. He was all set to have the best three years of his life.

And then Tamsin happened. She walked into the bar and every male head turned to watch her progress. She was beautiful, with thick brown curls that swung to the movement of her hips. Even in the standard student outfit of jeans and skinny t-shirt, she was movie star elegant. Sahan, who had been brought up to be courteous and always button his shirts right to the very top, never thought for a moment that a guy like him would have a chance with someone like her. Which was why, when she came over to talk to them, he assumed it was Nate she was interested in.

She was even more flawless up close and for the first time in his life, Sahan was lost for words. Small talk, which normally came easily to him, was a struggle. Yet, Tamsin didn't seem to notice. She smiled at him, touched his arm, complemented him on his long eyelashes. When she left, she passed him a piece of paper with her mobile number on it.

Sahan and Nate watched her leave.

'Wow,' said Nate. 'I think you've pulled.'

Sahan looked at the piece of paper in his hand and swallowed hard. Blood that had deserted his brain for more interesting destinations slowly returned. 'She was being nice,' he said. But he tucked the paper carefully into his jeans pocket.

He'd tried to call her, several times, but it was too much for him. Somewhere deep inside, he knew that his parents would be horrified at the thought of him being with a woman like that. It broke all the rules he'd been brought up with. The girls he knew would never approach a guy like that, let alone give him their phone number. Which was why, when he saw her in the student union shop a few days later, he tried to stammer an apology.

Tamsin laughed. 'You're so sweet,' she said. 'Tell you what, I'm not busy right now. How about you buy me a coffee?'

So they sat in the cafe, perched on the tall stools, elbows leaning against the round table in between them, and chatted. Every so often, their knees would touch and it was like a bolt of lightning to his stomach. After a few minutes, Sahan recovered his ability to speak. Tamsin was in the final year, a few years older than he was. She seemed to be bright and charming. Finally, she slid off her stool.

'Since you're quite shy,' she said, smiling, 'I'll do the asking. Do you fancy taking me out for dinner on Friday night?'

'Uh… yeah. I'm mean. Yes. That would be… That's great. Yes.'

Her smile widened. 'You're so cute. Come pick me up at seven.' She wrote her address and room number on the back of the receipt and pressed it into his hand. 'Don't lose that. Okay?' Her hand lingered in his.

'No. Of course.'

'Great. I'll see you on Friday night.' She left him staring at his hand and wondering if he could get away with never washing it again.

On the Friday, he walked down the corridor of her halls of residence at five to seven. After several hours on TripAdvisor, he and Nate had chosen a restaurant. He had even ironed his shirt. Nate, who had found out quite how sheltered Sahan's life had been so far, had given him a lecture on safe sex and made him take a condom. Sahan had said he didn't believe in sex before marriage. Nate had laughed and said it should be an interesting evening then.

It turned out that dinner involved a lot of wine. Sahan wasn't used to wine. It tasted heavy compared to beer and it was making him feel fuzzy, which wasn't unpleasant. Tamsin, two years older than him, was telling him about what she was going to do when she graduated. Sahan watched her red, red lips moving. She had done most of the talking that evening. He had tried very hard to pay attention and tried to make sure that his eyes focussed on her face whenever he was looking at her.

Tamsin reached across, her arm brushing his, and picked up the wine bottle. There wasn't much left.

'Oh.' She tipped the last of the wine into her glass. 'Let's order another.' Before he could answer, she had raised her arm to get the waiter's attention.

He didn't mind. Not really. But she could have *asked* him. He assumed he was paying for this meal, and even if he wasn't, surely it was good manners to check if he wanted more wine. Tamsin ordered another bottle. Sahan frowned. He was fairly new to drinking alcohol and his head felt muzzy. As the waiter turned to leave, he said, 'I'd like a glass of tap water as well, please.'

'You okay?' said Tamsin. She leaned closer. He could see down her dress now. Her chest gleamed in the restaurant lights, as though she had swept her breasts with glitter. Inadvertently, he thought of his father and his warnings against loose women. He forced his gaze back up to her face.

'Yes, yes, I'm fine. Just needed a glass of water. Thirsty... you know,' he said.

She laughed. 'Me too, which is why I ordered more wine.' She smiled at him. The skin around her mouth wrinkled in a strange way. He realised that the skin he had taken to be flawless was actually just a coating of make-up. Of course it was. Silly of him to not notice before. His father's voice rang out in his head. 'Be sensible. Foreign women are all fake glamour and no substance. They will use you and discard you. Dangerous creatures.' He squeezed his eyes shut and opened them again.

Tamsin was looking at him with her head to one side. 'Sure you're okay?' Her fingers made contact with his hand, warm but no longer thrilling.

Damn his father and his moralizing. He was ruining everything. The rush of emotion that he had started the evening with had fizzled out. This was not going as he had hoped. Still, she had done nothing wrong. He needed some time to think. 'I'm fine,' he said. What had she been saying? 'Um... you've got a job interview soon...'

'Oh yes,' she said. 'It's actually a second interview. There's a whole day of assessments.' Her hand moved away from his as she gestured. 'You know, psychometric tests and all that.'

He shook his head. 'I've not done that sort of thing...'

She explained. Partway through her explanation, the wine arrived and she poured herself a glass. He topped up his own. He wasn't sure he wanted any more. He was already feeling woozy. More wine wasn't a great idea, but he needed to have something to do. So he drank it anyway.

It wasn't late, but Sahan was unsteady on his feet from the wine. Tamsin, who'd had far more wine than he had, was steadier than he was, but not by much. They wove their way down the corridor of her hall of residence. It was quiet, everyone else must still be out. Tamsin tucked her arm through his, pressing her body close so that he could feel the squash of her breast through her coat. He knew he should be enjoying that, but couldn't muster any enthusiasm.

Tamsin lost her glamour faster than he'd thought possible. The meal, the glitter... that had started it, but the final stroke had come when they'd stumbled out of the restaurant and she'd leaned against a pillar and pulled out a cigarette. She had offered him one, showing a generosity that she hadn't shown with the wine. He had refused, but then had to put up with her second-hand smoke as they walked back to the halls of residence. The smell clung to them now, making his already queasy stomach turn all the more.

He had thought he knew about the world. Nate had tried to tell him that he was too naive, but he had been so sure that watching TV had prepared him. Maybe Nate had been right. Or worse... maybe his father had been. That thought sobered him up.

'Here we are,' she trilled. He tried to release himself from her, but she managed to open the door whilst still holding his arm.

'I... should go,' he said, when she dragged him in. 'Thank you very much for a lov—'

Her mouth pressed against his. He tried to protest, but opening his mouth only let her tongue in. She tasted of ash and smoke and tannin. He stood, paralysed by panic for a second, not sure how to push her away. When he moved, his hands were suddenly full of warm flesh and for a moment, he could think of nothing other than the sensation of a nipple hardening against his palm and the slide of her tongue against his.

She pushed, making his back slam against the closed door. She stopped kissing him for a moment. 'You,' she said, her voice low, 'are so damned cute. I could eat you.'

He didn't want to be eaten by her. He didn't want her cigarette taste in his mouth. She kissed him again. This time, he managed to move.

'T... Tams—'

She pulled his shirt out and thrust her hand under it. He yelped at the cold touch.

'Stop it.' He pulled her hand away. 'Please.'

'Aww,' she said. 'I've heard...' she nipped at his earlobe, making him flinch. 'That the quiet ones are the best.' Her hands scrabbled at his waist. She was undoing the buttons on his jeans. His insides lurched in panic. He batted her hands away, but she was too quick. Her cold fingers reached inside his underwear.

'No.'

'What's the matter, little man?' She looked down. 'Let's see what we have...'

'I don't—' He grabbed her wrist and tried to pull her hand away. Years of being taught to be polite made him try to explain. 'I don't even know you. I don't want to sleep with y—'

She pressed towards him and tried to kiss him again. Thoughts of explaining vanished in another rush of panic. Nothing about this was right. It went against everything he believed in, not just about romance, but about basic respect.

Her free hand groped into his underwear again and gripped his penis, making him yelp.

'Aw,' said Tamsin, squeezing. 'So soft? Don't you like girls?' Her other hand groped round to his bottom. He twisted and wriggled out her grasp.

'Leave me alone.'

She released him, pinching him as she drew her hand away. 'Oh fine.' She rolled her eyes. 'You shouldn't be leading girls along if you really like boys.'

He clawed at the door. It took him two attempts to get it open. He glanced over his shoulder and Tamsin was watching him, her lower lip pouting. 'Aww,' she said again. 'There's no need to get upset over such a tiny thing.' And then she began to laugh.

Her laughter chased him as he stumbled down the hall. He found the stairs and practically fell down them. He made it out of the building before all the food and the wine rose up from his stomach and splashed onto his shoes.

Now, every time anyone touched him or made him think of sex, he experienced that same wave of shame and terror and the urgent need to be sick. She had ruined his life.

When he finally told Nate and Cara the following day, Cara had wanted him to report Tamsin for assault, but Nate had pointed out that no one would take him seriously if he did. He understood that. If someone had told him that a guy like him would have had trouble fending off a slim, pretty girl like Tamsin, he would have laughed too. Cara and Nate had advised him to put it behind him and carry on, but Sahan couldn't. The shame and fear were such a potent mixture. He dreaded running into Tamsin, so he found excuses not to go out, until eventually people stopped inviting him.

Sahan got back to the house and slammed the door behind him. This was ridiculous. He couldn't let Tamsin haunt him forever. This had to stop.

Chapter Twelve

'What are you doing today?' Madam said.

Soma looked round from where she was watching the toaster. 'Madam?' It was Saturday. She had intended to stay in her room, watching television, like she always did on her day off.

'Are you planning to go into town?'

'No Madam. I thought I would watch some TV.'

A small frown appeared on Madam's forehead. 'You should go out, practise your English a bit. I know you don't need it, living with us, but you may as well learn something new.'

She *was* learning a new skill. Her ability to read English was improving. She could hear the words in her head when she read now and she could understand most of what people were saying on TV. Sahan had told her how to get English subtitles up on her screen, which somehow helped her understand things better. Watching TV was learning a new skill, but Madam didn't realise it. Or perhaps she wanted Soma out of the house.

'Okay Madam,' she said. She could walk to the shops at the far end of the avenue. She had been that way with Louie before, but she always turned back before the crossroads with the shop on the corner and returned back to the house. Maybe she should be braver. Besides, if Madam thought something was odd, she might start asking questions. That would be bad.

—

Half an hour later, she left the house, wrapped up against the cold, a hat pulled low over her hair, which was growing back nicely. Out of habit, she went out through the wicket door from the garage. She had never used the front door, so she had all but forgotten it existed.

The sun was struggling to show from behind the layer of cloud and the cold clung to her. She pulled the scarf tighter around her neck and set off, going in the opposite direction to the park. The avenue was lined with huge trees. As the weather warmed up, the trees had burst into leaf, so that the wide pavements either side were in dappled shade. What had been dry and bare in the winter was now soft and green.

During the week, the road was quiet, but today there were many more cars on the quiet side street. People too. A few passers-by said good morning. Soma fought back the urge to hunch further down into her coat and forced herself to nod and smile hello.

Huddling into her coat and not speaking was what Jaya would do. She wasn't that girl any more. She was Soma. Who could understand some English and cook lasagne. Soma could walk down the street like she belonged there, even without a pram to push.

A couple walked by, arm in arm. Maybe she should try and say 'hi' like the other people did. The couple got nearer. The woman made eye contact and said hello.

Soma said, 'Hi.' It sounded strange and high-pitched and foreign. But the couple didn't seem to notice. They didn't pause their walking, but they smiled and said 'hi' back.

Yes!

—

Yamuna packed a bottle of milk and some pureed food to take to the shops. What else did Louie need? She put the changing bag on the table and checked the contents. She needed more wipes.

Louie, who had been sitting happily in his high chair a few minutes ago, started to grizzle.

'What's up little man?' Yamuna approached him. He had been fed. He couldn't need a nappy change already, surely?

Bim came in, reading something on the iPad. He put the tablet on the work surface, filled up the kettle and put it on whilst simultaneously still reading. He didn't seem to notice either of them.

Louie was rubbing his eyes now. 'What's the matter?' Yamuna unclipped the straps and picked Louie up out of the chair. He didn't stop complaining. Yamuna balanced him on her hip and started replacing items into the changing bag. Louie nuzzled his head against her shoulder. Yamuna paused. Was he being affectionate? She should enjoy that. Yes. You were supposed to count the small wins. She should make the most of it. Packing the bag could wait. She turned her back on the table and looked at her son.

He sneezed. Mucus sprayed onto her face. Yuck.

Yamuna sighed. 'Bim, can you pass me a paper towel please?'

Bim didn't respond.

'Bim!'

'Sorry? Yes. What?' He looked up and seemed surprised to see her.

'Pass a paper—Oh. Never mind. Here. Hold your son a minute.'

She thrust Louie towards his father, who looked completely bewildered. Yamuna looked down and noticed that while Louie had been nuzzling her, he had left a trail of slime on her top.

Bim was staring at Louie like he wasn't sure what a baby was.

Yamuna snapped. 'Take him.'

Bim took Louie in his arms and held him awkwardly, as though afraid he would break. Normally, Yamuna would have helped him adjust his grip so that Louie was comfortable, but right now she didn't have the energy to care for a grown man as well as a baby. 'I'm going to change my top and get some wipes for the bag,' she called over her shoulder as she headed up the stairs.

In her room, she pulled her top off over her head and rummaged around until she found a clean t-shirt. Downstairs, Louie started to cry. Yamuna cursed under her breath and pulled on the clean top. Bim didn't know the first thing about babies. He barely cared about the child at all.

She ran upstairs to get more wet wipes. Why had she told Soma to go out? If Soma had been here, she would have kept Louie happy until they were ready to go out. No. She relied too much on Soma. The girl deserved her day off. She worked hard.

Yamuna clattered down the stairs and found Bim pacing the kitchen, trying to bounce Louie up and down to cheer him up. This seemed to annoy Louie even more. Bim's face was a study in confusion and mild panic.

Yamuna threw the wipes into the bag and sighed. 'Here,' she said, holding her arms out. 'Let me take him.'

Bim handed Louie to her with a look of relief.

Yamuna popped Louie on her hip and picked up the bag without looking at Bim.

'We're going to the shops,' she said. 'We will be back in a bit.'

She took Louie outside and, for some reason, he stopped crying. 'What?' she said to him. 'You just wanted to leave the kitchen?'

He looked at her, his bottom lip still sticking out.

She managed to get him into the car and strapped him into his car seat, before the first tears leaked out. Leaving the door open, she leaned against the car and had a little cry. She was tired of making excuses for Bim's vagueness. When they were first married, she'd thought the fact that he was polite and helpful when she asked for help was good enough, but now it wasn't. She organized everything for Louie, even if Soma carried out the actions. She didn't have the energy to have to organize Bim's paternal duties as well.

If she was a bad mother, Bim was a worse father. He didn't seem to realise Louie was there most of the time. Poor baby. Born to the most useless parents in the world. If only there was someone she could talk to. Before Louie was born, when she was pregnant and full of hope and vision, there had been her NCT friends and people at work, who gave her advice based on their years of experience. She had soaked all of that up, assuming that she would be the same as them and that Bim would notice her and their son. But Louie wasn't like other babies. He cried all the time. Yamuna, sleep-deprived and rattled, was snappy. Bim had got more distant, not less, and who could blame him? And worst of all, Yamuna was deficient in the one thing that everyone seemed to have – motherly love. She couldn't confess that to anyone. Least of all to those mothers who had all the natural instincts they needed.

There was only Soma to talk to now and she couldn't ask a servant for advice. Not if she wanted to maintain any semblance of being the boss. So she was alone. She had to weather this by herself.

Yamuna dried her eyes. She checked on Louie, who was intently chewing on one of the toys hanging from the car seat hood. Okay. She needed the pram base. Still fighting tears, Yamuna went back to get it. When she looked in the kitchen, Bim had already disappeared back to his study.

—

Soma got to the end of the avenue. Ahead of her, the bigger road loomed, with its busy traffic and small shops packed together in a confusing mass. She slowed down. Even from where she was, a few yards before the main road, she could tell that there were a lot of people around. Not just old people and mothers with prams, like there usually were, but people of all ages and shapes and sizes. Did she have to nod and smile at them all? What if one of them tried to talk to her? What would she do anyway? She didn't want to buy anything. Her heart beat faster and she felt the prickle of cold sweat on her back and neck.

She didn't want to do this. She knew the route to the park and never deviated from it. Once she stepped off this road onto another, she might get lost. How would she find the way back? She stopped walking, breathing hard.

No. This was a bad idea. She had been out of the house for about twenty minutes now. Madam had mentioned taking Louie out to Mothercare to buy him some new clothes. If she walked back slowly, maybe Madam would have gone. If not, she could always claim she'd forgotten something and had to come back. She glanced back at the main road, with its bustle and noise. No. It was too much. Even for the brave new Soma. She turned around and set off back to the house.

Still, she had done it. She had gone for a walk, outside the house, by herself.

She reached the house. It was hard to tell from the outside whether Madam was still in. Soma was so busy looking intently at the windows to check for movement that she didn't realise immediately that someone had called her name.

'Somavathi.' Kemasiri had appeared right next to her.

Soma shied away, startled. Where had he popped up from?

'I was calling you, didn't you hear?' he said. 'Your Madam said you had gone out. I thought you might not have gone far, so I thought I'd wait.'

'Uh. I… yes. Not far.' What now? She took another step back, away from him. He was dressed in a thick coat and had a hat pulled over his ears. Dressed for the outdoors, so he hadn't come as a driver with his master. Did that mean he had come especially to see her? What could he want?

As though sensing her confusion, he said, 'I have the day off today. Your Madam said that you were off today too.' He smiled, showing uneven, discoloured teeth. 'Maybe we can spend some of that time together.' His glance moved quickly, searching her face, his expression keen.

She couldn't think what to say to him. Spending the day with him was the last thing she wanted to do. If only she had kept to her nice, safe room. She could have pretended not to be in.

'It would be nice, to talk to someone in Sinhalese,' he said. 'Away from work, I mean. Just to chat.'

He was staring at her with an almost pleading expression on his face. She felt a pang of sympathy. It was lonely. Even with the pressure she had of being someone else, it was a strain to be subservient and helpful all the time. She understood his desire to talk to someone who didn't feel they could give him orders. A friend. But she couldn't do that. She didn't know him. Didn't trust him. Lonely, he may be, but there was something about him that made her uncomfortable.

He seemed to take her hesitation as a good sign. 'So, what about it? We can go for a cup of tea.' He was beaming at her now, as though sure she would agree. 'Come.'

She caught a whiff of cigarettes as he spoke. Her stomach squeezed.

'I... have some things I need to do,' she said. 'I'm afraid I can't.'

The smile winked out. 'What things to do?' he said. 'Your Madam said you had gone to the shops. You've done that now.'

'Other... things.' She backed a little further away, towards the garage. 'I'm sorry. I can't.'

He stepped forward, closing the gap again, bringing with him the smell of cigarettes.

'I'm sure you could spare a few minutes for a cup of tea. There aren't many other Sri Lankans around here. Not like us. I've come all this distance to see you.'

'It's very kind of you.' She looked around. A few people walked past; no one seemed to notice there was anything untoward. Her heart pounded, trying to escape from her chest. 'But I don't—'

He stopped advancing and glared at her. 'What? Am I not good enough for you to have tea with? Is that it?'

She had to think of something to mollify him. She didn't need enemies. 'I… have someone… back home.'

That gave him pause. She pulled her keys out of her pocket. That was a good excuse. A likely one too. Surely, he would go away now.

He narrowed his eyes. 'Which home would that be?' he said. 'Matara?'

Her mouth went dry. She had hoped he'd forgotten about that. She must sound more sure of herself. 'Of course.'

'Are you sure about that?'

What did he mean by that? He was watching her, eyes glittering, like a cat. Had he guessed? What did he know? Was he somehow connected to those letters?

Behind her there was a clank and a whirr. The garage door started to open. Madam was just leaving now.

Kemasiri glared at the slowly rising garage door and then back at Soma. His nostrils flared. He turned on his heel and strode off, muttering 'snooty bitch'.

Thank goodness. Soma ducked under the rising door and entered the garage, sidling in next to the car.

Madam slid her window down. 'What did he want?' she said, nodding to Kemasiri's retreating back.

Soma hesitated. Her first instinct was to say nothing, but if Madam knew that Kemasiri wasn't welcome, maybe she would provide some protection if he came back. 'He wanted me to have tea with him,' she said. 'I didn't want to.' She glanced at the road. He had disappeared around the corner. 'I told him to go away.'

Madam nodded, frowning. 'Okay. Good.' In the back of the car, Louie gave a little squawk.

'We'll be back in a few hours,' Madam said.

Soma stood back, leaning against the rough breezeblock wall, so that she was well out of the way. Once the car had pulled out, she dashed into the house and locked the door before the garage door had closed again. Leaning against the kitchen door, she resolved that she was never going out alone again.

—

Later that week, Soma picked up the post to put it on the stairs, like she always did, when a rough brown envelope caught her eye. Another letter from Sri Lanka. Her stomach dropped. She glanced across at Louie, who was sitting on the floor a little way off, contentedly playing with his toy giraffe. She sat down on the stairs, the letter in her hands. This one had been sent directly to her, rather than via the agency – the name written in Sinhalese above the address written in English. They were getting closer. They knew where she lived. Her pulse grew louder in her ears. She couldn't throw the letter away and pretend it had never showed up… could she? No. She would only wonder what was in it. It was probably best to read it now. Get it over with.

She checked on Louie again. He was okay. She took a deep breath and ripped the letter open. She scanned it quickly, searching for any suggestion that they were coming to look for her. There wasn't one. Relieved, she read it again. *Why didn't she write? Didn't she know her mother was worried about her? They missed her. Why had she not sent any money home? What was the matter? Why was she being like this?* Questions, questions. In them she saw the mounting confusion of a mother who was fighting against the conclusion that her child no longer wanted any contact with her.

She put the letter down and stared into space. They thought that Somavathi was okay, but that she had decided to disown her family. The pain of that was clear... Somavathi's mother had done nothing to deserve that. There was nothing she could do to make things better for her. It was too risky. At least this way they were spared the knowledge that Somavathi was dead. It still left open the chance that they would try to come and find her. But people living in a village like the one she herself had grown up in wouldn't be able to afford a flight... but if they knew someone who lived here... like Kemasiri?

Louie grizzled. He had dropped the toy and was wriggling on his tummy, trying to reach it. Soma checked her watch. Nearly time to go to the park. Soma took a deep breath and pulled her thoughts away from the knot of terror in her midriff. She had to focus on the fact that they weren't coming to find her. It was very unlikely anyone would come. She was safe. For the moment. She stuffed the letter into her pocket and stood up.

'Come on baby Louie.' She scooped him up and breathed in the baby smell of him, her relief making her appreciate him all the more. 'Let's go see your uncle Sahan.'

A few minutes later, she was pushing Louie's pram briskly through the park. She wished she'd thrown the letter away before she'd left the house. She could feel it, heavy in her pocket, poisoning the day.

Sahan was standing by their usual bench, reading something on his phone. He looked up when she arrived. 'Hello.'

She smiled in response. Sahan came round the side of the pram and peered in. 'Hello Louie.' He reached in and tickled the baby, who gurgled.

Soma realised she'd barely glanced at Louie since leaving the house. She couldn't let that letter distract her from her job. Louie was more important than anything. She watched Sahan and Louie pulling faces at each other and reminded herself that she was lucky to have this. The weather was warmer now and there was actual sunlight. Not the pressing hot sun that she was used to, but a gentle one that warmed without burning. It made everything better.

Sahan looked up and the sun caught his eyes, making them look a liquid brown. Soma drew a breath. Yes. She was lucky to have this. Even if it all came tumbling down around her tomorrow, she would at least have had it for a few months. A job, a safe place to live, her own room and Sahan, her special friend. This was a good life and it was *hers*.

'We should walk,' she said. 'Louie is very wide awake right now, but it is his nap time.' She started walking.

'I have a new book for you,' said Sahan. He fell into step beside her. He didn't speak, which was unusual. He looked thoughtful. It was almost as though the letter was spreading its influence to him too. She sneaked a glance at him. Had something happened? Had the people from

Somavathi's past somehow got in touch with him too? She tried to think if she'd seen any telltale brown envelopes arrive for Madam. No, she couldn't remember seeing that. But that didn't mean they hadn't.

'Is everything okay?' she asked Sahan.

He looked across at her, the small frown still on his forehead. 'Soma,' he said. 'Do you mind me meeting you like this?'

That wasn't what she was expecting. Where was this going? 'Of course I don't mind. You are helping me to read. We are… friends.'

'You're not allowing me to hang around with you and Louie because you're afraid to tell me not to?'

'No. I like… I like speaking to you.'

'If I am annoying you, you mustn't be afraid to tell me to go away.' He stopped walking and turned to her, making her stop too. 'You mustn't be afraid to tell me anything.'

'I'm not afraid of you.' She responded without thinking, but the minute she said it, she realised that it was true. He was a man and she wasn't afraid of him. 'I am not afraid of you,' she repeated, to check if she really meant it. She did. 'You're my friend.'

'A friend,' he said. He looked thoughtful for a moment, as though he was trying the idea on for size. Then he smiled. 'I'm glad to be your friend.'

They resumed walking. Soma shot another glance across at Sahan. Not only was she not afraid of him, but being with him made her feel less afraid of everything else. She had started off thinking he was handsome. When she was with him, she'd imagined she was in a film. It had been a harmless few minutes in a fantasy world. But now she had really got to know him, she could see beyond the Bollywood ideal to the complicated human being underneath and she still liked what she saw. He was kind and gentle and didn't push her to do anything. He made her feel safe. With that thought came another realisation. Friendship didn't cover what he meant to her. It was far more than that. She was falling in love with him.

And that was a bad thing, because it would have to end sometime.

–

By the time she got home, Louie was asleep. Soma quietly ran water into the kitchen sink. When it was half full, she pulled out the letter. This new life was hers. Not Somavathi's. She had made it what it was and it, in turn, had made her anew.

Her baby brother's death and what had followed had changed Jaya from a lively, chatty child who was consistently at the top of her class, into a withdrawn and frightened other person. She had escaped from that world. The decision to take Somavathi's passport had whipped her into a strange dream, where she'd shuffled past men with guns and sat on a flight, too frightened to go to the toilet. The high state of terror had burned inside her, shutting down all thoughts that weren't essential to getting her through the barriers undetected. It had seared her, cleansed her until she had become someone else. She wasn't Jaya any more. She wasn't Somavathi either. She was Soma. Someone entirely her own. And she was going to stay that way.

She tore the letter and envelope into pieces and dropped them into the warm water. Pushing in with both hands, she held the pieces under until they softened and blurred. She tore the pieces into even smaller bits and churned them about until the water was full of grey pulp. Scooping out the mush, she squeezed it in a fist, tighter and tighter until there was nothing left of Somavathi's letter but a hard, unrecognisable lump. Then she threw it away.

Chapter Thirteen

By the end of the Friday night shift, Sahan was ready to drop. A mild night always meant more customers at the restaurant and this one had been no exception. On the other hand, the tips had been good. He had learned long ago that a sincere looking smile could earn him almost an hour's wages in a few seconds. The leftover food had been divided up between the staff, so he had a nice bag of curry to take home. His bus was in a couple of minutes, so he grabbed his coat and ran out ahead of the other guys.

He left the restaurant through the back door and walked up the alleyway, the 'ten-foot' as the local guys called it, wanting nothing more than to go to bed.

'Hey, Sahan.' A shadow detached itself from the wall and Kemasiri stepped into the light. 'Want a lift home? I've got the boss's car parked around the corner.'

Sahan shook his head. Kemasiri made him uneasy, there was something about him that grated. He reminded himself that everyone was equal in this country and said politely, 'No thanks. I'll catch the bus. It drops me off very close to my house.'

Kemasiri fell into step beside him. 'Why would you want to catch a bus when there's a perfectly good lift available?'

'Because… it's late and I'm exhausted, okay. Maybe some other time.' He glanced at his watch. Still on time for the bus.

'Oh, I get it,' said Kemasiri, sneering. 'I bet you're going to see a girl or something.' He laughed, a dirty low chortle that set Sahan's teeth on edge. 'Don't worry, son. I can keep a secret. I'll drop you off.'

'No.' Again with the 'son'. He would not rise to it. Kemasiri might get off on weird power games, but he, Sahan, was better than that.

'Is she a white girl then? Someone you really want to keep secret from the family?' Kemasiri pulled out a pack of cigarettes. 'I see. I see. Can't say I blame you. Must be very tempting being at university with all that…' He paused to light his cigarette.

Sahan picked up speed, but Kemasiri caught up with him again.

'White girls,' Kemasiri said. 'Very pretty. And very accommodating, yes?'

He thought of Tamsin. Nausea. He didn't want to think about her. He most certainly didn't want to talk to this creep.

'We could go out one night, on the… what do they call it? On the pull?' said Kemasiri, through a cloud of smoke.

His breath was shortened. He had to get away before he threw up. 'No thanks.'

'Maybe some other night, eh? We should stick together, us Sri Lankan men. You know, get to know each other. What do you say?' He clapped Sahan on the shoulder.

The contact was too much. Sahan stopped and pushed the hand off. 'Look. I am tired. I don't want to chat. Leave. Me. Alone.'

Kemasiri recoiled as though Sahan had struck him. His expression changed. His eyes narrowed, making him look more like a rat than ever. 'I see,' he said. 'Like that, is it? You think you're too good to be friends with me too, fancy boy?' He jabbed a finger at Sahan.

'No. I—'

'Just because you have a rich mummy and daddy?' Kemasiri continued, his voice rising. 'You think people like me who actually need to work for a living aren't worth your notice?'

'Look, I didn't mean to offend you. I'm—' Over the other man's shoulder, he spotted his bus. 'I'm sorry, Kemasiri. It's been a long night. My bus is here.'

Kemasiri followed his gaze moved out of Sahan's way. Relieved, Sahan strode past him and got on the bus. When he looked back, Kemasiri was still watching him. That guy really had a massive inferiority complex. Weirdo. Sahan shuddered and turned away.

Chapter Fourteen

Louie had a temperature. The thought drummed in Yamuna's mind, over and over like a backing track. *Louie has a temperature. Louie has a temperature.* It nagged while she pipetted samples out of the fraction collector; while she put took readings from the spectrophotometer; while she checked her emails. Finally, when she'd read the same email three times and still failed to retain it, she gave in and phoned home.

She had instructed Soma to answer the phone, just on that day, in case it was her. She tapped her finger on the desk, waiting for Soma to pick up. The phone rang and rang and went to answerphone. Yamuna scowled. Why didn't the girl answer? She tried again. This time, Soma answered with a timid 'Hello?'

Yamuna didn't bother introducing herself. 'How is he?' she said, in English. Then, remembering, she asked again in Sinhalese.

'He's sleeping, Madam,' the girl said. 'I gave him some medicine as you said and now he's sleeping.'

'What's his temperature?'

There was a pause. 'It's lower.'

'How much lower? What number?' She had checked that Soma knew how to use the forehead thermometer before she left.

'I haven't had a chance to get the thermometer, but he feels cooler.'

Feels cooler? She had left instructions for his temperature to be recorded. Soma was supposed to call her if it got any higher.

As though reading her thoughts, Soma said, 'He's been asleep on my lap. I didn't want to disturb him. His temperature hasn't gone up…'

Excuses. She didn't need to hear excuses. Still, the girl was looking after her son. She needed to keep her on side. Yamuna took a deep breath. 'Okay. When he wakes up, can you please check his temperature? I'll call back in an hour or so.'

'Yes, Madam.'

'When he wakes up, make sure he drinks some water.'

'Yes Madam.'

After she'd hung up, Yamuna stared at the phone. It should be her, at home with Louie. Not the nanny. She wondered where this emotion squeezing her insides came from. Was it guilt? It must be. And worry. If anything happened to Louie… she would never forgive herself. It was her job, as his mother, to love him and cherish him over everything else. The fact that she felt nothing towards him… that was not a good thing, but it was largely irrelevant. She was expected to look after him. It was her duty.

She rubbed her eyes. She had tried. Really, she had, but when she thought about Louie, all she could think of was what a responsibility he was. She went about the daily business of looking after him, just as she would have done for any creature that depended on her, and waited for her endocrine system to realise she had become a mother. When weeks passed and that didn't happen, she'd wondered if there was something amiss with Louie. He was so grumpy and cried so much. But the doctors told her that her son was perfectly healthy. And then Soma had turned up and he was as good as gold for her. So the problem wasn't him. It had to be her.

With Soma's arrival, Yamuna had swapped nights disturbed by Louie's every movement for nights where she stared into the darkness, wondering what was wrong with her. How had her body produced this baby when there was such a huge part of her maternal make-up missing? How was it possible to be ambivalent towards her son?

She walked back into the lab, still thinking.

'Louie alright?' said her colleague, Jenny.

Yamuna shook her head. 'Still got a temperature.'

Jenny looked around. 'Do you need to go home? I can cover for you...'

Did she want to go home? She supposed she should. But that meant leaving work early. She would have to take it as annual leave. She could do that.

'You won't be able to concentrate here anyway,' Jenny continued. 'I remember when my two were ill, I was useless. Couldn't stop worrying about them.' She smiled. 'Go home Yamuna. When they're ill, all they want is their mummy.'

Not Louie. He would want Soma, not her. But Jenny had a point. She wasn't concentrating. Besides, going home would be what a good mother did. She wasn't a good mother, but she wasn't about to let other people know that. 'You're right. I will go home.'

'What do you need me to do for you? Anything?'

She quickly ran through what she was doing. She dealt with what could be put on ice and gave Jenny a short list of instructions for the rest. Within an hour, she was on her way out. Pretty convincing, she thought as she headed out of the building. Anyone would think she was a proper mother.

–

Soma sat on a cushion on the floor, with a pillow resting on her shins. Little Louie lay on her legs, head on the pillow, legs falling limp either side of her knees. She rocked her legs gently whenever he stirred, keeping him asleep. Poor baby. She reached forward and put a hand against his forehead. Still warm, but not as hot as before. She checked the bowl of water she had next to her. It was too cold to sponge his hands and feet down with now. She would need to move him to go and get some warm water. Carefully, she leaned forward and eased the pillow and baby off her legs onto the floor. Louie whimpered, but didn't wake. Soma quietly eased away, crawling along the floor a few yards before standing up.

She looked back at the sleeping baby. He seemed so lifeless, arms limp, knees flopped apart, but there was something about the way he was breathing that was better than before. This was proper sleep, not the fever-induced slumber she'd seen earlier. He was on the mend.

Soma tiptoed out and headed downstairs. Pausing to look at the clock, she noticed it was nearly the time when she and Louie went to the park. Sahan would be waiting for them. Except, Louie wasn't in a fit state to go anywhere. She couldn't take him out when he was so ill. Would Sahan wait for long? What if he thought she'd decided not to meet him? Soma sighed. If only there was a way for her to get in touch with him. She didn't have a phone of her own and she didn't dare make any calls on Madam's phone. If Madam found out about her and Sahan, there would be hell to pay. Sahan would be fine, but she would be sent home. That could not happen.

They had never spoken about the risk of Madam finding out, but it seemed they were both aware of how important it was to keep their friendship secret. Sahan had recently suggested that it would be good to be able to get in touch if he needed to tell her he couldn't come to the park. He'd suggested a code where he would call, let it ring three times, then hang up and dial again. This would tell Soma it was him. She could pick up the second time he called. It was a sensible plan, but they'd not had to use it yet. He might use it today, when he got tired of waiting.

If she was upstairs with Louie, she wouldn't get to the phone in time. She knew that because it had taken her ages to get down when Madam called earlier. By the time she'd dislodged Louie and got downstairs, the phone had stopped ringing. Thankfully, Madam called back. By the time she'd spoken to her and got back upstairs, Louie had been keening.

She took the cordless handset out of its cradle. May as well take it upstairs. Even if Sahan didn't phone, Madam might call again and it would be good to answer it without upsetting Louie too much.

She grabbed herself a banana and a glass of water and headed back upstairs to get a bowl of warm water. She knew from sitting with cousins that sponging down a child's hands, feet and forehead was a good way to get a fever down. It wasn't a problem in Sri Lanka, but here, the water was so cold, it was bound to wake him up if she tried it without making sure it was warm. She ran the tap for a while, dipping the inside of her wrist into the stream to test the heat. When it was finally warm enough, she collected some water into the bowl. Downstairs the front door thudded shut.

She was almost at Louie's room when Madam arrived at the top of the stairs. Madam glanced at the things she was clutching and frowned.

'I was going to wipe baby's forehead and hands down again,' Soma explained.

The frown cleared from Madam's face. A slight nod. 'That's a good idea,' she said. She followed Soma into the room. Soma headed for the little nest of pillows she'd made for herself and Louie on the floor and put down the things she was carrying next to it.

'Why is my son on the floor?' Madam demanded in a harsh whisper.

Soma looked down. Louie lay on the floor next to the cot. His top half was on the pillow and his bottom half on the carpet. Why did Madam sound annoyed? It wasn't like he was on a dusty floor. 'I rocked him to sleep on my legs,' she explained. 'He was asleep and I didn't want to move him too much.'

Madam knelt next to Louie and picked up the temperature strip that she'd shown to Soma that morning. She pressed it firmly to Louie's forehead. As if by magic the strip lit up a number, telling his temperature. Madam said 'Hmm.' Louie stirred and let out a thin wail. His eyes flew open, wide and unfocused.

Without thinking, Soma leaned forward and laid a hand on his tummy. 'Shh. Baba,' she said. Louie whimpered again and closed his eyes.

When Soma looked up from Louie, her gaze briefly connected with her employer's and she caught a look of intense dislike. Madam looked away so fast that Soma wasn't sure if she'd imagined it. Why would Madam dislike her? She did everything she was told. And she looked after Louie well, didn't she? He seemed happy. What possible reason could there be for Madam to not like her?

Could it be that Madam suspected something about Sahan? The thought made her catch her breath.

Madam went over to the other side of the room and looked through the notes that Soma had made through the day. She wrote something in the notebook, probably the latest temperature. The woman was obsessed with note-taking. It was almost as though she didn't believe in things unless they were written down. Perhaps she would take more notice of Louie himself when he learned to write. They could leave each other little notes.

Madam looked up from the book. 'He seems to be improving,' she said.

'He's sleeping a bit better now,' Soma volunteered. 'He was really floppy before. Like he was unconscious.'

Madam spun round. 'Why didn't you call me?'

Soma looked from the baby to his mother, confused. Madam had known the baby was ill. What good did it do to call her to say he was still ill? He wasn't worse. And now he was better. For a second she wondered if Madam perhaps loved the boy more than she let on? Perhaps she was worried? But then, she could have rung earlier.

Madam looked like she was about to say something else, but was interrupted by the phone ringing. Soma stared at it. Madam was here. So there was only one other person who would phone at this time. Sahan would have been waiting for her in the park for about twenty minutes now. It had to be him.

Another ring.

She couldn't speak to him with Madam here. If Madam picked up… would he have the presence of mind to pretend he'd dialled here by mistake?

A third ring. Louie cried.

Madam strode over to the phone. It stopped ringing. Soma picked up Louie and rocked him, using him to shield her face. It was Sahan. That was the signal. He would call back again and Madam would answer it. This was awful. Soma turned away, gently rocking Louie against her. She didn't want to be sent back. She liked it here. She loved Louie. And Sahan. She would never see Sahan again. Tears pressed on her eyes. She blinked them back and laid her cheek against Louie's hot little head.

'Strange,' said Madam. 'I wonder who—' The phone rang in her hand and she answered it. 'Hello.'

Soma risked a glance over her shoulder and saw that Madam was watching her through narrowed eyes. Oh no. She suspected.

'Hello? Hello?' Madam took the phone away from her ear and clicked it off. 'Very strange,' she said. 'They hung up.' She looked back at Soma. 'Does this often happen? Are there phone calls during the day that get cut off?'

'No Madam.'

'Hmm. Well, if it happens again, note down the time. I'll keep a record and see if I can find out who's making the calls.'

'Yes Madam.'

Madam stared at her for a few seconds longer, then sighed and rubbed a hand over her eyes. 'When baby settles, put him back in the cot, please. I don't like him being on the floor.' With that, she left the room.

Soma rocked Louie and hummed to him gently until he fell asleep again. Madam definitely suspected something. It would be another day or two before Louie was fit to go out, and then it was the weekend. She really hoped Sahan didn't give up on her in the meantime.

—

Sahan was sitting on the floor of his bedroom, documents and textbooks strewn in a semicircle around him. Soma had failed to show up again, but he knew from when he'd called Yamuna on the pretext of 'catching up' that Louie was unwell. It was the first time that Soma's job had got in the way of her meeting him. It brought home to him the fact that she *had* a job. She was only there, wheeling his nephew around, because she was employed by his cousin. Not because she was a friend or family. Suddenly the gulf between their situations seemed wider than ever.

He looked at the neat pile of letters and brochures that lay at the far end of the room. He was applying for jobs in earnest, not many of which were local. Soma was interested and supportive. He wondered how she felt about the fact that he might be leaving soon. Perhaps she didn't mind. What bothered him was how much *he* cared. He had spent weeks convincing himself that his interest in Soma was entirely platonic. He was homesick and wanted to hear someone say his name properly. He was teaching her to read. When his course came to an end, he would leave and forget about her. Who was he trying to kid? He could never forget her.

His thoughts were interrupted by someone rapping a rhythm on the door. There was only one person who knocked like that.

'Come on in, Nate.' He put the textbook down on his lap.

Nate wasn't alone. Cara followed him into the room. 'Bex told us what happened. What the fuck, Sahan? I thought you liked her.'

Ah. He had been expecting this conversation to happen a lot earlier. Perhaps Bex had kept it quiet for a while. 'Is she really upset?'

'Well, she's understandably a little annoyed.' Cara stood in the doorway, with her hands on her hips. 'No one likes to be rejected.' Nate put a hand on her arm and led her across to the bed, where they both sat down. 'Sahan, mate. We talked about this. You said you were ready to move on.'

'But I have exams and—'

'Don't give me that crap.' Cara leaned forward. 'We all know what this is about. It's been two years, Sahan. What Tamsin did was wrong, but it's not going to happen again.' She gave him a look full of sympathy. 'You can't carry on like this, Sahan. You can't let her have this hold over you.'

He didn't bother looking up. Since he'd met Soma, he thought of Tamsin less and less often. Why did Cara have to mention her now? Even the sound of her name made him feel sick.

Cara threw her hands up. 'It's not like anyone even knows about what happened. And even if they did, no one would care.'

Saliva rushed inside his cheek and he felt hot, but he didn't feel as nauseous as he normally did. Sahan swallowed. 'I know. I care.' He sighed. 'You must think I'm a huge drama queen.'

There was a pause. Cara sighed too and rubbed her eyes. 'No. No, you're not,' she said. 'I'm sorry.'

Nate slid down to sit on the floor beside him. 'Everyone's different. You were brought up with your dad's weird Victorian values and you've never been alone with a girl before. I'm not surprised it scared the crap out of you when she grabbed you.'

Sahan shuddered and crossed his legs. 'Yes, but compared to some of—'

'You can't compare trauma. What happened to you is a big deal to you,' said Cara.

'I thought you were past this, though. What's happened to make you think about it again?' Nate peered at him. 'Are you okay? You haven't been yourself lately. You've been disappearing off at random times in the afternoon. When you're here you're away with the fairies. What's going on?'

Sahan studied Nate. They had been friends since freshers' week. Cara had come on scene a couple of weeks later and now Nate and Cara were a unit. He trusted them like he trusted the members of his own family. He thought about how little he revealed to his parents nowadays. Okay, he trusted them more than his own family. When the Tamsin debacle happened it was Cara who helped him work out that independence meant testing the values his parents had given him and not adhering to them slavishly; it was Nate who had helped him come up with a plan to get him back on an even keel.

Keeping Soma a secret was difficult. He wasn't made for deception. Could he share his secret with them? Would sharing it make it more real?

'Sahan? Is it the stress of exams? I know it takes different people in different ways. Do you want me to find out about counselling? I know you didn't want to before, but if it's affecting your studies…?'

Cara's concern touched him.

'I have been moving on,' he said. 'Sort of.'

Cara and Nate exchanged worried glances.

Yes, Sahan decided, he could tell them. He could guess Nate's response. It made him smile. 'I think… I think I've met someone.'

Nate's face was a picture. 'Really? Wow.' He leaned forward and slapped Sahan on the back. 'You kept that quiet, you dark horse.'

Cara joined them on the floor. 'That's brilliant. Who is she? Where did you meet her?'

The last traces of Tamsin-induced discomfort vanished. His smile widened. 'She's called Soma. She's… amazing.' Even talking about her made him fizz inside. Nothing he'd felt before came even close to this.

'That's awesome,' said Nate. 'Totally amazing. So, when do we get to meet this wonder girl? Why don't you guys come out with us on Friday?'

'Um… I don't think that would be possible. I could see if she can come meet you lot around lunchtime on a Saturday.' Yamuna would expect Soma to be home of an evening. He knew his cousin. She wouldn't let a young girl living in her house go out at night without knowing who she was going with. And he wasn't ready to tell her about Soma yet.

'It'd be better to meet for drinks. It's less pressure that way,' said Cara.

'No she… er… works on Friday nights. Most nights, in fact.'

'Oh yeah? What does she do?' said Nate.

Sahan didn't answer. Now that he had let his secret out of its cocoon, he was starting to see the flaws in it. Like a precious painting held under glass for years that he'd suddenly noticed was disintegrating at the edges. 'She uh… she looks after someone's baby.'

Nate's laughter buffeted around the room. 'Classic! You've fallen for an au pair.'

Au pair was a fancy word and conjured up images of European girls with bright eyes and lip gloss. Soma was nothing like that. Back home she wouldn't have been called an au pair or a nanny. She would have been called a servant. An *ayah*, closer to the family than most, but still a servant. Sahan stared at the book on his lap, not really seeing it. Now that he'd articulated it, it was clear that there could be no future for him with Soma. There were strata upon strata between her social situation and his.

His parents would disown him. His heart constricted at the thought. Was she worth that? Surely, nothing was worth that. Nothing and… no one.

'Dude, what's the matter? Was it something I said?'

He looked up. 'No. It's… as you say, it's a classic cliché. My parents would never approve.'

Nate's smile faded. 'So?'

Cara said, 'Is that why you said you *think* you've met someone? Are you not sure how you feel? Or are you just worried about what your family will think?'

'I can't do that to them.'

Nate settled down cross-legged on the floor, getting into full mentor mode. 'First of all, from what I've seen, you guys are a tight family. Your parents will get over it, they love you. They can't stay angry forever.'

'They'll be so disappointed in me. It's not what they'd planned… they'll be so… hurt.'

'But they will still love you. Right?' Cara said.

If the press found out about Sahan and a servant girl, his father would be a laughing stock. His father would never forgive him. And worse, his parents would think that he didn't care about it. They would think he didn't love them. He couldn't do that to them. He just couldn't. He didn't respond to Cara's question.

'Right?' Nate prompted.

'Yes. But things won't be the same.'

'Well that's always going to be the case, isn't it? You're not going to stay the same guy all your life. They'll have to adapt.' He put a hand on Sahan's shoulder. 'We talked about this. Their value systems are based on where they are. You live in a different country now. You're bound to see the world differently.' He waved a hand. 'Take your restaurant job. You were so sure that taking it would mean that people saw you as some sort of failure. No one has. In fact, no one gives a shit.'

Sahan shrugged. 'I suppose so.' He hadn't mentioned his job to his parents.

Satisfied, Nate carried on with his argument. 'Second of all, it's probably not as serious as you think. I know you're new to this dating stuff… so you'll have to trust me on this. First love is… really powerful. But it's often short-lived. You might think you've found The One, but really, not many people meet the right person right from the get-go. So maybe you should chill out about things a bit.'

'Or,' said Cara. 'This might actually the The One. In which case you don't want to let her slip through your fingers.'

Sahan put his head in his hands. 'Guys, this isn't helping.'

Nate said, 'You're overthinking this. You overthink everything. Relax. Go with the flow. You're leaving this place to get a job soon enough anyway. Your parents need never know.'

Sahan wondered again how he could be such good friends with someone when there was this huge gulf of understanding between them. Nate's parents respected his right to choose his own path. Cara's parents didn't care what she did, so long as she was happy. Sahan's choices were limited to the paths his parents deemed acceptable. How could he expect them to understand?

Still, he had been rude to Bex and she was Cara's friend. Even if Cara didn't fully understand him, he knew enough about her to know that she was fiercely protective of her friends, himself included. He lifted his head. 'I'm sorry I upset Bex,' he said to Cara.

Cara made a rueful face. 'I should have warned her off. She can come on a bit strong, can Bex.' Her hand twitched, as though she was going to pat his arm, but she caught herself in time and lowered it. 'I genuinely thought you were ready to move on, Sahan. I didn't realise that you already had.' She smiled. 'This girl you're seeing. Does she make you happy?'

'She does.'

'Then, enjoy it. See where it takes you.'

He stared at her earnest face for a second. She genuinely wanted him to be happy. He smiled and nodded.

Cara grinned back.

'So,' Sahan said. 'Did you guys just come here to talk about my love life? Or did you want something else?'

'Nah. Just wanted to interfere with your life,' said Nate. 'Thought you might appreciate the distraction.'

Sahan laughed. 'I should really get back to studying.'

Nate rolled his eyes. 'We know when we're not wanted. Come on, Cara. Let's go see if we've got any Pringles left.'

Once they'd left, Sahan tried to concentrate on his books. Although it was a relief to talk to Nate and Cara about it, they hadn't really helped him gain any clarity. Were his feelings for Soma born of homesickness and the fact that she was completely unlike Tamsin? Or was this the real thing? How could he tell?

He would get into serious trouble if his parents found out. She was completely unsuitable for him. If this was a passing infatuation, really, he should get out of this relationship, before he got in any deeper. But the thought of not seeing her again was painful. Just a few days of not seeing her was hard enough. This didn't feel like a passing romance. It felt very real indeed.

He groaned and leaned back against his bed. Why was nothing ever simple?

Chapter Fifteen

Sahan escaped from the restaurant floor and ducked into the kitchen with relief. He'd been waiting on a group of young men who were too drunk and too loud to be good customers.

'They've gone,' he said. 'Didn't leave too much of a mess.' He pulled a face. 'Didn't leave much of a tip either.'

The cook was sitting in a corner, making use of a well earned break to check his messages. Through the open door to the pantry opposite, Sahan could see Deepthi was doing a stock check.

The cook looked up from his phone. He had a plate of singed garlic naan beside him. 'You eaten?'

'No. I'm starving.' Sahan grabbed a plate and started serving himself. 'It's quiet in there at the moment.' He felt grumpy and on edge. Trying to keep calm whilst being heckled and messed around by drunk customers was one of the biggest downsides to the job. Most of the time, he reminded himself that being a waiter was a temporary thing. But tonight had been especially bad. If he got on the engineering grad scheme he was interviewing for next week, he could stop working here. Forever. It wouldn't be a moment too soon.

'Your friend was looking for you,' said the cook.

'What friend?' Had Nate come to see him? Why would he?

'The driver guy.'

Sahan glowered. 'That guy is not my friend. Just because we happen to come from the same country, doesn't make us mates.'

'He gives me the creeps,' Deepthi observed. She came to the doorway of the pantry and leaned against the frame, clipboard by her side. 'He's always in here, trying to talk to me. He just can't take a hint and go away.'

'I think he's lonely,' Sahan said, feeling he should at least try to be sympathetic to the other man.

'That's no excuse,' said Deepthi. 'The way he looks at me… pretty much the same way you're looking at your food.' She gave a theatrical shudder. 'Ugh.'

'If it's any consolation, he gives me the creeps too,' said Sahan.

The shift in the cook's gaze alerted him before Kemasiri even made a noise. Sahan turned.

'Look, it's Mr Colombo Seven,' said Kemasiri. His grin was not reflected in his eyes. 'Hello, beautiful Deepthi. Stock take day, is it?'

Deepthi gave Sahan a look that said 'see what I mean'. 'Yeah,' she said weakly and went back to work, turning her back on them.

Kemasiri looked at Sahan, gestured towards Deepthi and made an appreciative face. Sahan ignored him.

Mr Ghosh came in from the main restaurant. 'Sahan. Customers. Get in there.'

Relieved to have an excuse to leave, Sahan put down the food and went back out again. He would eat later. He'd lost his appetite anyhow.

–

It was clearly the night for rowdy groups. Sahan ushered the last lot out of the restaurant and pulled the blinds down. It was past their normal closing time. Behind him, Mr Ghosh moved around gathering tablecloths for the linen hamper. Sahan grabbed a cloth and started to wipe down the chairs and stack them on the tables.

'You get off, Sahan,' said Mr Ghosh. 'Tell Deepthi to get in here and help me with the hoovering.'

He didn't need telling twice. He finished the table he was doing and went into the back to grab his coat and the bag of food the cook would have left for him. It was quiet in the back. The cooks had left a while ago. Deepthi was probably still in the stockroom. Bags in hand, he went across. When he reached the door, he stopped dead.

Kemasiri was in the stockroom. He had one arm up, leaning against the shelving in an exaggerated casual pose. Effectively trapped between him and the shelves behind her was Deepthi, chin up, eyes moving. When she spotted Sahan, a look of profound relief passed over her face.

Sahan saw the look in Deepthi's eyes and felt a surge of anger. 'What's going on?' He stepped into the stockroom, ready to pull Kemasiri out by his greasy hair.

Kemasiri didn't move his arm, but looked over his shoulder. Deepthi took the opportunity to dodge past him.

'You okay?' Sahan said, as she ducked past him.

She nodded tersely. 'Thank you.' She turned and shot a furious look at Kemasiri.

Kemasiri spread his hands. 'What?' he said. 'We were having a friendly chat, weren't we? What's wrong with that?'

Deepthi's face told Sahan everything he needed to know. He turned back to Kemasiri.

'Don't you dare come near her again, understand?'

'I don't know what you're talking about.'

'Don't bullshit me, Kemasiri. You stay away from Deepthi, or I'll tell her father. Trust me. You do not want to upset Mr G.'

'No,' said Deepthi, from behind him. 'You don't.'

Kemasiri narrowed his eyes. 'You should be careful going around accusing innocent people of things.' He looked at his watch. 'Anyway, my shift is over. Get out of my way so that I can ask Ghosh for my money.'

Sahan backed out of the stock room and let Kemasiri pass. As soon as the other man had disappeared into the main restaurant, Sahan turned to Deepthi. 'You're sure you're okay? He didn't try anything?'

She nodded. She was still clutching her clipboard to her. She looked down at it and lowered her arms. 'No. He didn't. Although, if you hadn't showed up...' She looked up again. 'Thanks Sahan.' She reached out and put a hand on his arm.

The contact made him flinch. 'I wouldn't like to see my sister being intimidated like that,' he said, moving his arm out of the way.

'Right.' Deepthi's brow furrowed. 'Don't tell my father,' she said. 'He's so overprotective, if he hears...'

'I won't tell him,' said Sahan. 'But maybe you should. That guy might try it again.'

'You think?' Her frown deepened.

'I do.'

'Deepthi. Where are you?' Mr Ghosh marched in from the restaurant. His eyes darted from Deepthi to Sahan and back again. 'What is going on here? You.' He pointed at Sahan. 'Why haven't you left?'

'I'm just going.' Sahan caught Deepthi's eye and nodded towards Mr Ghosh.

She sighed. 'Tha,' she said. 'There's something I have to tell you.'

Sahan left them to it and left the shop through the back door.

—

Soma hurried, not wanting to be late. Louie, now fully recovered and delighted to be out and about, waved his arms around and giggled as the pram bounced. Madam had adjusted the pram so that Louie now sat semi upright. He seemed to prefer that to lying down. It was the first time they'd been out since Louie fell ill and Soma half expected to get to the park and find that Sahan hadn't come. She hadn't dared answer the phone during the week, and then it was the weekend. What if he thought she was staying away on purpose? What if he had given up waiting for her?

When she saw him standing by their usual park bench, doing something on his phone, her knees nearly dissolved with relief. He looked up as she approached and the look on his face told her that she needn't have worried. He had turned up for her every day and would carry on doing so.

'You came,' he said, grinning at her. No one had ever looked so pleased to see her before. She felt warm. The tension that had gripped her for the past few days finally started to unravel.

'I'm so sorry. Louie was ill. That time when you called—'

He raised a hand. 'I know. I realised when Yamuna answered the phone. I know you weren't avoiding me.' He lowered his hand, slowly.

'I wouldn't do that.' She wondered if it would be okay to take his hand. They had met so often, and sat together, walked together, but they had never touched. It seemed... too presumptuous. Too much. 'I wouldn't do that,' she repeated.

They stared at each other. And something changed. A barrier she hadn't even been aware of dissolved.

'I will always come to the park,' he said, slowly. 'If I possibly can, I will always come.' His gaze was intense, as though he wanted to be sure she understood him. 'Always.'

She knew what he was telling her. Happiness flooded through her, worries washed away. This was something real. He felt the same way about her as she did about him. For the first time in years, here was something that could genuinely make her happy. Something right. Oh, she knew it couldn't last. He would tire of her soon enough, because he was a man. Men were unpredictable. Even her stepfather, always a little frightening, had seemed like a good husband for her mother until he'd started drinking in earnest.

Although she didn't think Sahan would stop being this kind, gentle individual, she could never be sure. But for now, he liked her and that was good enough for her.

She smiled at him, happiness seeping from every pore, and he smiled back.

Louie blew a raspberry, his current favourite pastime. The spell broke and Sahan laughed. 'Glad to see you're feeling better, little one,' he said, and tickled Louie with a finger.

The baby giggled and squirmed. Sahan looked up. 'I've got some new books...'

She couldn't sit next to him. Not today. She couldn't be so close to him and not touch him. She would never be able to concentrate on a book. 'Can we just walk today?' she said. 'Louie is awake and… it would be nice to walk.'

He nodded. 'Sure.' He strode along next to her as she pushed the pram. After a few moments, he put his hand on the pram handle. 'Shall I push him?' he said.

Surprised, she let him, moving out of the way. Then, in a fit of boldness, she put her gloved hand on his and left it there. He looked across at her and then away. Neither of them mentioned it.

'I should get a mobile phone,' she said. She had been thinking about this a lot in the past few days. The system with the phone worked well enough when Madam wasn't around, but when she was… 'You can call me sometimes then. And leave a message. Like if you can't come to the park. And I can call you.'

'That's a very good idea,' he said. 'And if Louie is ill, you can tell me, so I won't have to stand around in the park like a spare part.'

'I… don't know much about phones,' she said.

'How do you keep in touch with your family?' he said. 'Don't you call them?'

Hah. Who would she keep in touch with? 'I… write to them,' she lied. 'Not that often.'

He didn't seem to find that unusual. 'Oh, okay. Well, what sort of phone do you want?'

'I only have about twenty pounds to spend on it. I need to have money to make calls too.'

'That should be plenty,' he said. 'On Monday, instead of coming to the park, we can go to Princes Avenue. There's bound to be somewhere there you can buy a cheap phone. I'll help you choose.' He stopped and frowned. 'Actually, maybe Princes Avenue is too close to Yamuna's work. Let's go to Chanterlands instead.'

She had no idea where he was talking about. Seeing her expression, he explained, giving her directions. To do this, he had to move his hand out from under hers. When he had finished explaining and they resumed walking, he reached for her hand and placed it on the pram handle, underneath his own. And Soma thought her heart would explode with happiness.

That weekend, Kemasiri was not at the restaurant. Mr Ghosh must have fired him after he heard about the incident with Deepthi. Mr Ghosh was in a bad mood because he had to drive the takeaway orders out himself. It was a difficult night and Sahan was glad when the restaurant shut for the night, so that he could grab his bag of food and leave.

He was coming out of the alleyway when Kemasiri sprang out in front of him.

'You.' Kemasiri stopped him by pushing a palm against his chest. Even at this distance, Sahan could smell the alcohol mixed in with his cigarette breath. 'You'll pay for what you did to me, Colombo Seven. I will make you wish you'd never crossed me.'

Sahan tried to keep going. 'It had nothing to do with me. You tried to mess with the boss's daughter.'

'She wouldn't have run squealing to her father if you hadn't made her.' Kemasiri stepped in front of him again. 'You couldn't mind your own business, could you? You think you're so much better than me? Back home, you've got all the privileges, but over here, we're the same.' He closed the space between them and jabbed a finger at Sahan's chest. 'I may be just a driver, but you, Colombo Seven, are just a waiter. You think I can't hurt you? You think you're too big for that?'

Sahan felt a stab of alarm. He weighed up his chances if the other man got violent. He hoped things wouldn't come to that. Kemasiri jabbed him in the chest again. Sahan batted his hand away. 'Look, I'm sorry. I have to go catch a bus.'

'Scared of me, Fancy Boy?' Kemasiri squared up to him. Too close, too ugly to ignore.

Over Kemasiri's shoulder, Sahan could see his bus approaching. The sooner he got on it, the sooner he could put some distance between himself and this odious twerp.

'Yes, yes, I'm scared of you,' he said and pushed the other man out of the way. He pushed harder than he'd intended and Kemasiri stumbled backwards. Sahan carried on walking.

'Everyone has their secrets, Fancy Boy,' Kemasiri shouted after him. 'I will find out yours. And I will destroy you. This isn't over.'

'Oh yes it is.' Sahan muttered. He kept walking and hoped to goodness that he was right.

–

Soma ran the conversation with Sahan through her mind again as she prepared for Louie's bedtime. Madam had brought Louie back from the bath and dressed him, while Soma tidied up the room, putting toys away and collecting muslin burp cloths or bibs for the wash. This was one of the few times of day when she and Madam overlapped in their care of Louie. Soma tried to stay out of the way as much as possible.

The phone rang. Instinctively, she counted the rings. It reached three and kept ringing. It wasn't Sahan then. Madam, looking harassed, gave an exasperated tut and put Louie in the cot. The baby immediately protested, so Soma drifted across to calm him down.

'Soma.' Madam returned, holding out a phone. 'It's the agency. They want to speak to you.'

The bottom dropped out of her world. They knew. Somehow they had found out her secret and they were going to send her home. She couldn't breathe.

'Soma.' Madam gestured for her to take the phone.

Adrenaline kicked in and saved her, just as it had done on the flight over. Trying to keep her face from betraying her fear, she took the phone. 'Hello?'

'Is that Somavathi?' said a woman's voice.

'Yes.'

'This is Ira from the agency. You met me in Sri Lanka when we interviewed you.'

They had never met. She was talking about Somavathi. Panic rose. She thought fast.

'Yes. I remember, miss.'

'I wanted to check that you were all right. We don't normally do this, but your family said you hadn't been in touch and they were worried about your safety... Are you being treated well?'

It took a few seconds for this to make sense. Somavathi's family must have been so worried about the lack of response to the letters that they got in touch with the agency. They were checking on her. If they thought she was in danger, they might try to come and rescue her. First, she had to convince the company that she was fine. 'Oh yes, I'm well,' she said. Then, remembering that

Madam was listening, she added, 'Madam treats me very well.'

'You haven't been threatened in any way? Your passport is still with you? Just say yes or no.'

'Yes. Yes. I am happy here.'

There was a small sigh on the other end of the line. 'Your family say that you haven't been in touch...'

Her stomach twisted. She was hurting someone. But she couldn't do anything without risking this fragile new life she'd built. She couldn't do the right thing, because it meant her being sent back to hell. 'I... don't want to. I'm sorry,' she said. 'I don't want to write or call.'

A pause. 'Okay. I will let them know that you are safe and unharmed. That is all I can do.'

'Thank you.'

'Please can you hand the phone back to Mrs Gamage.'

She obediently gave the handset back to Madam and sat down next to Louie's cot. As she lifted the little boy onto her lap and gave him his bottle, she hoped that Madam wouldn't ask too many questions.

Luckily for her, by the time she had sung Louie to sleep, Madam had gone downstairs. What could she say if Madam wanted details? She could make up a lie about how she and her mother didn't get along. Or maybe even tell the truth of sorts about her stepfather... but that would lead to more questions. She had shut Jaya and her sad life out of her mind now and she didn't want to remember it. She rubbed her face and sighed.

She could only hope that Madam had forgotten all about the phone call by the next time she saw her.

If only she could do the same.

Sahan spotted her before she saw him. He watched Soma manoeuvre the pram across the road and back onto the pavement. It had only been three days since he'd last seen her, but he'd missed her.

She was wrapped up in layers of clothing again, despite the weather warming up. It wasn't quite the weather for shorts and t-shirt yet, but Soma looked like she was prepared for a blizzard. He watched her nod to people and smile shyly when they said hello. Even well wrapped up, she looked small compared to the people she passed. She wasn't that much shorter, but she had a certain compactness about her, as though she was trying to take up as little space in the world as possible. It made him want to put his arms around that space and protect her.

Their last meeting had changed something. He wasn't sure what had happened, but suddenly his doubts had shrunk to insignificance. For the first time since the Tamsin incident, he had touched someone and not felt anything other than happiness. Holding her hand felt... right. Even the insistent tug of wanting in his stomach had felt okay. Not shameful, not wrong, but normal. He was in love with this girl. He was allowed to want her.

Of course, his family would go ballistic if they found out. They would say that she was just looking for a way to climb up the social ladder by marrying him. But, he reminded himself, he was an adult now. When he finished his course, he would be a graduate. With any luck, he would get a job and be able to support himself, and maybe... but he was getting ahead of himself. He didn't know how Soma felt. She seemed to be shy and frightened and in need of looking after. But what if that was all she wanted? What if his family's views had a grain of truth? Socially, they *were* poles apart. She was a pretty girl, but one with no prospects apart from her job as a nanny. Her fear of Yamuna finding out about their relationship, innocent as it was, was evidence of that. What if he was her insurance policy?

As he always did when this thought intruded, Sahan pushed it away. There were things he needed to think about – the fact that his course was coming to an end, the jobs he was applying for which were based miles away, the social strata that lay between them. He would have to face them eventually, but not now. What he had with Soma, whatever it was, was too new and precious for practical reality to ruin. Not yet.

Across the way, Soma spotted him and her face transformed from worried to delighted. She smiled and gave him a tiny wave, not quite removing her hand from the pram. He stepped away from the bus shelter he'd been standing in and walked up to join her.

The street was busy, but there was room enough on the pavement for them to walk side by side. When the sun came out, it would be busier still as the students from the university ventured further afield in the good weather. Sahan liked this area of Hull. It was a good distance away from the city centre, closer to Cottingham and the university than to town. The street was crammed with independent shops and cafes, which, despite the preponderance of tanning salons and nail bars, made it more lively than the city centre with its chain stores. People bustled about, often in huge family groups, which made it noisy and friendly. It reminded him a little of Colombo.

He took Soma into a shop that sold unlocked phones and explained to the bored man behind the counter what they needed. Soon they were standing on the pavement, Sahan holding the pram, pushing a cranky Louie back and forth while Soma put away her purse. A couple of elderly ladies walking past smiled at him.

'It's nice how the men do their share of looking after the little 'uns these days. Our Pete never did a nappy with any of ours,' one said to the other as they passed.

Sahan looked from Soma to Louie. They did look like a little family, the three of them. The idea should have horrified him, but oddly, it didn't. Soma was changing him, he reflected. Somehow making him more himself.

She finished fiddling around with her bag and smiled at him. 'Will you show me how to use it?' she said.

'Don't you know? I thought everyone had phones these days, even in Matara.'

She shook her head. 'Not me.' They started walking again, heading back the way they'd come. 'We were too poor for that sort of thing,' she said. 'There was a phone at the shop though, you could use it if you paid a few rupees.'

To Sahan, whose parents had had to confiscate his phone during exam season, this seemed incredible. What different worlds they came from. 'That's...' he shook his head. 'I can't imagine that.'

Soma laughed. 'I know.'

He took the phone from her and turned it on. When they'd walked a little way, she said, 'How is your job search going? Did you send off that application you were preparing last week?'

'Yes.'

She seemed to be thinking about something for a few minutes. 'Is it very far away, that job?'

'Quite far, but only a few hours on the train, really.' He would be able to come back and visit her at the weekends, but it would be awkward. Soma wouldn't be able to disappear for the day with him every weekend. And she certainly wouldn't be able to come and visit him without raising eyebrows.

'Oh,' said Soma. The smile dropped from her face. Her shoulders dropped a fraction and she seemed to shrink into her coat.

'But we can talk to each other, now that you have a phone,' he said. 'Besides, I haven't got the job yet. You never know… I might not.'

'But that wouldn't be good either,' said Soma. 'You need to get a job to stay here. If it's far away, then…' She leaned forward to fuss with Louie's blanket, leaving the sentence hanging in the air. A reminder of the frailty of their relationship.

'We will manage,' he said, with more reassurance than he felt. 'We'll cross that bridge when we get to it.'

She didn't look at him, but carried on walking. He wished he could magic away his problems and pretend, just for a day, that everything was going to be okay.

The traffic on the road next to them was steady. Out of the corner of his eye, Sahan noticed the cars slowing down but didn't think anything of it. A horn beeped. He turned his head. A black car was pulling slowly past, despite the road being clear ahead. Odd. Perhaps they were lost. Thinking to help, he glanced inside the car… and froze. Kemasiri sat in the driving seat, staring out at him as the car crawled past. Seeing him look, Kemasiri nodded. A thin smirk lit his features and the car sped up and pulled away.

Sahan felt a chill run through him. He didn't like Kemasiri at the best of times, but that smirk… that frightened him. Kemasiri had recognized him. He had seen him with Soma, pushing Louie's pram, so he couldn't claim they'd merely bumped into each other. *Everyone has secrets.* Now Kemasiri knew his. The smirk suggested that he was planning to use the information somehow. What if he knew some way to get in touch with his family?

'Sahan?' said Soma.

He realised he had stopped walking. He looked at Soma's worried face. He couldn't frighten her with his crazy suspicions. 'Sorry,' he said. 'I got distracted for a minute.'

They walked along, chatting. He demonstrated how to use the phone and put his own number into the contacts under S. He then swapped with her, giving her the phone and taking the pram again, so that she could practice calling him.

Finally, they reached the house, walked past the front door that Sahan always used and came to a halt by the garage.

'I… will go in here,' Soma said, gesturing to the entrance that Sahan knew led to the garage. You could enter the kitchen through the garage that way, without having to lift the pram over awkward steps. 'Will I see you tomorrow?'

'I can call you this evening,' he said. 'After nine o'clock… if you like.'

She beamed. 'Oh. Of course. With my phone, you can call me.'

'That is the idea.'

She flushed a little, adorably. 'I would like that very much.'

'In that case, I'll speak to you later.'

Sahan stopped at the side gate and watched her take the pram up the sloping path. He was glad she didn't suggest he come in. Going into his cousin's house without her knowledge felt too great a betrayal. It also made an unwelcome link between Soma and his life back in Sri Lanka. But if he was serious about how he felt, he would have to let her into his other world sometimes. It was too great a leap to think of introducing Soma to his family, but perhaps they could do more than just walk around a park. Maybe they could have one day, when they forgot the world and pretended it all okay. 'What are you doing this Saturday?' he called, suddenly. 'I know that Yamuna gives you Saturday off.'

Soma frowned. Her gaze did a quick sweep of the street behind him, as though checking for spies. 'I will stay in and watch television. As always,' she said.

'Come to York with me,' he said. 'We'll catch a bus and go and sightseeing.'

She looked worried. Scared, even. He had a sudden wave of emotion. He wanted to cocoon her, keep her safe. 'Don't worry. I'll be with you. You'll be perfectly safe.'

'But—'

'You can't spend all the time in that house by yourself. You'll go mad.' He smiled. 'Come on. It'll be fun. I'll text you the bus times. You'll be back home in time for Louie's bedtime.'

She pushed the pram back to the gate, so that she could speak in a low whisper. 'What will I tell Madam?'

'Say you're being adventurous and going into town to do some shopping.'

'She might offer to take me. She sometimes does.'

He grinned. 'No, she won't. They're going to Sheffield this Saturday. I know because I was supposed to go with them. So, you'll be in the house alone all day.'

She fussed with Louie's blankets for a minute, not looking at him.

'I won't let anything happen to you,' he said. 'I promise.'

When she looked back up at him, her eyes were huge and trusting. 'Okay,' she said. 'Let us do that.' She glanced back at Louie. 'He's going to wake up and want his food in a minute. I must go in.'

'I'll call you tonight,' he said.

'I would like that.' She gave him a happy grin and turned back towards the garage.

He watched her disappear through the wicket door into the garage before he set off for the bus stop. The warm glow he always felt after spending time with Soma buoyed his steps. By the time he got home, he'd forgotten all about seeing Kemasiri that afternoon.

Chapter Sixteen

The mobile phone was a wondrous thing. It cost money to make phone calls, so Soma didn't use it for that, but it didn't cost anything to receive calls. Sahan called her well after Louie had gone to bed. They had arranged the whole trip to York via quiet conversations late at night.

Conscious that she was leaving not only the house, but the whole town, Soma left a note for Madam with her number, explaining that she had gone out. She hadn't told Madam about the phone, but there was no reason to hide it. If anything, Madam would be relieved that she could contact her.

With luck, she could be back before Madam got home and no one would know she'd even been out. Sahan texted her to say he had caught the bus, so she went out of the back door as always and ran to the bus stop.

She repeated, 'Return ticket to York please,' over and over under her breath until it was time to say it out loud to the driver. The woman driving the bus understood her without any problem. Soma went to take the seat Sahan was saving for her, feeling triumphant. She'd spoken to an English person and managed it.

It was strange sitting together like this with no Louie to provide a reason for her being there.

'So here we are,' said Sahan, after a few minutes. 'This is strange.'

She looked across, glad he felt the same. 'It is. But it's good.'

'It's weird seeing you without Louie,' he said. 'You've got your phone?'

She pulled it out of her pocket to show to him.

'You've got a phone and now you're able to take the bus out to different cities. You'll be a native in no time,' he said.

She giggled and some of the awkwardness disappeared. She could do this. In the past few months she'd done more new things than she could even count. This was just another one. All she had to do was relax and let the day go as it would. She could see a new city. Learn more about this amazing country. Being able to have Sahan with her while she explored only made things even better.

They talked all the way to York. They had talked before, but this time it was different. It was just the two of them. No Louie. No careful space between them. The bus went round a corner, and pressed her shoulder against his. She blushed and looked up at him through her eyelashes, suddenly shy again. He smiled at her. His fingers moved across to hers and they held hands rest of the way there.

–

He didn't let go of her hand when the bus stopped, or even when they alighted on the busy pavement. Soma looked around. The streets in York were narrower than the ones in Hull and seemed much busier. She felt a moment of panic, but Sahan squeezed her hand and that made everything better again.

'Where shall we go?' said Sahan, smiling.

'I don't know.' It was all bewildering to her.

193

Sahan got a book out of his bag. There was a map folded into the back of it. He opened it up, fold upon fold upon fold, until it was several times the size of the book.

'There's lots to see. How about we walk through the Shambles? If we go this way, we can make our way to the cathedral.'

The places were just words to her. He showed her the map. She nodded. She didn't really care, so long as she was with him. They walked through the narrow cobbled street, with mashed together houses leaning over them on either side. At one point they walked through a square, where a man was juggling fire whilst riding a sort of bicycle with only one wheel. They stopped to watch and her mouth fell open. She had seen fire jugglers before, but it had been at night and she had the vague memory of being held on her father's shoulders so that she could see.

She glanced across at Sahan, who had let go of her hand to applaud. She felt her world opening up, like the map in Sahan's book; getting wider and taller with each unfolding page. There was so much she didn't know about. So much to learn. The places she'd seen on the little TV were real. It was terrifying and exhilarating at the same time.

The juggler leapt off his cycle, put out the fires on his juggling pins and took a bow. Sahan threw some money into the man's hat. Then he picked up Soma's hand again.

'Shall we go on to the cathedral?'

When she nodded, he started walking, leading her along streets that were less narrow, but just as crowded.

'Sahan,' she said. 'What is a cathedral?'

'It's a big church,' he said. 'Is that okay?'

She shrugged. She had seen churches before. There was a small one in the town near where she lived and bigger ones in Matara. She tried to remember if she'd ever been inside one.

'Here we are,' said Sahan.

She looked around, expecting a blocky, whitewashed building.

Sahan laughed. 'There,' he said, pointing.

She looked up. And further up. The building wasn't a church, it was a palace, soaring up towards the sky covered in delicate decorations that looked too intricate to have been carved from stone. 'Oooh,' she breathed. 'It's beautiful.'

'Wait till you see inside,' he said.

—

He could have watched her for hours. They were walking through the vast nave of York Minster. Sahan had been there before and admired the elaborate bosses on the ceiling and beauty of the stained glass windows. But Soma was seeing these things for the first time. He was towing her along, holding her hand, because she was walking so slowly, looking at everything. The church had been built to inspire wonder and it was certainly doing that. Soma was transfixed.

He was glad he'd brought her here. Being away from Hull and Louie made Soma different. She seemed to have relaxed a little, opened up. When he was with her in the park, there was always something jittery about her. It was as though she was expecting Yamuna to jump out of the bushes at any moment. In fairness, he felt a bit like that too.

But here, with the threat of discovery so remote, Soma was wide-eyed and delighted with the world. She had seen so little of it. Things he took for granted were new discoveries to her – British street food, bendy buses, enormous book shops, doughnuts. Doughnuts! He had bought her one from a street vendor, just to see the expression on her face when she bit into it. When she looked at him, with her eyes shining, he felt… invincible. How could he ever have thought this was passing phase?

He looked down at his hand, wrapped protectively around her smaller one. He was holding a girl's hand and he wasn't feeling any of his usual reactions. In the back of his mind, Cara's voice corrected him, 'woman, not girl'. Woman, then. Still no nausea. That had to mean something, didn't it?

Looking up, he spotted the time on the ornamental clock. It was nearly quarter past the hour. 'Soma,' he said. 'Look at the clock.'

'Hmm?' She turned and glanced at it, tearing her eyes away from the stained glass window. 'It's very nice,' she said.

'No. Watch.' The clock hit quarter past and a mechanism whirred.

He watched the delight on her face as two knights came out of the clock to strike the bell. He didn't think he'd ever felt this happy.

–

Finally, it was time to go and they sat on a half wall, waiting for the bus to take them back to Hull. Soma wrapped her scarf around her throat and face snugly and made Sahan laugh.

'You look like you're hiding,' he said.

She had forgotten she was meant to be hiding. She gave him a quick glance and was relieved to see his eyes sparkling. 'I'm not,' she said. 'I don't want to get cold.'

'It's not that cold, honestly,' said Sahan, still laughing. 'You should loosen that scarf a little bit. Let me see your face.' He reached across and tugged a loop of it down, revealing her face. His hand grazed her cheek and she felt his touch somewhere deep inside.

His smile fell away. His gaze held hers. Had he felt it too? Sahan took a breath and his fingertips touched her cheek again, the softest, gentlest caress. The thrill was so intense, she could barely breathe. Her whole existence narrowed to focus on him; his eyes, his mouth, the delicious warmth of his fingertips against her skin. The moment stretched. Was this what it was like to *want* to be touched?

The bus pulled in at the stop.

'The bus. We should…' Sahan's voice sounded deeper. He cleared his throat and moved his hand away. 'We should get on.'

'Yes. Of course.' She sprang to her feet and followed him. They sat together again, close together, hands intertwined. Neither of them spoke on the way back although Soma felt every touch, every shift of muscle. She wanted to memorize it all.

When the bus finally arrived back on the approach to Hull, she rang the bell at her stop, stood up and left him sitting there. Once she was off the bus, she turned to look at him through the window. He raised the hand that she had been holding only a few seconds before and waved. She smiled and waved back. The bus pulled away and he was gone, leaving her alone.

She walked back in a hazy cloud, barely noticing anything around her. She could feel the ghost pressure of his hand still in hers and on her face she could still feel his touch as though she had been branded by it. She let herself into the house and was relieved to find that her note was still there. She had just scrunched it up when she heard the garage door scrolling open. Madam was home. Quickly, she hung up her coat and scarf and took off her shoes.

Yamuna came in, carrying a sleeping Louie. 'He fell asleep in the car,' she whispered to Soma. 'We may as well put him to bed now.'

If Madam noticed that she was glowing with happiness, she didn't mention it. Soma took the sleeping baby in her arms and took him upstairs. She laid him gently in the cot, and leaned over to kiss him goodnight. Then, because she thought she would burst if she didn't tell somebody, she whispered in his little ear, 'I went to York with Sahan today. I love him.'

–

Sahan lay on his bed, fully clothed and wide awake. He tucked one arm underneath his head and held his other hand up to look at it. He could still feel the shape of Soma's hand in his. He closed his fist around the feeling, trying to hold it there. Today was the first time he had seen Soma without Louie to give her context. Without the pram, she seemed somehow smaller, more accessible. Seeing the guarded look in her eyes when she'd first got on the bus slowly melt away had made him feel as though something inside him was melting in response.

It was the first time in years that he had been able to bear contact with someone. He had held her hand, bumped into her, touched her cheek without a single flinch. Not a hint of repulsion. All too familiar longing stirred, but without the usual dousing of shame.

He wanted to hold her. It would be okay with Soma. She was different. There was something about her shyness, her vulnerability, her ability to be amazed and over-whelmed by the world. She was different to the worldly wise, hard-bitten girls from his course. She was sweet and kind and… pure. And it was okay to fall in love with her.

–

'I think Soma has something going on that she doesn't want us to know about,' Yamuna said, as she got into bed. It was one of those rare evenings where both she and Bim were going to bed at the same time.

He was sitting up, reading a copy of the *FT* and scrib-bling notes on a pad of paper. He said 'mmm,' without looking up.

'First, she didn't tell her family where she was, so they had to write through the agency. Then, there was the whole thing where the agency wanted to check that she really was here. Now she's got a new mobile phone. She didn't tell me, but I can hear her, whispering in Sinhalese in her room. And she's been wandering around with this stupefied look on her face.' She turned to look at her husband. 'Are you listening?'

Bim lowered his paper with exaggerated patience. 'Does it matter?' he said. 'Everyone has a mobile phone these days and she's probably using it to phone home.'

'It does matter.' She held up her hand to tick off her points. 'She's been here four months and she's never wanted to call home before. I asked her. Even showed her where to get the long-distance phone cards. Secondly, why the secrecy? Why the daydreaming? I think she's got a man.'

'So? She's a grown woman.'

'A grown woman? Have you seen her? She looks like she's about twelve. I have serious doubts about how thoroughly that agency checks people's age.'

'You said they showed you photocopies of a birth certificate and passport.'

'They did. But those were photocopies. What if they were clever forgeries?'

Bim lowered his paper again and finally looked at her. 'You think the agency is a bunch of master criminals now?'

Was he really so obtuse that he didn't see a problem? 'But Bim. Who is this man she's met? Clearly, he's Sri Lankan, because she speaks Sinhalese to him. How did she meet him? She doesn't go out at the weekends, so she must meet up with him when she's with Louie. I don't want Louie exposed to strange men.'

Bim shook his head. 'I think you're worrying about nothing. Where would she meet a Sri Lankan around here?'

'I don't know. Unless it's someone she knew already. Maybe she had a boyfriend who moved to the UK and she followed him here.' Yamuna chewed the inside of her cheek. 'What if she lets him in the house when we're out? What if they sleep together when Louie's around, Bim?'

Finally, Bim frowned. 'Do you seriously suspect that the girl is bringing a man into this house?'

'Yes. That's what I've been trying to tell you.'

'Well... you could ask her.' He held up a hand as she started to protest. 'Even if she doesn't tell you anything, her reaction will tell you something.'

Yamuna opened her mouth to argue again, and then shut it. 'Actually, that's not a bad idea. Not asking her, but I could ask Sahan. He knows the other Sri Lankan students at the uni. Between them, they'll know all the other Sri Lankans around here. Especially the young ones. He might be able to find out who this guy is that Soma's so taken with.' Having a plan of action made her feel better already.

'Isn't Sahan busy studying for his exams?' said Bim. 'Besides, you don't know that there is a man involved, yet. All you know is that she's got a mobile phone. That's not the same thing.'

'I know she's up to something,' said Yamuna. 'I can feel it in my bones. I'm going to find out what it is.'

'Speaking of mobile phones,' said Bim. 'There's something wrong with mine. I keep having to plug it in to charge by lunchtime. I must get a new one.' The newspaper came back up and he resumed reading.

Yamuna glared at him. He was engrossed in his paper again. He blatantly didn't care. She turned away from him, annoyed. Sometimes, she got the impression that he only kept her and Louie around to say he had them. Like pets or houseplants. Wife, tick. Son and heir, tick. He had what he wanted now. It didn't matter how they felt about it, so long as he could wheel them out when he needed them.

What had her life come to? Getting married was supposed to make her life better, not make her feel more and more irrelevant.

She shook her head and curled up with her back to him. What was done, was done. There was no undoing it now.

She would have to catch Sahan and ask him to find out some information for her. Really, the only place she could think of where Soma would meet someone her own age was the university, which was only twenty minutes' walk away. She wondered idly what she'd do once she found out who this guy was. She frowned. She herself had always been too plain, too serious to get any attention from attractive men, but had seen enough hearts broken to know that the sort of man who insisted on sneaking around out of sight was the sort of man who meant trouble. Soma was young and she was in a strange country. A girl like that was easy prey. If this man was looking for a girl to take advantage of, Soma would be perfect.

The thought that Soma could bring a man into the house and put Louie at risk bothered her. Could it be? Despite her irritation at Soma, she still had to admit that the girl seemed to care for the baby. Yamuna had never seen her do anything that could harm Louie. Even the whispered conversations she'd heard were late at night, well after Louie went to sleep. No, she decided. Whatever else there was to worry about, she didn't have to worry about Soma neglecting her baby.

Chapter Seventeen

Soma cleared up Louie's breakfast and put slices of bread in to make toast for herself. She could feel Madam watching her. The hairs on the back of her neck prickled with awareness. Why did Madam dislike her? Soma examined her behaviour. She always did her jobs. She was diligent. So why?

She turned to look at her employer, who looked away, a small frown line between her brows. Soma took a deep breath. She should find out what the problem was. 'Madam?' she said, carefully. 'Have I done something wrong?'

Madam looked up. 'That's a strange thing to say.'

'If I have made a mistake, of I'm doing something wrong with Louie, please tell me. I will make sure not to do it again.'

The frown line deepened. 'Soma. I can't think of anyone who looks after Louie better than you do.'

'Then why don't you like me?' The question burst out of her before she could stop it. As she said it, she realised it was important. Madam was important. Soma blinked. When had that happened? Why? She only needed Madam to not suspect her of anything. She didn't need her to like her. Did she?

Madam looked surprised. It was a few seconds before she said anything. 'You are a diligent worker, Soma. I have no reason to dislike you. Unless you are hiding something from me. Are you?'

Thankfully, the toast popped at that moment, giving Soma an excuse to turn away. 'No Madam,' she murmured. Her heart hammered. Did Madam *suspect*?

–

Sahan didn't often go into the centre of Hull during the day. There wasn't any point. He could get most things he needed from near the campus. For anything bigger, there was always the internet. But the sunshine was glorious and he couldn't bear to sit in his room studying any longer, so he tagged along with Nate and Cara to go and see the music festival in the Queen's gardens. It was busy, with groups of people, mostly families, sitting in the park. Flowers provided a riot of colour in the borders. A jazz band was on in the bandstand. The plaza at the end of the park was full of food stalls. The whole place had a low key buzz about it. It was wonderful to lie back on the grass and think about something other than hydrodynamics. Sahan let the jazz wash over him and shut his eyes to dream about his afternoon in York with Soma.

'Oi lazy arse. We're going into town to grab something from the pie stall, you coming?' Nate poked him with the toe of his trainers.

Sahan opened an eye. There were more people in the group than before. 'Uh. Yeah. Okay.' He sat up. The new people were mostly Cara's friends. One of them was, uh oh, Bex. She nodded to him and looked away. He felt a twinge of guilt. He could have been nicer. Or at least been clearer. Still, it was done now. He scrambled to his feet and dusted himself off.

They set off in a straggled line, past the bright flower-beds and fountains. The various food stalls were bustling, giving the place a festival atmosphere. People fell into step with others and somehow Sahan was left walking next to Bex.

'Um… how's it going?' he said.

She glanced at him sideways. 'Not bad. You?'

'Oh you know, studying.'

She nodded. 'Right.'

What did you do when there was awkward silence like this? He cleared his throat. 'Look I'm sorry about…'

She made a brushing off motion with her hand. 'It's fine.'

'I—' But he was interrupted by someone saying 'Sahan?'

They had reached the open space of Victoria Square, where some children were playing in the open fountain under the stern gaze of Queen Victoria. He stopped and turned to see Yamuna approaching from one of the many paths that fed into the square. Behind her was Soma, pushing Louie. His heart kicked up a notch. He resisted the urge to look at Soma and tried to focus on his cousin instead. 'Yamuna, hi.'

'How are you? We haven't seen you in a while.' She smiled at him, but her eyes darted to the group of friends behind him. He had to be careful. Everything about this meeting would make its way back to his parents. He had to be absolutely sure not to give anything away about Soma.

'I've been… studying. Exams start next week.' Not looking at Soma was unbearable. He could feel the pull of her, standing quietly behind Louie's pram. He forced himself to keep his eyes on Yamuna. 'How are you? How's Bim?'

He didn't hear what she said in response. He couldn't bear it any longer. He moved to the side of the pram and made a show of peering in at Louie. 'And how's Louie?' Louie, who was used to seeing Sahan, beamed at the sight of him and wriggled happily.

Sahan risked a glance up and found himself looking into Soma's eyes. Warmth rose from the core of him and he could barely breathe for wanting to touch her. He tried to convey in his single glance that he was happy to see her. That he missed her. That he wished he could speak to her now and not pretend not to notice her. He saw her breath catch and it thrilled him. She took a deep breath and looked down. A smart reminder to Sahan that Yamuna mustn't find out. He took the hint and straightened up.

For the first time, he noticed that his friends had stopped too. Yamuna was still looking at them curiously. 'Oh, Yamuna, these are my friends. Nate, Cara and... uh... Bex.' Damn. Why had he hesitated at Bex's name? He took a quick glance at Soma to see if she'd noticed. She was still studiously ignoring what was going on and fussing with Louie.

'Hi. I'm Sahan's cousin,' said Yamuna.

'I've seen you around at the uni,' said Cara. 'Are you studying there?'

Yamuna laughed. 'No. I'm flattered you think I'm a student, but no, I'm staff. I'm a post doc in the Biological Sciences department. What are you studying?'

'History. Medicine. Drama.' Cara pointed to herself, Nate and Bex in turn.

Yamuna politely enquired how things were going. Soma continued to avoid eye contact and fuss around with Louie. Sahan stood there, shifting his weight from one foot to the other, in agonies of awkwardness. Finally,

Yamuna said, 'I guess I'd better let you get on. Sahan, you should come round one evening. I'll make dinner.'

Oh, the relief. 'Yes. That would be great. I'll call you later,' he said. Yamuna nodded her goodbyes to the others and peeled off on her way. As she pushed the pram past him, Soma looked up shyly and gave him a little, secret smile. He felt it in his gut. He smiled back and watched them as they hurried away.

'Hey, that was her, wasn't it?' Nate nudged him hard enough to make him jump. 'The girl you were talking about. That was her.'

'Shh. Keep it down.' He checked to see if Yamuna had heard, but she was still hurrying away, well out of earshot. 'Yes,' he smiled. 'Yes, that was her.'

'Wow,' said Bex, quietly. 'The way you looked at her. No wonder you're not interested in anyone else.' She smiled, and for the first time that day, it reached her eyes. 'If someone looks at me like that just once in my life, I'll be a happy woman.'

Sahan grinned back at her, glad the ice had melted. 'Someone will, Bex. Someone will.'

They started walking again. 'And your cousin doesn't know about you guys? Why keep it a secret?' Cara said.

'She's their nanny. It's not the done thing to fall in love with the nanny, really. If my parents found out, they'd kill me.' He saw Nate and Cara exchange glances. They didn't really see a problem, he knew. Thankfully, they didn't launch into the argument about cultural norms and class snobbery. The three of them had wasted too many evenings on that already.

'So what are you going to do when you graduate?' said Bex, who had made no secret of the fact that she was going to go to London when she finished.

He didn't really want to think about that too much. He had originally thought of working in the south of England for a bit, then applying for jobs in the Middle East, where the money was good. But now... now he wanted to be somewhere near Soma. Hull wasn't really an option, not unless he found something in one the big chemical firms in the area, but there were places like Leeds and Sheffield within an hour's commute. He was confident he would pass his course with at least a 2.1, but he needed a work visa to go with his job, which immediately put him at a disadvantage.

'I'm applying for jobs...' he said. 'I might get lucky.'

'What if you get a job miles away from here?' said Bex. 'What will you do then? Long distance relationship?'

Cara laughed. 'Or you could elope with her and get married in secret.'

Sahan laughed too, but at the back on his mind, the thought nestled in.

—

Soma sat by Louie's bed, waiting for him to go to sleep. By the glow of the nightlight, she watched the shape of his little body as he moved around, trying to fight sleep and failing.

The image of Sahan with his white friends kept resurfacing in her mind. It was the first time she'd had a glimpse into his life. She'd seen him striding along in the sunshine, chatting to a girl who was far more glamorous than she could ever be and her heart had leapt to her throat. When he'd looked at her, his eyes speaking volumes in that one glance, her whole body had felt as though it would burst into flames and she'd felt, for the briefest of moments, that they had something special. But then he had looked away, snatched back into a world where she didn't belong. Where he spoke English and sounded exactly like his friends – a world where people had degrees and owned houses and had big, office jobs.

Oh, she knew her connection to him was tenuous. She was only a distraction to him for a few short months. But that didn't stop the thought of being so far from him ripping holes in her heart. He was applying for jobs in places she could barely pronounce. Places that were too far away for her to have a hope of seeing him again. She couldn't ask him not to go. That was where his future lay. Not with her.

People like her didn't end up with people like him. That was just the way the world worked. She sighed. He would call her later. No matter how she felt, she would be cheerful and back him in whatever decisions he was making. What else could she do?

–

Yamuna called Sahan that night. 'I need to ask you some-thing,' she said.

His breath caught. Had Yamuna noticed the look that had passed between him and Soma? If Bex and Cara had spotted it, then it wasn't such a stretch to think that Yamuna had noticed it too. What did he say if she asked him outright? He would have to lie. He steeled himself. 'Sure. What is it?'

'Do you know if there are any Sri Lankan guys at the uni? Students, I mean?'

Okay. Weird question, not what he was expecting. Phew. He relaxed. 'A few, why?'

'I think Soma has a boyfriend. A Sri Lankan one. She's only been here a few months and already she's sneaking around with someone. You know what these people are like,' said Yamuna, her voice dripping with disapproval.

'Wh—?' Soma wouldn't cheat on him. 'Uh. What makes you think that?'

'She's got a mobile phone in her room. She hasn't told me about it, which is fairly suspicious in itself. Anyway, she's usually on it, whispering in Sinhalese. I've heard her when I go to check on Louie.'

Thank goodness. That was all it was. 'You listen outside her door?' Oh god, what had she heard? He tried to think what they'd talked about – they'd mostly talked for the pleasure of hearing each other's voices. But what if Soma had said his name? Maybe Yamuna was using some elaborate double bluff to make him incriminate himself.

The pause at Yamuna's end was a dead giveaway.

'You do, don't you?' he said.

'She lives in my house and looks after my son. I have a right to know,' said Yamuna. 'It didn't do any good, though. She speaks so softly, I couldn't tell what she was saying.'

Another wave of relief. 'You think she might be seeing someone from the uni?'

'Well, I'm not sure, but even if he's not a student there, someone there is bound to know something.'

'And you want *me* to find out who it is?' Oh the irony. He tried not to grin, in case she could hear the amusement in his voice.

'Yes. Can you do that for me? Ask a few questions? After your exams are over, obviously. Your education comes first.'

'I don't know, Yamuna…'

'Sahan, if she's seeing some man when I'm not at home, I need to know. She's supposed to be looking after Louie.'

'She would never do that!' It came out before he had time to censor it. He quickly tried to recover the situation. 'I mean, I get the impression she's very fond of Louie. She wouldn't put him in danger.'

There was a pause. 'You're probably right.' Yamuna had the grace to sound embarrassed.

'What will you do, if you find this guy? Assuming there is a guy.'

'Try and put a stop to it, I suppose. I mean, she's only young and… vulnerable, really. I feel responsible for her while she's under my roof.'

'You don't own her, though,' he said. 'She is an adult and entitled to a love life… you don't have control over her life.'

Yamuna sniffed. 'That's not really your concern.'

Sahan said nothing. Yamuna had effectively just told him to stop interfering with grown-up conversations.

'Well, anyway, can you ask around?'

'Sure. I'll see what I can do.' What else could he say? He would have to tell Soma that Yamuna was suspicious. They would have to be even more careful. At least they never met in the house.

'Oh, by the way, Sahan.'

'Yes?'

'You are keeping your focus on your studies, aren't you?'

Wait; where did that come from? What was she trying to say? Was this a subtle way of saying she knew? Play it cool. He had to play it cool. 'Yes,' he said. 'Why?'

'I just wondered. It was nice to meet your friends today.' Yamuna paused. 'Especially that nice girl, Bex.'

'Bex?' What? 'Yamuna *akki*, what are you saying?'

'I'm just saying, remember what you came for. Education first. Your exams are more important than anything else.'

'Okay. I know that. Thanks.'

After he hung up, he stared at his phone for a few minutes. If Yamuna thought he was interested in Bex, then that was a good thing. It made it less likely she would suspect the truth.

Chapter Eighteen

Soma's first reaction when Sahan told her of the conversation was one of hope. Was that what Madam had been referring to when she asked if she was hiding something? It must have been. She put her hand over her heart, which was slowing back down after the flash of panic.

'Oh. She knows about the phone.'

Relief was followed by another thought. Did Madam suspect about Sahan, too? She thought back to all the things they'd said. 'Wait a second.' She put the phone down, opened her bedroom door and checked outside. No one. She bolted the door and returned to sit on her bed. 'She doesn't know it's you, does she?'

'No,' he said. 'I'm pretty sure she doesn't.'

'What would happen if she figured it out?' They had never properly discussed their relationship, despite how often they spoke to each other and the way they'd held hands on their one day out. Maybe this was because he didn't want to admit there was anything there. Soma was well aware of how unsuitable she was for Sahan. She couldn't help how she felt, but it seemed too much to hope that he would feel the same way about her. Oh, he gave every appearance of being interested in her too, but really, when it came to choosing, there was no chance he would choose her above family and comfort. The fact that

Sahan took so long to answer her question was proof of that.

'I don't know,' he said. 'It wouldn't be good.'

'She'd tell—' Even though she knew Yamuna wasn't lurking outside, she turned her face to the wall and whispered. 'She'd tell your parents, wouldn't she?'

'Yes, most likely.'

'What would happen then?' Part of her didn't want to know the answer. The other part of her wanted to know that she was right. If she was forewarned, maybe it wouldn't hurt so much when it finally came. Time was running out for them. Sahan's exams were starting in a few days. He was bound to get a job soon. He would be leaving Hull and she would be staying. Then there were those letters... if they came looking for her, she would have to run.

'I don't know.' He sighed.

For a moment they sat in silence, listening to each other breathing. Each preoccupied with their own thoughts.

'Soma,' said Sahan finally. 'I don't want to lose you. I... don't know what to do.'

His words electrified her. She forgot about facing the wall and secrecy and flopped back on her bed, a smile beaming out. 'Oh Sahan.'

'Shhh. Don't say my name!' But there was no anger in his voice.

'I love you,' she whispered, trying to get a world of emotion into a single whisper. 'I've never felt like this about anyone before.'

He gave a low laugh. 'Is that because you've never met someone who was boyfriend material before?'

He was teasing, and she knew it, but it still bothered her. He didn't know how right he was. She had never been loved before. Used, but not loved. Her smile faded. She hated that she had to hide things from him.

When she didn't answer, he said, 'I've never felt this way about anyone else either.'

The smile returned. This wasn't going to be easy, but if they loved each other, they could find a way. Love always found a way, didn't it? 'Listen,' she said. 'The important thing right now is your exams. You get through them first. Once they're over, we'll think about what happens next.'

He sighed. 'Yes. I suppose I should get back to work. You look after yourself, okay? Keep out of Yamuna's way. Perhaps we should stop calling each other every night. We could text each other instead and talk at the weekends.'

'Okay.' She hated the idea. Texts had to be in English and it took her ages to write one, but if he felt it helped him with his studying, then she wasn't in a position to complain.

'Will you text me?'

He laughed. 'I will. When these exams are over, would you like to go out for the day again?'

'Oh yes, I'd love it.'

'Brilliant. Let's do that.'

'What shall I do about Madam? Should I say something?'

'No. Don't do anything. Just keep acting normal.'

'I'm scared,' she said. If only she could tell him why.

'Don't be,' said Sahan. 'You're not doing anything wrong.'

That made her feel terrible. He had no idea how wrong he was. But, she reminded herself, neither did Madam… which was the more important thing.

They said protracted goodbyes and Soma carefully put away her phone. It had become her favourite possession.

It connected her invisibly to Sahan and, to her, it was as precious as life itself.

Soma padded over to the small mirror that hung by the door and looked at her reflection. She had changed. Apart from the pallor that seemed to mute everything in England, her face had changed. Where before she had been thin to the point of being bony, her face was now fuller, and her eyes looked less enormous compared to the rest of her features. Her hair was still short, but no longer boyish. Somehow, it made her look older, which was useful, given that she was supposed to be twenty-five.

She turned her face from side to side and examined it. This face belonged to Soma. It was right that it wasn't the same as Jaya's. She wondered what would happen if she ever needed to be Jaya again. What proof did she have? The thought made her give a sniff of laughter. She now had so much paperwork with Soma's name on it that it was easier for her to prove her identity as someone else than it was to be herself. As far as everyone in England was concerned, she was Soma and Soma was the one that Sahan loved.

He had asked her, in a roundabout way, if she had ever had a relationship before. She had answered, truthfully, that she hadn't ever had a boyfriend. The boys in her village had all been friends, almost like cousins and when she finally got to work at the sewing mill, her supervisor had taken a very stern view of her young charges fraternizing with the opposite sex. By then Soma was too scared to look at any male, man or boy, anyway.

The thought of *him* made her skin creep. She rubbed her side without thinking, soothing the tiny scars. Should she tell Sahan? All that belonged to Jaya and she wasn't that person any more. Jaya was a poor, damaged soul. Sahan deserved someone better than that. Someone like Sahan deserved someone better than Soma too, really.

Even in the short time that she'd known him, she'd realised that Sahan was not like other men. He actually looked at her face and listened when he talked to her. In all the weeks they'd met at the park, he had made no attempt to 'accidentally' bump into her, or put his arm around her or touch her in any way until that day in York. Finally Soma had met someone who seemed to want to know her as a person first. That was one of the things that had made her love him.

She hadn't lied, but was letting him think she was sweet and untouched any better than lying? What happened when things went further? When it came to it, Sahan would realise that she wasn't a virgin. As much as she'd like to think that it would make no difference to him, it *would* matter.

Would she be able to tell him about what had been done to Jaya at some point? Could she ever be completely honest with him? Could she really live a life where he never called her by her own name?

–

After he hung up from speaking to Soma, Sahan couldn't concentrate on his reading. He was sitting on the floor again, leaning against his bed. In various places around the room, he had stacks of books. He tipped his head back so that he couldn't see the mundane reality of exams, but the glorious hope in the posters on his wall. He relived the sound of her saying 'Sahan', happiness thrumming down the line. She sounded happy and that made him happy. He closed his eyes and pictured her face smiling at him over a teacup in York, her eyes shining as she talked about how much she loved the York Minster. She made him feel… bigger, better than he really was. More alive. As though, until he'd met her, he'd only been playing at being a person and mere contact with her made him more himself than he'd ever been before. For her, he was enough.

So this was what it was like to be in love. All the songs, the books, the films that were written about this feeling, they were all right, yet none could do it justice. Sahan grinned. None of them even got close to the real thing.

After a few minutes daydreaming, he sat up again, focusing on the real world. If he wanted to be with Soma, he had to think of a way to make it happen. He pulled a notepad towards him and started to make a list of what was in his way. He wrote in quick bullet points, making notes in Sinhalese, so that Nate couldn't find them and rib him about it later.

His parents would not approve.

Hers might not either. She rarely mentioned her family. Even when he asked, she would quietly sidestep the subject. He added a note to ask her about them.

He had no money of his own. Neither had Soma.

He had no job to go to and it was unlikely he could stay in Hull. Soma would have to go home in a little over a year, when her visa expired.

Sahan looked at the list of seemingly insurmountable problems. At the end, in small, tight letters, he added 'Tamsin', then immediately scribbled it out. He couldn't let that woman ruin his life any more than she already had. Soma was healing him of the damage Tamsin had done. He could feel it. It was time he forgot that Tamsin even existed.

He tore the page out and started a new page. Options. He could tell his parents – there would be hell to pay and they would be very upset. He pictured his mother's disappointment. He could probably live with his father's anger, but he couldn't face hurting his mother. But that aside, what would they do? It took him only a few seconds to work that out. They would make him come home. Cut him off from her. They would make Yamuna send Soma home, forcing her out of her job with a pay-off. Under no circumstances would they let him remain anywhere near her. He crossed that option off his list.

He could leave Soma and hope that time would heal his pain. After a moment of staring at the sentence, he crossed that out too. He couldn't face that either.

He could marry her anyway, in secret and tell his parents about it afterwards, when it was too late to do anything. He tapped his pen on the paper, mulling over this option. His parents would be very, very angry. They had never understood that they couldn't impose all their values on him. They might expect disobedience and reck-lessness from Priyanka, but he had never fought them before. They would never see it coming. He thought of his mother again and felt a squeeze in his chest. Might she forgive him in time? His father would be furious – for the betrayal of trust and the damage to his political career. His selfish actions could well cost his father a place in parliament. Would he be able to live with the knowledge that he'd hurt his parents so badly?

He might even do irreparable damage to his relation-ships with more distant relatives. Yamuna might support him though – after all, they got on quite well and she liked Soma well enough to trust her with Louie… And his sister would think it impossibly romantic, if a bit stupid. Maybe she could help talk their parents round to forgiving Sahan for his betrayal. Once they met Soma, they'd know that she wasn't a gold digger or some awful clingy creature. They'd love her too, eventually. Who wouldn't?

The more he thought about it, the more the option seemed the most plausible. His parents would get over it, he was sure. Especially if he showed them that Soma would be an asset to his future, rather than the catalyst for ruin.

If he could get a job, then rent a place big enough for two... He looked around his room. He didn't have that much stuff. Soma wouldn't either. She didn't seem the hoarding type. So somewhere small would do for the both of them. But he still needed a job to pay for it. And for that, he needed to pass his exams. He sighed, tore that page out of his notebook, put it with the other one, and went back to his books.

Chapter Nineteen

With two exam papers down and only a few more to go, Sahan was too tired and numb to find any real food, so he made himself a bowl of cereal for lunch. His phone rang. He fished it out of his pocket and spotted an unfamiliar number. As he answered it, Nate ambled in. Sahan walked over to the window in order to have some semblance of privacy.

'Hi Sahan, this is Gary Crowmarsh from Winterbrook Engineering. You had an interview with us last week.'

His mouth went dry. If they were rejecting him, they would have just sent a letter. Did this mean…? 'Um… hi.'

There was an awkward pause at the other end, then Mr Crowmarsh cleared his throat. 'Well, basically, we would like to offer you the job, if you still want it.'

'Oh. Wow.'

'We'll send you a letter, which should arrive by tomorrow. If you could let us know whether you want to accept the job in the next few days, that would be great. If you have any questions, of course, you have my number. Or you can email me. Do you have my email address?'

'Yes. I have your business card.'

'Excellent. Well, I'll look forward to hearing you soon then.'

'Um. Yes. Thank you. Bye.' He hung up and stared at the phone. 'Shit.'

'Bad news?' said Nate, as he put bacon in a frying pan.

'No. Good news. I've just been offered a job!' He was still having trouble believing it. He had almost given up hope of finding a job that would let him stay in the UK.

'Hey, congratulations!' Nate grinned. 'That's great. You going to take it?'

Sahan nodded.

'So where is it, this job? Somewhere local?' Nate added an egg to the pan. He maintained that protein was the only way to keep your strength up during exams. He seemed to have gone off vegetables entirely.

'Teesside. I don't even know what it's like to live over there. I mean, is it colder than it is here?'

Nate pondered this for a moment. 'I can't say I've ever been up that far north,' he said. 'But I'll tell you, people are pretty friendly around here. They'll probably be just as friendly up there. I reckon, the further away people get from London, the happier they become.'

Sahan grinned. Nate's suspicion of London was always a source of amusement. 'You'll be heading to London soon, you wait.'

'No chance, mate. No chance.' Nate brought his plate of protein over and squirted chilli sauce on it. 'Does this mean that you're going to be able to keep seeing the lovely Soma? Teesside's only a few hours away by train…'

'I haven't thought it through that far. I guess it's a workable option.'

Nate pointed his wooden spatula at Sahan. 'This makes it crunch time, my friend. Do you like this girl enough to take on your family? Or not?'

Sahan sighed. 'I don't know, okay? I like her. I really, really like her. But…' He pushed away his bowl of cereal, all appetite now gone. 'You know what, I can't think about this right now. I have revision to do.'

'You know you're going to get a first anyway. You can do this shit with your eyes shut.'

Sahan walked away.

Back in his room, he texted his parents and asked them to get on Skype.

It took him a few minutes to tell them about the job. There was a moment when they both stared at the computer screen, frowning. Sahan wondered what was wrong. Then his mother let out a huge sob. His father gave a cheer. 'Well done son! We are so proud of you.'

His mother, tears pouring down her face, said, 'It's exactly what we hoped. We are so proud. So proud.' She lifted her arms as though she wanted to hug him and, pausing, turned to grip his father's hand instead. He put his free arm around her.

'Yes, yes. Well done, Sahan. It's wonderful news. I knew you could do it.'

Sahan smiled, then, feeling his excitement should reflect his parents', forced a grin.

'Is it a good offer?' said his father, settling back into sensible mode, although the smile didn't quite leave his face.

'Not bad, I think.' Sahan told them what had been on the job advert. 'Subject to my passing my degree, obviously.'

'Ah, but that's not going to be a problem.' His father waved this aside with absolute faith. His mother nodded, still smiling and dabbing her eyes.

'Once you're settled,' his mother said, 'we can slowly start looking for someone for you.'

He remembered just in time that he was on video and kept his face neutral. He didn't respond to his mother's comment but talked instead about how Teesside had an airport and train connections. He was babbling, but his parents were too happy to notice.

By the time Sahan signed out of Skype, his parents had his entire future mapped out. He shut the lid of his laptop and stared ahead. He could almost see his life from now on. He had the degree and the offer of a steady job. His parents would introduce him to a stream of 'suitable' girls – bright, educated, middle class Sri Lankans. He would have a tidy, conventional life, married to someone who was perfectly adequate, but nothing special. He thought of Yamuna. When she had married Bim, most of the extended family had jumped in with comments about how Yamuna had 'done well'. She was comfortable with Bim, of course she was, but even Sahan could see that she wasn't happy. He had hoped that the birth of Louie would lift that resigned look from his cousin's face, but if anything, she looked worse.

Was that the sort of life he wanted? Married to an unobjectionable woman? Living in the suburbs with their unobjectionable children? The thought of touching someone brought with it a hint of nausea. Why was that happening again?

He closed his eyes. He could see the house, the kids… but the only woman he could see next to him was Soma. Soma. Her sparkle, her eyes. The thrill of his fingertips brushing her cheek. The warmth and safety of her smile.

He had spent his whole life doing exactly what his parents wanted him to do. They had chosen his A-level subjects for him, tipping him inexorably towards engineering because of its employment prospects. They had 'helped' him choose the right university course, conveniently in a town where his cousin lived, in case he needed anything (and so that she could keep an eye on him). Every decision he made was weighted in some way by his family and his love for them.

But by controlling his life in the name or protecting him, they'd left him unprepared to fend for himself. Having been sheltered from making his own stupid mistakes early on, his first encounters with the unfamiliar had knocked him sideways. He had never really tested his boundaries either. He had been happy to drift along doing what his parents told him because it was easy. There was no need to fight them, when he had no objection to what they wanted him to do. But now, he wanted something they could not countenance. The question was, was he willing to disappoint his family in order to be with Soma?

Sahan carefully moved the computer off his lap. Yes, he decided. Yes he was. He grinned and looked at the paperwork around him. Before he did any of that, he had to pass his exams first. Still smiling, he picked up his books again.

—

Soma sat on her bed, the phone pressed to her ear.

'Provided my exams go well, I'll be able to move up to Teesside in about eight weeks' time,' Sahan said.

'So soon.' Her heart creaked. She thought she'd accepted that he would have to leave. He had a job to go to. Of course he would leave. But, she realised, she had been hoping that somehow he wouldn't. That perhaps he would have found a job nearer. Or decided to carry on studying. Anything to keep him near.

'You can come with me,' he said, as though it was obvious.

'Wh—' Her heart picked up speed. 'Really?'

He laughed. 'Yes, really.'

She forgot to breathe. It took her a second to realise that, in her elation, she'd stopped talking. 'Sahan…'

He chuckled again. 'I've never felt this way about anyone before. I want us to be together, properly. Not just for stolen afternoons in the park. I want to explore my new home with you.'

'Oh. I would like that.' Images of herself walking next to Sahan, proud and free, like the girl in the shampoo commercial, flashed through her mind. She put her hand up and found her hair. It was no longer heavy and flowing. It was short and choppy. Reality crashed back in. 'But what about baby Louie? And my work? I can't just leave them.' It was as though all her hopes had been raised, only to be dashed against the same rocks again and again.

'If we want to be together…' The line rustled. She wondered if he'd sighed or merely changed position.

'I do want to be with you. I do. But if I run away with you… Madam will report it to the police and… and she'll worry.' How odd. She had run away before without any concern for those she'd left behind. She had no great love for Yamuna Gamage but, she realised with sudden clarity, Madam had treated her well. She had been happy, comfortable, respected, in this house. Things she hadn't been for a long time at her mother's house. Her eyes drifted up to the small bolt that Sahan had affixed to her door. And safe. She was safe in this house.

'We're going to have to tell her,' said Sahan.

'What? No. She'll go mad. She'll… send me home. People like you don't marry people like me. Your family—'

'Let me worry about my family,' said Sahan. There was a hard edge to his voice that she had never heard before. She wished she could see him, look into his eyes.

'I think,' Sahan continued, 'that we can persuade Yamuna and Bim to help us.'

'Why would they do that? I'm their servant. I look after their son.' Sometimes it was like they lived in different worlds. It was alright for him. The worst they could do to him was stop talking to him for a while. For her, on the other hand, things would be different. 'I don't want to lose this job.'

'Soma,' said Sahan quietly. 'You can't have it both ways.'

She knew that. But he was asking her to give up this safe place and go away with him to somewhere unknown. What if it went wrong?

'Soma,' Sahan said, after a few moments of silence. He sighed. 'I need to see you. We can't discuss this over the phone. My exams will be over in a couple of days. We'll meet up in the park and work this out, okay?'

He made it sound like it was a real possibility. Did she dare hope it was?

'Okay,' she said. 'Sleep well. I hope you remember everything you need to in your exam tomorrow.'

'Soma.'

'Yes?'

'Think about it.'

As if she was going to be able to think about anything else. 'I will.'

After she hung up, she lay on top of her bed, the phone clutched against her heart. Sahan loved her. He wanted to be with her. Emotion swelled in her chest and brought tears to her eyes. She loved him and he, the boy from Colombo Seven, loved her back. It was the most incredible feeling.

He said he was going to work out a way for them to be together. She couldn't see how, but he was clever and knew more about the world than she did. He would think of something.

She had never dreamed that a girl like her could be with a boy like him. A sudden thought intruded. But what if it did work out? They would have to go back to Sri Lanka and be seen together. What if someone found out that she wasn't who she said she was? Who *Sahan* thought she was! She would lose this new person that she had become. The betrayal would be so great, she would lose him too. Should she tell him? He would be so upset. Sahan was an honest person. He would hate that she'd lied to him. If she told him, she would lose him. But if she didn't tell him and he found out some other way? What then? That would be worse. She couldn't bear that he would think badly of her.

No, she couldn't tell him. That would risk ruining everything before it even began. She would have to keep this going like she had done for so long. The longer she kept it up, the more she became Soma.

She had to take each day as it came. Whatever happened in the future may not be easy, but right now, it was worth every agony.

Chapter Twenty

The post dropped through the letterbox while Soma was getting Louie bundled up to go out for their walk. Sahan was going to be out with his friends, so they wouldn't meet him, but Louie would appreciate the sunshine, so they were going out anyway. As she grabbed her own light jacket, she glanced at the pile of envelopes and froze. A brown envelope peeked out from under the mass of white ones. Hands trembling, she picked it up. It was addressed to her – Somavathi. No, no, no, no. There was no place in her life for this. If she went with Sahan, this would stop. She scrunched up the letter and rammed it into her pocket.

She was distracted as she stamped to the park and Louie, sensing that her attention wasn't fully with him, was cranky. He grizzled and grumbled. For once, Soma was too preoccupied to stop and take him out and cuddle him better. She marched the pram up and down the paths. She ran the pram over a rock and jolted it. Louie started to cry. Soma stopped.

'Oh baby.' What was she doing? As if there was anything in that letter that was more important than Louie. 'I'm sorry, bubba.' She put the brake on the pram and picked him up. It took a few minutes to calm him. A couple of women walking by smiled at her sympathetically. Soma half-smiled back. She had been so wrapped up in what the letter could bring that she'd left a perfectly nice day behind to go live inside her fears.

When she leaned forward to put Louie back in the pram, the letter crackled in her pocket. She took it out and looked at it. There could be nothing in there that was good. She was not giving this life up. She had come too far to let the letters ruin things. There was a rubbish bin not far away. Without opening the letter, she tore it up and threw it away. She felt better immediately.

'Come on then, baby,' she said to Louie. 'Let's have a nice walk.'

–

Louie was asleep by the time Soma wheeled the pram back to the house. She had walked a fairly long circuit and, when he fell asleep, decided to bring him back so that she could have a little sit down and drink a cup of tea before he woke up again. She wheeled the pram up to the garage door and pulled her keys out of her coat pocket.

'You're home. At last.'

She gave a little squeak and spun round. The man Kemasiri stood behind her. Where had he come from? Had he been hiding, waiting for her? Her mouth went dry. Something about this man set her sixth sense screaming. 'Uh… Sir and Madam aren't home. If you come back—'

'I haven't come to see them.' Kemasiri stepped closer. 'It's you I came to see. I need to talk to you.'

He was standing too close. So close that she could smell the cigarettes and alcohol on his breath. That smell. Her heart picked up pace. Her first thought was for Louie.

Soma edged sideways, so that she was in front of the pram. She slid her hand into her pocket, looking for her phone.

'Ah, ah.' He grabbed her hand, his grip strong. 'You're not going to do that. We are going to talk.'

'Wh— what do we have to talk about?' Her mind whirred. The letter. Had it contained something that could have warned her about this man? She should have read it. She didn't doubt for a moment that this man was dangerous. The malevolence in his eyes was obvious now. What did he want? Would he hurt her? Or worse, would he hurt Louie? The suburb was quiet at that time of day but if she screamed, surely someone would come? But if she screamed, she'd wake Louie. While he was asleep, he was safe. If he woke up and started howling, there was no telling what this maniac would do.

'Here's a funny thing,' said Kemasiri, stepping even closer. 'I've been thinking. What kind of person fails to respond when their name is called? Strange, no?'

Soma said nothing. Her stomach dissolved in fear.

'And… even stranger… you weren't sure of the name of your own home town… but when I described a man I'd made up… you said you recognized him.' He smiled, like a fox baring its teeth. 'Now I think, little girl, that you've never been there in your life. And I suspect that your name is not Somavathi, which is why you didn't respond when I called you.' He brought a finger up to the collar on her coat and ran it down along the zip. 'So what I want to know is… if you're not Somavathi. Who are you?' His finger came to rest above her breast bone and even through the layers of clothing, it made her skin crawl. 'And what else are you hiding?'

'I…' She tried to step back, but the pram was behind her. 'Please don't hurt me.'

'Oh, I won't hurt you,' he said. 'Not if you give me what I want. Now, I could tell your employers that you're not really Somavathi. And what do you think they would do?'

She shook her head. No. No.

His eyes gleamed. 'People will start to look for the real Somavathi. And they'll take you away and lock you up until you tell them where you hid the body.'

'I didn't—'

'And that precious, fancy boyfriend of yours. What do you think he would say?' He gripped the zip head with forefinger and thumb and pulled, undoing the zip tooth by tooth. 'Do you think he would like you so much if he knew what a dirty little liar you are?'

Tears sprang to her eyes. 'Please. I don't have much money—'

'Who said anything about money, pretty little one?' He put a finger under her chin and lifted her face up. She looked into his face and saw greed. She knew that look. Her skin prickled. Bile rose hot in her throat. She would have screamed, but she knew from experience it only made things worse.

'Please.' Tears escaped. She tried to pretend they weren't there. 'Please. The baby.' If she could get into the house with Louie she might be able to get to her phone. Kemasiri had her wrist at the moment, but if she could persuade him to let go, maybe she could punch in 999 on her phone. This was an emergency. They listened to all the calls, didn't they? Even if no one said anything, or was speaking in in another language?

Kemasiri paused, eyes gleaming. 'What about it?'

'He… he should be inside. He might wake in the cold.' It wasn't even cold, but it was the best she could think of.

'Don't think you can get away that easily. I know how minds like yours work.' He let go of her hand and plunged his own into her pocket. He pulled out her phone. 'But you're right. This is no place for us to chat. You let us in. I'll follow with the baby.' He spun her sideways and pushed her away from Louie. 'You behave and the baby will be fine.'

He wouldn't hurt Louie? Would he? Hands shaking, she unlocked the wicket door and pushed it open. Oh, why hadn't she been more alert? She might have spotted him and gone back to the park. If only Madam would come home early. She walked slowly through the garage.

'Hurry up girl,' said Kemasiri.

There was nothing she could use as a weapon. The garage was used as a garage only. Anything else was tidily put away in cupboards. She would never find a weapon without Kemasiri noticing. And he had Louie. Defeated, she opened the door that connected the garage to the kitchen. Once the door was open, she made a dash into the house. There was a phone at the end of the kitchen. And knives. It would take Kemasiri a moment to get around the pram. That was all she needed.

She lunged across the kitchen. But he was too fast for her. He leapt after her, grabbed her wrist and slammed her back against the wall. She struggled, but his hands were like vices as they pinned her arms up, either side of her.

'Don't try your tricks with me, girl. You think people will come to help you? What do you think they'll say when they find out who you really are? Or who you aren't? Do you think they'll let you stay?'

She froze. This was no idle threat. He didn't need to hurt her. Because he could destroy her with just a few words. A whimper escaped from her throat.

'And do you think that precious boyfriend will stay with you when he finds out about your lying?' His eyes gleamed and she was suddenly back in the dark hut, pinned under the alcoholic breath of her tormentor. Points of pain on her ribs and thighs. All the fight left her. All she could hope for was that it would be quick. It was never painless. She squeezed her eyes shut turned her head away.

When he sensed she was no longer fighting back, Kemasiri released one of her hands. It flopped down to her side, useless.

'Ah now,' he said. 'No need to be like that. We can be so much better than this.'

She could smell him. Cigarettes and arrak. Old lessons came back to her. Don't fight. Don't scream. No noise, no fighting or things got worse. *Look what you made me do, little bitch.*

'Look at me,' said Kemasiri, his voice wheedling now. 'We can come to an arrangement. I won't tell anyone your dirty secret. And you be *nice* to me.' He traced the corner of her mouth with a rough fingertip.

She squeezed her eyes shut tighter and wished she was somewhere else. Mustn't flinch. Mustn't try to run away. If she stayed still would he be happy? Would he do what he wanted and leave before Louie woke up? Tears leaked down her cheeks. Tears were okay, but no noise.

'What is this crying?' Kemasiri pressed a palm to the side of her face and wiped a tear away with his thumb. The touch made her shudder. Not wanting to annoy him, she held herself as still as possible, while he stroked her cheek.

Suddenly, in the middle of the horror, there was a sound. The front door opened. A blast of cold air along the hallway. Soma's eyes flew open and she twisted her head round to see who it was.

Bimbisara Gamage stood in the hallway, mouth hanging open, frozen in surprise. For an instant Soma's gaze locked with his. She saw his eyes widen and she knew she'd made a connection. 'Help me,' she mouthed.

A beat. No one moved. Then Mr Gamage roared, 'What the hell is going on?'

Kemasiri leapt back, releasing her. 'I'm sorry, sir. She said you wouldn't be back, sir.'

Mr Gamage seemed to swell up. For such a small man, he took up a lot of room in the hallway. 'You. Get out of my house.'

Soma slumped back against the wall, not sure what to do.

'We didn't mean any harm.' Kemasiri backed away. 'She was so keen and we—'

'OUT!'

In the garage, Louie woke up and started to cry. The sound brought Soma back to life. She looked from Mr Gamage to the garage. 'No,' she gasped and ran into the garage and picked up Louie. She didn't trust Kemasiri not to hurt the baby. But Kemasiri was backing out, still explaining to the furious Mr Gamage that Soma had seduced him and that they'd been a couple for weeks.

Once Kemasiri was outside, Mr Gamage locked the garage door and advanced on Soma. He didn't look directly at her. 'Are you hurt?'

She held the screaming child against her. 'No sir.'

'He attacked you?'

Now that he finally looked at her, she couldn't respond. If she said yes, then Kemasiri would find out and make good on his threat to tell her secret. She was lying about who she was, but he would make people think she was a murderer as well. She would go to prison for the rest of her life. Her heart pounded. What to do? What to do?

Bim's eyes narrowed. 'Soma? When I came in, it looked like... did he attack you?'

If she said yes, this life was over. If she said no... the fear would never be over. Her head began to buzz again. What was best? What was worst?

'Give me my son,' Mr Gamage said.

She handed him the baby.

'Go up to your room. Stay there until Madam returns.' He took the howling child, in an inexpert grasp and bounced him.

This made no impression on Louie's crying. Soma hesitated. 'Sir, it's not—'

'Go.'

She turned and fled. In the tiny bathroom, she scrubbed the traces of Kemasiri off her cheek and arms. She checked the landing anxiously, even though she knew no one had followed her, before she dashed across to her room. Downstairs, Louie still howled. She threw the bolt into place, rammed a chair under the door handle and tore off the clothes he had touched. Then, more slowly, she put on clean clothes. She climbed into bed and sobbed. And sobbed.

—

The sound of her phone ringing made Yamuna jump. She had been reading a journal article while waiting for the centrifuge to finish spinning down her samples. When she saw her home number flash up on the caller ID, her chest went cold. Louie.

'Hello. What's happened?' she said in Sinhalese, assuming it would be Soma.

'It's me.' Bim's voice. 'I need you to come home. Now.'

'What's wrong?' She scrambled off her chair, already reaching for her coat. 'Has something happened to Louie?'

'Louie? No. He's fine. Just come home.'

She could hear Louie crying in the background. 'He doesn't sound fine. Bim, what's going on?'

'I'll tell you when you get here. Just… Come.'

Yamuna ran to her colleague. 'Something's wrong at home. I've got to go.' She quickly outlined what to do with her samples. 'They'll keep until tomorrow in the cold room.' She grabbed her stuff and ran out of the door.

It was hard work concentrating on the drive home. She got there without any memory of the journey apart from burning impatience. She pulled the car into the garage and burst through the door. Bim was sitting at the kitchen table, Louie in his highchair. Both were covered in something which had once been a banana. They seemed unhurt.

'What happened? Where's Soma?'

'Soma is upstairs,' said Bim. He stopped trying to feed Louie and leaned back. He sighed. 'I don't know where to start.'

Yamuna pulled out a chair and held a hand out so that Louie could grab at her fingers. 'Why don't you start with why you're home?'

'I forgot my phone charger, so I came home to pick it up. I walked in the front door and found Soma in the kitchen, with a man.'

'What!' Yamuna smacked her hand down on the table with a loud crack. Louie, surprised, started to cry.

'I'm sorry, I'm sorry, baby, shhh. Here. Here, play with this.' She handed him her car keys, which she knew he loved. Mollified, he took them in his pudgy hands. 'What do you mean, with a man? What man? What were they doing?' She knew it. There *had* been a man! Yamuna felt a stab of satisfaction that she had been right.

'Kissing... I think.' Bim was staring into the middle distance, his mouth turned down at the corners.

'In our house? In front of our baby? I'll... I'll kill her. Where is she?' Yamuna started to rise.

Bim raised a hand. 'No. Sit down. There's more to it than that.'

'More?' What more could there be?

'She... I don't know. There was something about the situation that was... not right.'

'Well, obviously. She abused our trust. She—'

'No. No. I mean...' He shook his head. 'I don't know if she wasn't...' His gaze darted towards Louie, who was busy covering the keys in a layer of goop, and dropped his voice. 'I'm not sure she was entirely willing.'

It took a few seconds for this to sink in. She sat back down, slowly. 'You think she was attacked?'

'I don't know. I asked her and she wouldn't say...' Bim shook his head. 'The guy – I've seen him before. I think he's the Pereras' driver. He implied that they were seeing each other, but—'

'If he assaulted her, why wouldn't she say so? She wouldn't try to protect him, surely.' Yamuna tapped her fingers on the table. 'I saw him talking to her a few weeks ago. She said she'd told him to go away, but she must have been lying. I knew there was something going on. I knew it. All those whispered conversations, the walking around smiling to herself… it wasn't a student. It was him. I can't believe the cheek of it, bringing him here. To this house.'

'You think they *were* seeing each other then?'

Yamuna stood up. 'One way to find out. I'll ask her.'

Chapter Twenty-One

Soma knew from the knock on the door that it was Madam. And she knew that she was in trouble.

'Soma. Open this door at once.'

Her hands shook as she dragged away the chair and pulled back the bolt. What use was a bolted bedroom, when he could wait for her by the garage? She turned the doorknob, but instead of opening the door, retreated back to sit on her bed.

Madam pushed the door open and stood in the doorway. 'Did he force his way into the house?'

Soma tried to speak, but what could she say? Who would believe her? Her own mother hadn't listened when she tried to tell her about her stepfather, why would Madam take her word over Kemasiri's?

Even if Madam was different, even if they did believe her, what good would it do? He would tell them she wasn't the real Somavathi and the enormity of her deception would come out. She would be sent to prison in a cold cell in England somewhere. 'I'm sorry.' Tears rolled unchecked down her face. 'I'm sorry.'

Madam frowned. 'Is that a yes or a no? Did he force his way in?'

She couldn't go to prison. This was her life now. She couldn't lose it like this. If she wanted to keep it, she had to let Kemasiri get away with it. Soma shook her head.

Although she couldn't look at Madam's face, the sharp intake of breath told Soma everything. 'So you let him in. How long has this been going on?'

Her chest clenched. Her arms trembled. She said nothing.

'Look at me, Soma. Don't lie to me. How long has this been going on?' Madam's voice was quivering with anger.

She looked up and into Madam's hard expression and a small hope that she'd not even been aware of, died.

'I know you've had a boyfriend for a while,' Madam said. 'I know about your phone. I thought you were conscientious enough to keep your private affairs away from my son.' Her voice lost its hard edge. 'Soma, I am disappointed in you.'

Somehow, that was worse.

'Madam I—' Soma looked down at her hands, twisting together on her lap. She couldn't mention Sahan without dragging him into this whole mess. He wouldn't want her now anyway. She would be sent home and she would never see him again. 'Are you going to send me back?' There was nowhere for her to go.

'I haven't decided what to do with you, yet,' Madam said.

Soma looked up. 'Louie?' He would need his food soon. And if he had the banana that had been set aside for his meal, he would need a bath soon, too. 'Is Louie okay? Does he want his food?'

Yamuna drew a breath. 'Louie is fine.' She looked at Soma for a moment, her head to one side. 'Take a few minutes to get yourself together,' she said, her voice less angry now. 'Then come down.' With that, she turned and went downstairs.

Soma bolted the door again. The difficulty of her situation was becoming clearer. If he couldn't blackmail her into sleeping with him, then Kemasiri would tell Madam her secret, or an embellished version of it. She had no doubt at all that Madam would believe him.

But if she gave in to Kemasiri's demands, there would be no end. There had to be another way. But where could she go? There was no miraculous passport delivered into her hands this time. Her first thought was Sahan, but what could he do? He was a student. His parents had money, but Sahan didn't. His parents would never allow him to shelter a servant girl, let alone one who was in trouble with the law.

She reached into her cardigan pocket for her phone. It wasn't there. A few minutes of frantic searching later, she remembered that Kemasiri had snatched it from her. Had he thrown it down when he assaulted her? Was it somewhere in the kitchen? Or had he taken it? This thought made her stomach clench. Her link with Sahan, the only way he could contact her, was in Kemasiri's pocket. It felt like a violation almost as bad as the physical one.

There had to be a way out. She had come this far, she must be able to think of something. She was shaking violently now. She climbed into bed. Pulling her knees up to her chest, she rested her head on her kneecaps and tried to think things through. Despite her best efforts, Madam didn't like her. She didn't know why, but she knew it as a fact. Madam thought she'd been having an affair with Kemasiri. Madam was going to send her home. If she were sent home, what would happen?

She had some money now, she could start again, get a job at a sewing mill like she had originally planned. Only now, instead of a necklace to pawn, she would actually have foreign money she could use to pay her rent for the first few weeks. Maybe being sent home wasn't such a terrible thing. But how soon would it happen? She had some money in the bag under her bed, but how did she get the rest of her money from the bank? When Madam had shown her how to use a cash point, she had also explained about there being a limit to how much she could take out. She would have to go into the bank itself to get the rest. And then where could she keep it? The idea of walking around with that much money on her person was terrifying.

What if Kemasiri told Madam the truth about her? Then what? Again, she was sure Madam was not her friend. She would hand her over to the police without blinking an eye. For a minute, she wondered if she could appeal to her employer's husband for help. Mr Gamage was a distant figure whom she avoided if she could. He seemed like a nice man, but he would always listen to his wife. She thought back to that one moment of true connection she had had with him, when, trapped by Kemasiri, she had looked up and made eye contact. He had seen her. Really seen her. He had saved her, but then she'd lied to him. He might have offered her sympathy, but she'd shut the door on that when she denied being attacked. He wouldn't step up to defend her corner if his wife wanted to go to the police. No, there would be no help from there.

She could run. She had a bag packed and a small amount of money at the ready. But she didn't know where she'd go. And she couldn't bear the thought of leaving Sahan. She beat the heel of her hand against her forehead. Stupid, stupid, stupid. She should have kept her distance from people and not got attached. *Why* had she fallen in love with him? It was a stupid thing to do. Now she had ties that were difficult to sever.

Soma groaned. The only person who could help her was Sahan. The idea of being sent away was bad, but the idea of being separated from Sahan was unbearable. Tears welled up again. What would Sahan do when he found out about all this? Madam was bound to tell him. He would believe that all the while she was spending time getting to know him, she had also been seeing Kemasiri. Would he even want to talk to her after that? What man would?

But perhaps if she could tell him the truth…? He was a kind man. If she told him everything – what she did, how the lie took hold until it was too late to go back on it, how she had been Soma for so long that she no longer thought of herself as Jaya, how she loved him, truly, with every drop of her blood… If she told him all of it, maybe he would understand. He cared about her. It had to be worth trying. She thought of his smiling face. Yes. She would try. Maybe he would understand. Maybe he would help.

Sahan had his last exam that day. He said he was going out with his friends afterwards. He wasn't that far away, but she didn't know where to find him. If only she could contact him. But how?

She knew his phone number; she had memorized it, merely for the pleasure of knowing it by heart. The nearest phone was on the landing on the second floor. Did she dare tiptoe down to it and make a call? Would that make Madam angrier than she already was? Soma went to stand by the door and listened. She opened the door a crack. She could hear Madam in the kitchen downstairs. She opened the door further and crept out, her feet making very little sound on the carpet. The voices downstairs didn't pause. Feeling bolder, she crept down the stairs and across the landing, pausing frequently. She picked up the handset, thankful that it didn't beep on the other units. Pressing the keys would make a noise. She stood there, paralysed with indecision. How could she make the call without Madam knowing? There was a crash downstairs, followed by Louie shouting. She noted with relief that he sounded annoyed, rather than hurt. She had a few minutes before he stopped.

She quickly tapped out Sahan's number. It rang a few times and went to voicemail. 'It's Soma,' she whispered. 'Something's happened. I don't have my phone. Come and find me. It's—'

Madam said, 'I'll get him a clean top.' Footsteps as someone came up the stairs. Soma rammed the phone back in its holder and fled back to her room.

–

'No more exams! Or lectures!' Sahan took a swig of his beer. He was in the corner of a booth in a pub, wedged in between Nate on one side and another male friend on the other. They had been there some hours now and no one was entirely sober.

Nate turned his attention to him. 'So, Sahan, me old mucker. What are you going to do now?'

'Well, depending on whether I get the results—'

'Oh shut up. You'll get a first. Everyone knows that,' said Nate.

'Take it as read.'

For once Sahan didn't argue. It was too good an evening to be negative. He had his whole future gleaming ahead of him. 'In that case, I'm going to start work at the end of the summer.'

'And the girlfriend situation?' Cara nudged Nate back out of the way, so that she could see Sahan. 'What are you going to do about that?'

Sahan grinned. It seemed strange to hear Soma referred to as his 'girlfriend'. He had only been out with her on one date, really, but he had seen her several times a week for so long. He knew her so well. 'Girlfriend' didn't begin to cover how he felt about her.

'Yeah, Sahan,' said Nate, slurring a little. 'What are you going to do? You're going to be in Teesside, she's going to be here…' He spread his hands apart to illustrate his point.

He hadn't told anyone what he intended to do. He had mentioned to Soma that she should come with him, but he hadn't actually come out and asked her. Perhaps now, in the presence of his friends, was a good time to voice the thoughts that were buzzing inside his head. 'I think…' he said, 'I'm going to ask her to marry me.'

This raised cheers and applause around the table. A dozen questions were fired at him. Cara's was clearest. 'Are you going to run away together?'

That was a distinct possibility. How and when would need to be worked out. He was fairly sure he could talk Yamuna and Bim round. He needed to sound them out.

'That is one option,' he said.

Cara gave a loud whoop. 'I knew it! I knew it!' She punched Nate in the arm. 'See, I told you, true love will always win!'

Nate gave a theatrical sigh and shook his head at Sahan. 'She's going to be insufferable now.'

Sahan laughed. Nate raised his glass in a toast. Sahan joined in as they all drank to his future. He had never been so happy.

'Have you called her yet?' said Cara. 'Have you told her how your exam went?'

'No.' He was intending to call her later in the evening, when she finished work.

'Well call her, man, call her. Come on.' Nate made urging motions with his hands. 'Ask her to marry you.'

'What, with you lot all shouting? I don't think so.' But he pulled his phone out of his pocket anyway. It was eight o'clock. 'Bloody hell, is that the time?'

'Call her. Call her.' Nate started banging on the table. The others took up the chant. Sahan stood up, laughing. People let him out.

It was still light outside in the encroaching summer and the evening was warm. Sahan felt a moment of pure contentment. His exams were over, he had a job to go to and he was in love. He walked a little way into the car park and was surprised to realise he wasn't as steady on his feet as he'd thought. He grinned happily. When he got several bars of phone signal he dialled Soma's number.

After a few rings, someone answered the phone. Surprised, Sahan said, 'Hello, it's me.'

There was no answer. He could sense someone at the other end of the line. 'Soma?' Still nothing. 'Soma? Is everything okay?' The line went dead.

Sahan stared at his phone, where the call had clearly been terminated. What was that all about? Had Yamuna got hold of Soma's phone? Shit.

He noticed for the first time that he had a message. He must have not heard it ring with all the noise in the pub. Almost without thinking, he played it. It was Soma, breathlessly telling him that something had happened and she'd lost her phone. Suddenly he was completely sober. He played the message twice and felt alarm rising in his chest. What had happened to her? Had she been mugged? He checked the message again and saw that it had come from Yamuna's home phone, which meant that Soma had made it home safely. That was something, at least.

He called Yamuna's house.

'It's me. Sahan. I'm… calling to tell you I've finished my exams.'

'Was that today? I'm sorry Sahan, with all the drama I completely forgot. How did it go?'

'What drama?'

Yamuna made a disgusted noise. 'It's been a mad day,' she said. 'Bim came home to get something he'd forgotten and he found the servant girl kissing some man.'

The last trace of warm fuzziness vanished. 'What?'

'I don't know, Sahan. It's all such a nightmare.'

'What do you mean? What's going on? What man?'

'I knew she was carrying on with some man. I told you, didn't I? I was right. Bim came home and— ugh. I don't even want to think about it. I trusted her with my son.'

The man Soma had been seeing was him. Was there someone else as well? He felt his world twisting around him. 'What man?'

'Oh, not someone you know. He's the driver of one of Bim's friends. Sri Lankan guy.'

'Kemasiri.' That would explain it. He thought of Kemasiri's outburst a few weeks ago. And Kemasiri knew about him and Soma. Had he attacked her because he was annoyed with Sahan? Or was he angry with him because they were both seeing the same girl? No. He didn't believe that. His Soma would never do anything so duplicitous.

'What? Who?' Yamuna's bewildered voice dragged him back to the present.

'Kemasiri. The driver. I know him.'

'Oh. Right. Well, he claims she's been seeing him for a while. She doesn't deny it. Louie has been a nightmare child all afternoon and—'

'Wait. Where's Soma? Why have you got Louie? I'm confused now.' He needed to know what was true and what was not. He didn't put it past Kemasiri to lie. He thought of the man looming over Deepthi… he could even imagine him assaulting someone. But Yamuna seemed to think that Soma was in on it. Why wasn't Soma saying anything? *He needed to know.* Even if it destroyed him, he had to know. 'Look, Yamuna, I'll come over and give you a hand with Louie, so that you can sort this thing out.'

'Oh, would you? That would be brilliant. Bim is being so odd about the whole thing; it would be really useful to be able to talk to him without Louie being there.'

He started walking. 'I'm on my way.' He hung up.

Furious, he called Soma's phone again. Again, someone answered.

'Kemasiri,' he shouted. 'What have you done to her, you bastard? If you have a problem with me, you take it up with me. You do not have the right to go and attack an innocent girl.'

Kemasiri chuckled down the phone. 'Innocent? That little whore? You poor, wretched idiot. She took you in so well, didn't she? Didn't you know? Her name isn't even Somavathi. Everything she told you is a lie.'

'Wh—' but Kemasiri had gone. Sahan rang back, but the phone had been turned off. He paused at the bus stop. How long would the bus be? It was quicker to run.

Chapter Twenty-Two

Soma heard Sahan's voice downstairs and her heart kicked up a notch. He was here. He had come at last. She slid off the bed and pressed her ear against the door. Yamuna's voice, muffled by distance and the door, gabbled away for a while. Then came Sahan's voice, low and soothing. Footsteps, two sets, came up the stairs. Soma's heart pounded at the thought that Sahan was only a few feet away on the other side of the door. He had got her message. He had come. Now if only she could persuade him to help her.

She heard Yamuna and Sahan – and Louie, judging by the noises – go into the nursery. She went back to sit on her bed. She had Sahan to help her, but she needed to know what she wanted him to do. Her main thought was that she had to make sure that Kemasiri didn't tell people about her past. How could she do that? In a flash she realised that Kemasiri had merely guessed at her secret. If she had brazened it out, he would have had to back down. But she'd acted like a guilty person and now his thoughts had been confirmed. He might even think that she'd killed the real Somavathi. Stupid, stupid, stupid Soma.

Now that he knew it was true, he could make a lot of trouble. If he accused her, her identity would be scrutinized. Okay, she had all of Soma's papers with her, but if they looked very carefully at the passport photo, or examined her signature using an expert, like they showed on TV, then she would be caught for sure. And sent to prison. If the newspapers printed a picture of her, someone would recognize her and she would be sent home. No. She couldn't get caught.

Kemasiri wouldn't stop. She knew about men who made demands. They got drunk on their own power and carried on making bigger and bigger demands. If she gave into Kemasiri even once, she would never be free… and she would lose Sahan.

Soma buried her head in her hands. If she didn't have Sahan, what did she have? An employer who thought she had abused their trust and paperwork based on a lie. If she went home, she would have even less. She didn't even have her original identity documents any more, they had all been swept out to sea. Even if she did go home, she couldn't prove she was who she really was, unless her mother vouched for her.

She rocked slowly back and forth, taking comfort in the childlike action. None of that really mattered to her. What mattered was Sahan. She thought of how the news, given from Madam and Sir's perspective, would have sounded to him. Did he believe that she would voluntarily go with another man? Would he take her side at all? Tears slid into the gaps between her fingers. If he rejected her, she may as well give herself up to her fate.

She didn't know how long she sat there, rocking. There was the sound of footsteps on the landing – Madam's – and a whispered conversation. She heard Sahan's voice. Soma stopped rocking and sat still, straining to hear what was going on. She heard a single set of steps, the tread light and measured, which must be Madam, going down the stairs. Sahan didn't follow her. He must be staying up here to talk to her. Her heart rose from the mire. If he wanted to talk to her, he must be on her side.

With her ear pressed to the door once more, she waited until Madam was on the ground floor. She opened the door a crack and peered out. Sahan was standing by the open door to Louie's room. When he saw her, he put a finger to his lips and pointed into the darkened room. She nodded.

Sahan retreated into Louie's room. Cautiously, Soma tiptoed out and followed.

Louie's room was lit by a Thomas the Tank Engine night light. In his cot, Louie was snoring softly. Sahan stood in the shadows, waiting. She went to him and, despite her earlier concerns, threw her arms around him. It was the closest contact she'd had with him and she felt him tense. He patted her back awkwardly. She let him go and took a step backwards. 'I'm glad you came.'

He reached out and took her hand. 'What happened?'

Soma curled her fingers around his. He wasn't angry, then. He hadn't pushed her away. He was just being Sahan. She explained quickly and quietly that Kemasiri had waited for her, that he'd attacked her. 'Madam thinks I encouraged him. I didn't. You have to believe me.'

His eyes gleamed blue-black in the night light. 'Yamuna says she asked you if he attacked you and you wouldn't say he did. Why not? Why don't you tell her what you told me?'

'I can't. He'll...' She couldn't tell him, could she? She knew about secrets. You told one person and then it became their secret and you had to rely on them keeping it. Could she trust Sahan not to give her away? He was a good man. He would help her, wouldn't he?

'Well, tell me, then. Whatever he threatened you with, we won't let that happen. We'll tell the police about him. We will protect you.'

She twitched at the mention of police. Even in the dark, he noticed and frowned.

'Soma? The police here aren't like the police at home.'

Which only made it worse. She said nothing. She could feel the change in tension in his hand. He was worried now.

'Soma? What is going on?'

She was losing him. She had to tell him. She had to trust that he wouldn't use the information to hurt her.

'I... did something. Kemasiri knows and I don't want him to tell Madam.' Perhaps he would take her word that it wasn't anything too terrible. The real Soma was dead. She didn't need this future. It was better that someone had it than to waste such an opportunity. Would he understand that?

Another tremor in his hand. 'What did you do? Did you take something? Yamuna's not a bad sort, you know. If I talk to her, I'm sure we can sort this out. Whatever it is, it can't be that bad.'

Except it was, wasn't it? Governments didn't like it when people lied. Powerful people got annoyed and then bad things happened. They would think that she'd killed the real Somavathi and how could she prove otherwise? Sahan's features, already indistinct in the dim light, blurred even more as fresh tears welled up.

'Soma?' His voice was hardening. 'Soma, what did you do?'

'It's not anything terrible. I didn't kill anyone or anything.' Tears spilled and ran down her face.

'Well what is it then? Just tell me.' His voice was still low, and it sounded like an angry snake.

She tried to stifle a sob. His hand slipped out of hers. She tucked her hand against her body. This was where it ended. All the lies, all the pretending, it had brought her here. To a dimly lit room, where she had to tell the love of her life that she wasn't the innocent he thought she was. That she had done a terrible thing because it was less terrible than the alternative. Karma always got you in the end and this was where it had got her.

He was watching her, his head to one side, his eyes almost lost under his frown.

She had to tell him. She could lie, but it would only bring her back to this point, over and over until she told him the truth. A sob escaped. 'I stole someone's passport. I was running aw—'

'You did what?'

'There was a bus crash and the real Somavathi was dead. Her passport and everything was in her bag and I—'

Soma heard the hiss as he sucked in his breath. She reached out to him.

'You're not Soma?' He stepped back, hands raised, warding her off. 'Who *are* you?'

'My name is Jaya. But I'm Soma now. I haven't been Jaya since that day.' This wasn't coming out the way she'd planned. 'Sahan, please, let me explain.'

He kept retreating. Away from her. It was only a few feet, but may as well have been a thousand miles. He was deep in the shadows now, but she'd already seen the look of horror on his face. She'd lost him.

With Louie safely ensconced upstairs with Sahan, Yamuna knocked on the study door.

'Come in.' Bim was sitting at the desk, his email open. 'One second.' He finished typing his email and minimized the window. 'Okay.' He turned round.

Yamuna wearily lowered herself into the other chair in the room. Bim usually used it to sit and read reports; it was more comfortable than the office chair he was sitting in now.

'Bim. We have to do something.'

Bim laid his hands on his knees with exaggerated care. 'I called Mr Perera and told him that his driver was here and that he may have assaulted our maid.'

'And?'

'He said he'd speak to the man and get his side of the story.'

'Which will be that he's been seeing Soma for a while. That's what he said to you, isn't it?' said Yamuna.

'Yes, but I want to be sure we have the facts.'

'What other facts are there, Bim? I spoke to Soma. She doesn't deny any of it. I don't know what else you need to know.' Yamuna ran a hand over her face. She felt ragged. Louie was such hard work. It was as though he had picked up on her own mood and amplified it.

'Did she actually *say* she's been seeing this man? Or did she just not deny it?' Bim leaned forward, looking at her intently. It was the closest scrutiny she'd had from him since they got married.

'What difference does it make?' The fact that Bim was trying so hard to fight Soma's corner irritated her beyond belief. This man, who treated his wife and child as though they were background noise, was suddenly massively interested in minute details about a girl who had almost nothing to do with him.

Anger and pain that had been suppressed for so long, boiled up inside her. Her voice rose. 'I don't understand why you're taking her side!'

'And I don't understand why you're not!' His voice rose to match hers. 'If it was anyone else, any other girl who might have been harassed, you would be the first one to stand up and say that she should be believed. You. Why will you not believe this girl?'

'Because she isn't saying anything! It's only you that seems to have a bee in your bonnet about it. And… she—' Anger morphed into despair. It was all too much. 'Arrgh.' Her voice cracked. The room blurred and swam. 'It's not fair!' Yamuna, for the first time in her married life, burst into tears in front of her husband.

'Y-Yamuna.' The chair creaked as Bim stood up. Yamuna buried her face in her hands and sobbed. A hand rested on her shoulder. Bim knelt on the floor next to her. 'Yamuna.'

Awkwardly, he put his arms around her and pulled her towards him. She sobbed into his shoulder, the unaccustomed contact making her cry even harder. After a few moments of holding her gingerly, he said. 'Hey, hey. What brought this on?'

'Louie loves her more than he loves me. I'm a rubbish mother. Louie doesn't love me. You don't care. I thought I didn't have to be much of a wife if I was a mother to your children, but I'm awful at being that too. Louie doesn't love me like he loves Soma. And I don't feel anything towards him. I've failed at everything.' Her whole body shook as she subsided in another volley of sobs.

Bim said nothing for a long moment, then his arms tightened around her and he pulled her close.

'You're wrong,' he said. 'You're wrong.' He stroked her hair with one hand. 'It's not you. It's my fault too. You were so strong and capable, I thought you didn't need me. Louie... I didn't know what to expect with Louie and when he came, you handled it. Like you handle everything. I had no idea you felt this way.' He pulled away from her and lifted her chin. 'I'm so sorry.' He leaned across, pulled a tissue out of the box that sat on the desk and handed it to her. 'I had no idea and I should have.'

She blew her nose. Her body shook with another dry sob. When she finally looked up at Bim's face, she saw a tenderness that she had never expected to see. He looked so sad. So contrite. 'It's not your fault,' she said, almost by reflex.

'Oh, but it is. You're right. I haven't given you and Louie any attention.' He sighed. 'I'm not a young man, Yamuna. Getting married was a huge shock to me. I thought we would move into a bigger house together and then things would carry on as normal. I didn't expect... I don't know. I didn't expect things to change so much. Stupid of me, I suppose.'

'But our wedding was a transaction. You needed a wife. I needed a husband. We both wanted a child.' She swallowed another sob. Bim passed her the box of tissues.

'I didn't *need* a wife,' he said. 'I wanted one. I didn't want to grow old and find myself alone in the world. And I wanted to have someone to leave all this to. But I didn't want to put any effort into making it work. I'm sorry. I was a relative stranger to you when we got married and I let us carry on like that.'

'We tried, didn't we? When we first got married.' It seemed so long ago now, even though it was barely two years. They had done all the usual things. Going away for weekends, that sort of thing. It hadn't been easy and neither of them had been comfortable with it, but they had done it. Ticking off a list of things they expected newlyweds did. When she got pregnant with Louie, it had been a relief. Not only because she'd wanted to be a mother, but because it meant they could stop pretending to be in love and get on with other things instead.

'But I stopped trying after a while.' Bim settled down on the floor. 'Yamuna. When I asked my parents to find me a wife, there were a lot of women who were suitable. A lot.'

She nodded. She didn't doubt it. He was rich. He had no dodgy past, no obvious disfigurements. He was an inoffensive, quiet, rich man, who was willing to take a wife who was older than most brides out there. Who wouldn't be interested?

'Do you know why I chose you?'

She shook her head. 'Because I have a PhD?'

He smiled. 'That you were intelligent helped. No, I chose you because I thought you were the best investment. You're clever, charming, adaptable and so utterly capable. I thought, this is a woman who I can rely on; no matter what life throws at us, she will help me deal with it.'

'You chose me as an asset?' It was hardly the sexiest way to be described, but this was Bim. To him, everything was either an investment or a waste of time. An asset, to him, was the best thing you could be.

He looked sheepish. 'I suppose, yes. But the thing is, I forgot that a marriage isn't a business transaction. I needed to work at it too.'

She gave him a small smile. 'You forgot to work your assets?'

He grimaced. 'Something like that.' He reached forward and pushed her hair back off her face. 'I'm sorry. I'll try and do better from now on. Can you forgive me?'

She nodded. 'Of course I can, Bim. But you can't blame yourself. Most of it is my fault. I... I've failed as—' Tears welled up again.

Bim pulled her close to him and hugged her. She felt so pathetically grateful that she started sobbing all over again.

'Yamuna,' he said after a few more minutes. 'Do you think, perhaps, you're a bit depressed? It's clearly not been easy for you.'

'But Louie does hate me,' she said. 'And I look at him and I feel... trapped. Not love. Just this feeling of being trapped.'

'I think that can happen,' he said. 'It was in that American baby book you made me read.'

'You actually read it?' She had assumed he'd put it in his briefcase and forgotten about it.

'Of course I read it,' he said. 'I just didn't think I had to *do* anything with the information.'

She stared at him, completely baffled. How could he think that he didn't have to do anything about raising a child? He was the boy's father.

'See, I told you, I'm not so good at real life,' he said.

That made her smile. 'We're a funny pair,' she said.

He nodded. 'How about we both agree to try doing things differently? I promise I will try and come home earlier each night, so that I get to see Louie on weeknights, not just at the weekend. And you, my lovely wife, you must promise me you will go and see the doctor to check if you have postnatal depression. Deal?'

'Another deal?'

'Yes. I see. I'm sorry.'

'No, it's fine. You're right. I promise. It's a deal.'

'Good. I'm glad we got this straightened out.' He smiled at her and, to her great surprise, gave her a gentle kiss on the cheek. What happened now? Was that the end of the discussion? Did they go back to him hiding in his study and her dealing with things?

'Now, about what we were discussing before,' said Bim. His smile disappeared, to be replaced by a worried frown.

Yamuna sighed. 'Yes. Why don't you tell me what happened? From the beginning.'

He sat back and rubbed his eyes. 'The look on her face.' He shuddered. 'I came in. She was pressed up against the wall. He was stroking her face and she... She looked at me. Her face. Yamuna. She was terrified.'

'And that's why you think he was attacking her.'

He nodded. 'He was very close to her. She wasn't struggling or anything, but it looked to me like she was very, very frightened. Which makes me think he threatened her with something worse than physical violence.'

Yamuna stared. 'Worse than forcing himself on her? What could be worse than that?'

'I don't know. Maybe he threatened to hurt someone she loves. Blackmailed her in some way. There is more to this than meets the eye, Yamuna, and I don't think the girl is to blame.'

Yamuna took this in. 'What if he threatened to hurt Louie?' Her blood ran cold.

'Could be,' said Bim. 'But if that was it, she could have told you.'

'Something or someone from home, then?' Yamuna sat back and frowned. Pieces of the puzzle started fitting together: the nights when she'd heard Soma cry out in her sleep; the need for the bolt on the door; the reluctance to write home.

'Now I come to think of it, there are a few things that don't add up. The agency called a few weeks ago to check she was okay because her people hadn't heard from her and were worried. She doesn't really talk about home, either. And when she first came here, she seemed to be really frightened of something. I thought it was the shock of moving to another country, but maybe there was more to it than that.' Could it be? Had she been so wrapped up in her own small miseries that she had completely failed to notice something so vital?

Bim nodded, his expression far away. 'Perhaps home has something she'd like to forget.'

–

In Louie's room, the wall at his back stopped Sahan's retreat. This couldn't be happening. He couldn't name half of the feelings that were churning inside him, but they all made him want to be sick. He couldn't breathe. Soma. His lovely, sweet Soma, was a fabrication. She wasn't real. This girl had lied to him, had made him fall in love with her and was now asking him to lie to his cousin, so that she could carry on with her lie. What a fool he had been. What a fool.

His face burned and his heart was drowning in bile. He had been here before. Taken in by a girl that he'd thought was good. But Tamsin had merely toyed with him. He hadn't been in love with her. This. This was much worse.

She was still standing in the glow of the nightlight. 'Sahan.' The sound was barely a whisper. As it left her, she crumpled. He stared at her, on her knees, sobbing into her hands and revulsion turned to anger. She had played him for a fool. For all this time, she'd been laughing at him, stringing him along. Even now, she was hoping that tears and a display of misery would make him relent. Well, that wasn't going to happen.

Half an hour ago, he'd been willing to bet anything that she had been wronged. That she was a victim. But here she was showing him just how good a liar she was. She had played a part and played it so well that he'd fallen for it without the slightest hesitation.

He had thought she was the kind of woman he could make a life with. She was no better than Tamsin. Another wave of nausea. He retched, hot liquid climbing his throat. He dashed out, passing the sobbing girl without a downward glance.

Chapter Twenty-Three

Sahan did not sleep well that night. His thoughts circled around one another; memories of home, memories of Soma, memories of the awful, plunging despair. Finally, at six o'clock, when it wasn't quite dawn, he hauled himself to his feet, pulled on the jumper that served as his dressing down and shuffled quietly downstairs.

Sitting at the kitchen table, nursing his coffee, he forced himself to consider what Soma had told him. He had looked online to see if there had been a bus crash at the time she had come over. All he'd found were a few lines – *bus ran off the road, several dead* – the victims were not identified or discussed. At least that bit was true. It made sense. Two girls, one noted missing, the other on her way to the UK. When Soma's passport was used, the authorities would have assumed that she'd survived and the other girl was the dead one. But it still left the fact that Soma wasn't who he thought she was.

It hurt, it still did, but he had to rise above that and think about how it affected his future. The future he had pictured was gone. He needed a new one. One without Soma in it.

He thought of her face, turned up to gape at the stained glass window at York Minster. She had looked so amazed, so happy, so young. How old was she? He had always thought she looked young for her age. He'd put it down to the short hair and the fact that he wasn't used to seeing girls without a layer of make-up any more. But it could be because she really was very young.

Then he felt revulsion towards himself. Had he inadvertently fallen in love with her because she seemed unspoilt and young? What did that make him? He shuddered. Had he been lying to himself as well? This thing he called love…

The sound of footsteps disturbed him. He looked up to see Cara, dressed in a crumpled jumper and t-shirt pulled on over pair of pyjama shorts. If it had been any other girl, he would have felt awkward and not known where to look, but he was used to Cara. Sometimes he even forgot that she was a girl.

'Morning.' She put the kettle back on. 'What time did you get in last night? We didn't hear you.'

'Really late,' Sahan said, looking down at his coffee.

The kettle bubbled and clicked off. The sound of hot water pouring into the cafetiere. The smell of scalding coffee. Mugs clinked. Cara was making coffee for herself and Nate to have in bed.

Sahan's parents liked that he lived with Nate. They would have had a blue fit if they knew that Cara stayed over. Sex out of marriage, and girls wandering around wearing big t-shirts and no bra – these were not things that existed in their world.

Sahan rubbed his brow. His eyeballs ached, gritted over by tiredness and the pressing urge to cry. Things had been going so well. What had he done for it all to come crashing down like this?

He had hoped that Soma would lead him back to a place where he was comfortable. If his personal life was calm and settled, if he had a home that was comforting, like Yamuna's home was, he had no problem at all with England. He loved the TV, he loved the lack of mosquitos and the way things worked like they were supposed to. Okay, the weather could be better, but that wasn't so bad. It wasn't like he was super fond of sweat.

He had pictured himself and Soma together in a cosy little flat, maybe, in time, with a family... The loss of it hurt like he'd lost a limb.

Oh, Soma. A tear escaped and landed with a little *plip* in his cooling tea. Except she wasn't Soma. She was someone else. Someone young and duplicitous and strange.

'Sahan? You alright?'

Sahan opened his mouth to say he was fine, but the words didn't come out. Cara and Nate were the only people who knew, really knew, about him. They knew about Tamsin. They knew about Soma. They knew what Sahan's family expected of him and knew that Sahan loved them too much to rebel against them. Sometimes Sahan felt that they knew him better than he knew himself.

'Oh love, what's happened?' She sat down in the chair next to his and leaned on her elbows. She didn't touch him. He appreciated that.

He had to tell someone. He couldn't talk to his family. He couldn't talk to Soma. He had to tell someone something before this corroded him from the inside out. Sahan drew a deep breath. 'I'm not seeing Soma any more. We split up.'

It was a translation into Cara language. It said 'I'm going through something that happens to other people'. Not a lie. Nowhere near the real thing either.

Cara's hand flew to her mouth. 'No.' She shook her head, slowly, as though letting the idea settle. 'You really liked her. I'm so sorry, Sahan. It's... you must be gutted.'

'Yes.' Gutted. Insides torn out and thrown on the scrap heap. Yes. That was what it felt like.

'What happened?'

Sahan took a deep breath and did a rapid mental translation. 'My cousin told me that Soma has been seeing someone else.'

'Oh. Ouch. Is it true?'

'Soma says... not.'

'Okay.' Cara nodded slowly. 'And you don't believe her?'

When he hesitated, Cara drew a breath. Sahan said, 'I don't know what to do any more.' He pushed his mug away and buried his face in his hands. 'I just don't know.'

'Sahan... I saw the way you looked at her.' Cara sighed. 'The important thing here is, do you trust her? If you do, then you know what to do. If you don't... then do you want to spend the rest of your life with someone you can't trust?' Cara patted his shoulder gently and moved her hand away. 'Whatever you decide now, you're going to be stuck with it for years to come.'

Cara didn't know the half of it, but she was right. Whatever way he chose to go, the future would be fixed. The consequences of what he did now would stay with him forever.

—

Soma knew she was dreaming, but she couldn't do anything about it. It was worse than a nightmare. It was a memory. It felt so real; the pandan weave of the mat digging into her back; the sweat and arrak smell of the man who was kneeing her legs apart; the sharp heat of the cigarette tip he held between two fingers of the callused hand that held her down – part vice, part warning. If she struggled, that cigarette tip would be pressed against her ribs, her breasts, her thighs, where no one would see the burn marks. *Don't make me hurt you, girl. Stop struggling.* Pain under her right breast. *Look what you made me do, little bitch.*

Soma shrieked and woke up. Lights. Bed. She checked herself – no burns. A dream. Just a dream. He hadn't found her after all.

Footsteps thundered up the stairs. 'Soma.' Madam knocked on the door, too loudly. She would wake up Louie.

Soma leapt out of bed and unbolted the door.

Madam looked past her into the room, then straightened to look her in the face. 'Bad dream again?' she said. She didn't sound angry.

Soma nodded. Madam seemed to relax.

'Okay,' Madam said. 'You're okay?'

She nodded again.

Louie started to cry, a sleepy, confused wail. Both women stepped towards the nursery. Madam put her hand up and stopped Soma. 'I'll go see to him,' she said. 'You… go back to bed. Get some sleep.' She frowned. 'Or watch telly. I'll… I'll deal with Louie.'

A few minutes later Soma watched, astounded, as Madam walked out of the room with Louie in her arms. Madam wasn't the sort of woman who let the baby snuggle beside her while she slept, yet here she was, taking the boy downstairs with her. Soma leaned out to watch them disappear into the bedroom. What did that mean? Was

Madam finally taking the time to get to know her son? Was she finally going to give him the motherly love and attention he needed? Did that mean that Soma, his mother surrogate, was no longer needed?

She retreated to her room and sat down on the bed. Crying and feeling sorry for herself wasn't helping. She had to work out what to do. She had survived before. She could survive again. Staring at her door, Soma worked out her options.

What she had done was wrong. She knew that. She also knew that she couldn't tell Madam or Sir about it. She had no doubt that Madam would inform the authorities. No amount of begging would save her.

If she 'confessed' to Kemasiri's version of things, Madam would sack her and send her back to Sri Lanka. At least she'd be going back as a free woman. She could go back to being herself... except she had no identification papers to say she was who she was. All her ID was floating somewhere, eaten up by the sea. It was now easier to be Soma than to be herself.

Through the gap in the curtains, she could see the moonlit sky. She went over to peer out. Being at the top of the house meant she had a bird's eye view over the misty rectangle of grass that was the garden. She would miss this, if she went. This room. This view. Louie. She would miss him almost as much as she would miss Sahan.

Sahan. The look on his face, that tiny step back from her, had told her all she needed to know. He was repulsed by her. The pain of it was almost physical, a twisting in her insides that would never, ever go away. She had thought that what her stepfather had done to her was the worst thing that could happen to her. In those scant seconds, without even touching her, Sahan had hurt her more. He didn't love her. He loved the idea of loving someone he shouldn't. She would have found that out eventually, but things had been pushed to the point early. Perhaps it was for the best to have found out now. And now there was nothing to stay for.

Sudden fear ambushed her. She had told him the truth about what she'd done. Could she trust him? Whatever she had thought before was clearly wrong. He didn't love her. So could she trust him to keep her secret? He was Madam's cousin. Wouldn't he feel obliged to tell her? In telling Sahan, she had not only wrecked her heart, but she'd wrecked her safety too.

For a moment, she was unable to move, paralysed by what had happened. She had come all this way, had this massive adventure, only to be undone by her own stupid heart.

She had to pull herself together. She couldn't crumble now. Whatever happened, she would survive this. Surviving was what she did. The first thing she had to do was to persuade Madam to send her back. She could rebuild her life once she was back in Sri Lanka.

—

Yamuna opened her eyes. In the crook of her arm, Louie snuggled into her, asleep again after downing a bottle of milk. Bim was moving around quietly, getting dressed. She watched him through half closed eyes. Their conversation the night before seemed a long time ago now and he was a stranger again. Was he right? Was she depressed? If that was the case, was the stalemate that was their marriage really *her* fault?

He looked up from buttoning his shirt and caught her watching him. For a minute she felt shy. He smiled, came over and sat on the side of the bed. 'I haven't forgotten what we talked about,' he said. 'I will be home early tonight.' He leaned over and looked at the sleeping baby. 'What are you going to do today?'

'I'm going to call work and tell them something's come up. I can't leave him here with her.'

Bim raised an eyebrow.

'I want to believe her, I do… but if there's the slightest amount of doubt…'

Bim nodded. 'Probably wise,' he said. 'Can I leave it to you to call the agency? What will you tell them?'

They had decided the night before that whatever had happened between Soma and Kemasiri, they couldn't allow Soma to stay. If Kemasiri was telling the truth, they couldn't trust her. If he was lying, Soma was in danger, which put Louie in danger.

Yamuna nodded. 'I'll do that. I want her to go as soon as possible.'

'I'll call Perera again and have another word about my suspicions about his driver. If that man did try to attack Soma, he may well have tried it on with other people too.' Bim shook his head. 'I can't believe she invited him in. I just can't. She was so terrified.'

If he had attacked the girl, Yamuna knew she would have to go to the police. She couldn't in good conscience let a rapist go free. On the other hand, they couldn't go around accusing people without any proof. 'I'll talk to her about it,' she said. She looked over at Louie. 'Louie will miss her.'

Bim looked at her, thoughtfully. For a long moment he said nothing. 'Yes,' he said, finally. 'He will. You might, too.'

She frowned. 'Me?' Why would she miss the girl? 'I'll find other childcare for Louie.' She had heard good things about the nursery next to the university. A few people from the faculty had children there. Okay, they couldn't teach Louie Sinhalese, but perhaps that was too much to hope for anyway. She made a mental note to call them.

'You trusted her,' he said. 'With all those other nannies, you were always so tense before you left. With Soma, you could hand him over and leave him.'

'That's because she loves him.' She hadn't intended to say that. But now that the words were out, she knew they were true. Soma did love Louie. And Louie loved her back. Which meant that her boy was happy. It made a difference to her to know that.

Bim nodded, as though she'd confirmed something. He sighed. 'I'd better go. I have to be in Doncaster in an hour and a half.' The bed moved as he stood up. He turned to go, then turned back. 'I'll be back early, I promise.' He reached forward and touched his palm to her cheek.

The strangely intimate gesture took her by surprise. It took a second for her to relax into it. Bim made a rueful face as he withdrew his hand. 'I'll see you later.'

With that, he was gone. Yamuna stayed looking at the door, at the space he had occupied, the residual warmth from his skin still on her cheek. How odd it was to be touched by her husband. They had slept together, but it had been a purely functional thing. A transaction, almost. But the tenderness of being touched. Gently, reverently. It was new. She liked it.

Louie twitched in his sleep. A little fist went up in the air and then descended, slowly, until it came to rest against her ribs.

She looked down at the top of her son's head. He did love Soma. When she left, it would break his little heart. He was young, she rationalized, he would forget within a week. But inside her something felt heavy. He wasn't even a year old, and she was introducing him to loss. To heartache. The idea of hurting him hurt her.

She reached across, careful not to disturb him, and touched a soft black curl of hair. Her finger hovering just above his skin, she traced the perfect curve of his cheek, the brush of his eyelashes, the pout of his little lip. She breathed in the baby lotion and milk smell of him. It was as though she were seeing him for the first time. Her son. An innocent mix of her and Bim. His eyes, his hands, her smile. For once, Louie was not crying, not fretting, not trying to get away. He lay, content, in her arms and he was a miracle.

My son. The words arrived in her mind, suddenly full of meaning. My son. Her eyes filled with tears. She didn't brush them away as they meandered down her face and neck. All this time, she had been blaming herself for not caring, for not feeling what she thought she ought to feel. But the love had been there all along, masked by exhaustion and a new mother's inability to deal with the upheaval. She had tried everything to make herself love him and when it all failed, she had tried to hide from him, when all she had to do was take the time to look at him. To appreciate all that he was. To know that he didn't care that she wasn't perfect. He didn't care that she didn't know what she was doing. All he cared about was that he was held and loved. She had been so blinkered. How could she have got it so wrong?

Silently, keeping herself in check so that she didn't disturb Louie, Yamuna cried for the months she had lost.

Chapter Twenty-Four

'Soma.' Madam stood by the door.

Soma had been sitting on the floor with Louie, who was lying on his tummy and playing with a toy. She didn't have much longer with him. She wanted to treasure every moment she had. 'Yes Madam?'

Madam came and sat down next to her. 'Soma, I might be able to help you, if you tell me what happened…'

'Yes Madam.' Soma took a deep breath. She had to do this. 'What he said was true, Madam. He… he is my boyfriend.' It was hard to suppress the shudder that ran through her. She hoped Madam didn't notice. 'I deceived you.' More than they would ever know. 'I know what I did was wrong.' She forced herself to look into Madam's face. 'I understand that you have to send me home now.'

There was a pause after she said it. Soma could almost see Madam's mind turning this over. Perhaps she shouldn't have pushed it. She should have waited and let Madam come to the conclusion herself.

Unable to hold Madam's gaze for more than a few seconds, she looked at the floor. To her left, she could hear Louie, feel the tug of him, but she didn't look at him. If she did, she would start crying again. Getting Madam to send her home was the right thing, the only thing, she could do. It was the only way she could get away from Kemasiri. But it meant she had to lose Sahan and to lose

Louie. At the same time. She felt the pain swell in her chest and blinked hard to keep the stinging tears at bay.

'Soma,' Madam said, at last.

Soma looked up. Madam was frowning. Did she suspect? Did she know? *Had Sahan told her?*

'Soma, I don't for a minute believe that you are friends with that man,' Madam said. 'What are you hiding from me?'

She suspected. But she didn't know. So Sahan hadn't betrayed her. Soma's mind flashed back to Mr Gamage's face. The understanding in his eyes. He would have told his wife what he saw. That would explain the questions. But if Madam found out, would she help? No. One person knew her secret, she couldn't risk any more people knowing. She raced through options in her mind. What could she say that wouldn't lead to more questions?

'He threatened you, didn't he?' Madam said.

Madam knew the answer to that already. There was no point lying about that part.

'Yes,' Soma whispered.

'What did he threaten to do? Now we know there's a problem, we can help.'

But she couldn't tell her. She stared at the floor and said, 'Madam, I'm sorry. I can't tell you anything more.'

'Does it... have anything to do with Louie?' Yamuna's eyes darted sideways to look at Louie. It was all Soma could do not to look at him too.

'No Madam. It does not have anything to do with Louie. Or you. It is... personal.'

Madam's lips pressed together in a line. There was a moment of angry quiet.

Her throat was tight. She tried to swallow, but her mouth was dry. 'Are you going to send me home, Madam?'

'I don't know. I'll have to think about it.'

'Yes, Madam.'

There was a cry. Louie had pushed the toy out of his reach. Both women instinctively moved across to help him, but before either reached him, he pushed his toes into the rug and crawled, commando-style towards the toy. The women looked at each other, all other discussion forgotten for the moment.

'Has he done that before?' Madam whispered.

'No.' Soma looked back down at Louie, so proud of him that a smile pushed its way onto her lips.

'Oh, Louie,' said Madam. She scooped the boy up and hugged him. 'You clever boy.'

He wriggled in her arms. Madam's gaze met Soma's briefly before she dropped her head to kiss her son.

Downstairs, the phone began to ring.

Soma held out her hands to take Louie. Madam hesitated for second, holding Louie close. Then she slowly relaxed and passed him across. There was something deliberate about the movement. It was a gesture that said, 'I trust you'. Soma took the little boy in her arms and cuddled him. She hoped Madam never had a chance to realise that although Soma could be trusted with the baby, she hadn't been entirely honest.

–

'Ouch.' Sahan had forgotten to use a cloth to protect his hands and burned himself on the sizzling chicken korai.

'Again?' said Mr Ghosh. 'Go home, Sahan. You look ill. Come back when you're better.' He waved Sahan away.

'But—'

'We'll manage. Go.' His boss turned and went back into the restaurant.

Sahan rubbed his eyes and winced at the pain in his fingers. After a night of no sleep, he was clumsy. He was only two hours into his shift and had already spilled one dish and burned his hands twice.

'He's right, you do look like you're coming down with something,' said Deepthi, who was tying an apron around her waist, so that she could take over Sahan's tables. 'You going to be okay getting back home?'

Sahan nodded. 'Yeah. I'm just… tired.' He yawned and gathered his things. 'I'll see you tomorrow, hopefully.'

Deepthi waved distractedly and pushed the trolley containing the food order out to front of house.

It wasn't time for the bus yet, so he may as well walk. Maybe the exercise would help him think. Sahan stepped out of the back, deep in thought.

Logically, he knew the right thing to do, the sensible thing to do, was to let Soma go; to distance himself from her and her deception as much as he could and forget all about her. Soma had lied to him. Not just a little lie, but one that touched everything he knew about her. Could he ever really believe a word she said to him now? That was no basis for a relationship.

He had known all along that his parents would not have approved. So now he had the perfect reason to let the whole thing drop and never think of her again. He could get on with his life. Build a career in England. He was young. He would meet someone more suitable, get married, have a family. That picture in his head of a small family unit could still come true. It would just be with someone else.

All that made perfect sense to him, but the idea of a life with someone else made him feel hollow. He couldn't face it. He sighed.

'Finally,' a voice said in Sinhalese.

Sahan looked up to see Kemasiri, leaning against a wall, waiting.

'You.' This man. He was the reason for all this.

Soma said Kemasiri had worked out her secret. An image of Kemasiri leering at them out of the car sprang to his mind. If ever there was a man who could blackmail a young woman; that would be Kemasiri. The tiredness was replaced by sudden anger.

'Not so wonderful now, eh Colombo Seven?' Kemasiri said. 'I told you – everyone has secrets. Your little piece of skirt has been lying to you from day one and you fell for it.'

Anger flared. Even in his state of confusion, the need to protect Soma burned bright. Whatever Soma had done, Kemasiri had still threatened her. Blackmailed her. If he could work out a way to stop that, then at least one good thing would have come out of this debacle.

Sahan carried on walking, knowing the other man would follow.

'Lying to me about what?' he said, trying keep his voice casual. His mind worked furiously. Kemasiri was a man who preyed on other people's secrets. He was keeping his boss's secret about his mistress, so he could be secure in his job as a driver. He was now blackmailing Soma. But her secret was only a problem if anyone believed Kemasiri in the first place...

Kemasiri gave a 'hah' of satisfaction and fell into step beside him. 'Your girl, who you think is so innocent,' he said. 'She's a fraud. She's not called Soma. She's not even from where she says she's from.'

How much *did* he know? 'If she's not called Soma, what is she called?'

'It doesn't matter what her real name is.' Kemasiri's eyes gleamed with triumph. 'What matters is that she's lying. Nothing she's told you is true. She's not even the age she says she is. You've been screwing a child.'

Ugh. Sahan almost winced. This guy thought Soma was a child. Yet he would have had her anyway. Nausea rose in his throat. Sahan took a deep breath. 'I don't believe you.'

'She—what?' Kemasiri glared at him. 'What?'

The confusion in the other man's voice made Sahan look up. He saw a flash of uncertainty in Kemasiri's expression. He stopped walking and turned to face Kemasiri. 'I don't believe you. You say she's lying about who she is. I don't believe you.'

Kemasiri floundered. 'She doesn't always answer to her name. She says she's from Matara, but she doesn't even know the place.'

Sahan shook his head in mock astonishment. 'That's your proof? Basically, that she doesn't want to talk to you?'

'No. It's not. You're... you're an idiot blinded by her charms. Any fool with half a brain can see that she's not...' He twitched as though unable to contain his frustration. 'You ask her. You ask her and see what she says!'

So he had no actual proof. He had relied on Soma's feelings of guilt when he'd preyed on her. Soma must have let her guilt show. Once she'd done that, Kemasiri had had power over her. Which he had used. Without hesitation.

Soma wasn't a hardened liar. She was someone who had acted on the spur of the moment and found herself unable to go back. And he, Sahan, hadn't given her the smallest chance. The anger he felt was only partly aimed at Kemasiri. Some of it was aimed at himself.

Sahan stepped closer to Kemasiri. 'You stay away from her. And me,' he growled. Kemasiri's eyes widened and the sneer dropped from his face.

'I'm guessing,' Sahan continued, 'that this isn't the first time you've tried to blackmail someone. That there are other women you've assaulted. If you come anywhere near me or Soma, or anyone connected with any of us again, I will make sure she goes to the police to press charges.'

'You wouldn't. You can't risk—'

He stepped even closer. 'Wanna bet?'

Kemasiri took a step backwards. Hah. He had him. Kemasiri was a bully and a fraud. He wouldn't risk his own activities coming to light. Before Kemasiri could come up with a reply, Sahan pushed the man back and walked away.

The night was cooling as he marched down the road. The walking and adrenaline was helping clear his head.

He thought of Soma, wrapped up against the cold, hesitantly reading children's books, her face tight with concentration. Soma gaining confidence, reading chapter books, her lips moving as she formed the words. Soma, who had started off as a servant girl who he'd been helping and somehow ended up being his first and last thought each day.

He remembered the feel of her hand in his. The shock of feeling her skin underneath his fingertips. The long forgotten need to touch and be touched. Soma had made him feel emotions he'd never expected to feel again.

Something clicked inside. He loved her. Whatever her real name was. Whatever she had done, it didn't matter. She was the girl who'd held his hand, who'd taken weeks to slowly, slowly relax in his company. She was that girl and he loved her. There could never be anyone else.

His father would be furious at him, but what if… what if his father was wrong? The thought stung him. Until now, his father had been right. The first time Sahan had tried to break away from the lines his father had drawn, he had met Tamsin. He had taken it to be a lesson that his father knew best. But it wasn't. It was just an event. Shit happened.

That image of a perfect family wasn't what *he* wanted. It was what his parents wanted. But he wasn't them. He thought about his life here: the ropey student digs; the part-time job; the friends – the son of a canning factory supervisor and the daughter of a long distance lorry driver; in an interracial relationship, no less. His father wouldn't have deemed Nate or Cara suitable people for Sahan to hang around with, but Sahan couldn't imagine a world without them in it. All this time he'd been so worried about what his parents wanted that he hadn't stopped to consider whether he agreed with them. Now, finally he knew that he didn't see the world the same way they did. They wanted him to be just like them, but he wanted something different. He wanted Soma.

But Soma had lied to him.

But why? It was as though his brain was finally waking up. Details nagged him. He tried to think what she'd told him the night before. She had stolen a passport to come to England, but why? It couldn't be for money, that wasn't the sort of person she was. If it wasn't that, then why? What was she trying to get away from?

He had been so wrapped up in his own feelings that he'd forgotten to ask the most important question.

Chapter Twenty-Five

Soma heard the doorbell, but didn't move. She was standing in the kitchen, sorting Louie's clean clothes into piles, ready to be taken upstairs. She felt as though she'd been given a precious reprieve for a few days. Losing Sahan had been bad enough. To lose Louie just as abruptly would have been too terrible.

She heard Madam answer the door. The voice that responded to her greeting was Sahan's. The world stopped. Sahan was here. Sahan. She had thought she would never see him again. But he was here? Had he changed his mind?

His voice carried on, talking to Madam. She couldn't make out his words, but she could tell that whatever he was saying made Madam happy. There was no sign of his trying to come into the kitchen to see Soma. Her hopes, which had started to rise, froze. Madam was his cousin. Of course he'd come over to see her. He would have known he could come and talk to Madam without ever venturing upstairs into Louie territory. If she hadn't got behind with her washing chores, she wouldn't even be down here.

A tear rolled down her cheek and splashed onto one of Louie's t-shirts. Soma sniffed and dried her cheek on her shoulder. She needed to get over this. It was cruel for Sahan to come to the house like this, but he didn't owe her anything. Whatever she might feel for him, he clearly didn't feel the same way about her. People like him didn't fall in love with people like her. She'd known this all along. If only her feelings would respond to reason.

Footsteps came towards the kitchen. Soma knew from the measure and weight of them that it was Sahan. Behind him came Madam.

What should she do? She wanted to look at him, but what if he looked at her like he had done the night before? She couldn't bear that. She could feel him coming closer. She bowed her head. Her heart throbbed in her ears.

He came in, but didn't acknowledge her. He and Madam continued talking. Madam turned her back to reach for the coffee.

Soma shot a glance at Sahan from under her lashes, terrified to see his expression.

Sahan wasn't scowling. His gaze caught hers. There was an urgency in his eyes, as though he was trying to tell her something. Almost imperceptibly, he shook his head. She quickly looked back down at her work.

Sahan and Madam were speaking English, but they weren't talking about anything to do with her. They were discussing somewhere called Teesside, which was near where Sahan's new job was going to be. Soma tuned it out, too distracted by the pounding of her own heart. Sahan was back. He didn't hate her. He had come back.

She wished Madam would leave, so that she could talk to Sahan. What could she do to get her away from them? How could she engineer a few minutes alone with Sahan?

As though her prayers were heard, the phone rang. 'What now?' Madam sighed. She looked upwards for a few rings and sighed again. 'Bim's not going to answer it, is he?'

'You get it,' Sahan said. 'I'll get the coffee.'

The minute Madam left the room, Soma looked up. Sahan didn't move from where he was, but put a finger to his lips, cautioning her to stay quiet until his cousin got to the phone. She tried to stream all her questions to him using just her eyes, but all he did was shake his head.

When she heard Madam say 'hello', she darted across the room to him. 'You came back.'

He nodded. A small smile. 'There's one thing I need to know, before anything else. How old are you? Really?'

Oh. Of course. He might be back, but it was silly of her to expect nothing to have changed. 'I'm twenty-one. Twenty-one and two weeks.'

His eyebrows drew together. 'It was your birthday two weeks ago? You... never said.' He stared at her for a second.

'I...' Of course she never said. What did he expect her to have done?

'I suppose you couldn't do that...' He shook his head. 'This is going to take a bit of getting used to.'

Did that mean he was willing to try getting used to it? Hope rose, warm and golden, in her chest. She could never go back to being her old self, but perhaps she didn't have to.

'Sahan.'

'Yamuna told me she's not sending you home.' He pulled out a small phone, the same make as the one Kemasiri had stolen. 'Here. I've put some credit on it. We don't have long to talk now.'

She took it and slipped it into her cardigan pocket. 'Thank you.'

He nodded, his mouth lifting up on one side.

'I thought... I thought you hated me.' Tears threatened again.

'You lied to me. I don't even know your birthday,' he said, sounding weary rather than angry. 'We have a lot to talk about.'

She nodded, there was no denying that.

Sahan glanced towards the door. 'Soma, there's something else I need to know,' he said urgently. 'On the night of the bus crash. Why were you on that bus in the first place?'

She stared at him. In her rush to explain, had she missed out the thing that started it all? She had. 'I was running away from my stepfather.' she said. 'Because he hurt me the way Kemasiri tried to do.'

–

Her words struck him like a physical blow in the stomach. His view of her shifted again and he knew he was right to have come back. If only she'd told him that last night, he would have understood straight away.

She was watching him, her big eyes wide and fearful. A tear leaked out and ran down her cheek.

'It's okay,' he said. Gently, he put his arm around her and drew her closer until she was leaning against him, awkwardly. 'I had no idea,' he whispered into the top of her head. 'I will look after you, Soma. Don't be afraid. I will never hurt you.'

She bowed her head and was quiet for a long moment. When she looked back up, he was surprised to see her eyes were dry. Her gaze met his. 'I'm not afraid of that,' she said. 'If you'll let me, I will look after you too.'

There was something fierce about her expression, a determination he hadn't seen before. He smiled. 'I'd like that.'

They heard footsteps on the landing. Soma sprang back, swiping the tears off her face with the back of her hand. She hurried back towards the pile of washing.

'No. Wait.' Sahan caught her hand.

'But Madam—' She tugged her hand away.

'She has to find out sometime.' Sahan took a step closer and put his other hand out, so that hers was sandwiched between his two warm ones.

At that moment, Yamuna appeared in the doorway. 'What the hell is going on here?'

—

Yamuna stared at the two young people. Soma looked terrified. Sahan looked determined. Was Sahan holding Soma's hand against her will? For a second, she was genuinely baffled as to what she was seeing. 'Well?'

Soma glanced at Sahan and he smiled at her. Soma seemed to relax. She stopped pulling away and took a small step towards Sahan. They both turned to look at her.

Fragments fell into place in Yamuna's mind. 'You two,' she gasped. 'You're together.' Her first feeling was relief that Sahan wasn't another person that she needed to protect Soma from. Close behind that came the shock. 'Sahan. What are you doing? What will your parents say?'

Sahan shifted his weight. 'I... think we need to talk.'

Yamuna didn't know which one of them to glare at first. Sahan, who really should know better. Or Soma, who seemed to be a different person every time she looked at her. 'I'll say we do.' She made a decision. She couldn't deal with this on her own. 'You,' she said to Sahan. 'Come with me. We're going to see Bim.' She turned to go upstairs, then turned back. 'You,' she said to Soma. 'Stay here.'

Chapter Twenty-Six

Bim made everyone sit down in the living room so that he could make sense of what was going on. Yamuna tried to untangle her emotions. Sahan's parents would be furious. What was he thinking?

Yamuna glared at him. 'But... how? *How* did this happen? You were supposed to be studying. And—' She shook her head. 'This is ridiculous, Sahan. You can't run off with the servant girl. It's madness.'

'She's not just a servant girl. You trusted her with your son!'

'I *pay* her to look after my son. I suppose I might have expected it of her, but you... I expected better from you. Your parents didn't send you all the way here so that you could mess up your future.' Her voice was rising. She couldn't believe he would do this. Someone as intelligent and well-heeled as Sahan needed a wife in the same league. Not some girl who could barely speak English. It was so idiotic. And what would his parents say? They would blame her. She was supposed to have been looking after him.

Bim laid a hand on her arm. 'Let's look at this calmly,' he said. 'Sahan, start from the beginning. Tell us the whole story.'

Yamuna sat back, her arms folded. Sahan told them the story – of meetings in the park, of English lessons, of isolation and homesickness and of love, blossoming in whispered snippets. Yamuna watched her cousin's face as he talked. She had always seen him as the teenager but she realised now how much he had changed. He had been a shy and anxious boy in those first days. She remembered the time she'd met up with him a few weeks after he'd moved from her house to student digs. He had looked so ill that she'd offered for him to come and live in her house. He'd recovered, but remained nervy.

Since Louie's birth, she had stopped noticing anything else, and that included Sahan. Now that she was looking at him again, she saw that he was calmer; still serious, but somehow less wired. When he spoke about Soma, his face softened, a smile tugging lightly on his mouth as he spoke. There was something beautiful about the effect it had on him.

She stole a glance at Bim, who was listening to Sahan, his face impassive. She had seen that face before. It was Bim's business face, the one he used when he was absorbing information, reserving judgement for later. He nodded at something and said, 'I see.'

Yamuna realised she'd missed the last few minutes of conversation. She hurriedly focused.

'We'll be married then, which will make all the difference,' Sahan said, his attention on Bim.

'If you were planning to elope, why are you telling us this?' said Bim. 'Why not just go?'

'You guys are important to Soma. And to me.' Sahan looked from one to the other. 'And we didn't want you to worry.'

'Or call the police?' said Yamuna.

Sahan acknowledged that with a nod. 'That too. But mainly, it would be nice to have you on our side. My parents are going to be angry, for a while…'

'Angry? They're going to be furious,' said Yamuna. 'With you and with me for letting you do it.' She threw her hands up. 'Surely, you can see this is madness? She's poor, uneducated and just a nanny. How will you ever be able to take her for a meal at your parents' table?'

'I am not my parents,' he said firmly. 'All of what you're saying is true, but I have thought about this and I'm sure.' He raised his eyes to her. His jaw was set. Yamuna had never seen that look on his face before. This was not a whim. He really was serious.

She looked across at Bim, who said, 'Ask Soma to come in.'

Sahan sprang to his feet and disappeared.

'What do you think?' said Yamuna, her voice low so that Sahan didn't hear.

'I think he's serious,' said Bim.

'Can we stop them?'

He raised his eyebrows. 'The question is, should we?'

Taken aback, she didn't respond.

'This means several things,' said Bim. 'Firstly, the man you thought she was seeing was Sahan, not the driver guy. This suggests that that man did attack Soma. Whatever he said or did to the poor girl must have been pretty horrific if she couldn't tell us. Secondly, Sahan knows what happened. That must have been fairly difficult for him too, yet he's here, telling us he wants to be with her, which means he must care for her – it's not a casual affair.'

Yamuna opened her mouth to argue, then shut it again. He had a point. If Sahan was unsure about how he felt, he would have had a good excuse to break things off when he was told that Soma was seeing someone else. The fact that he'd not jumped to any conclusions and given everything so much thought suggested that his feelings for Soma were genuine.

'But how can we know she's not using him? After all, she's come from nowhere. She couldn't hope to marry a boy like Sahan if she were back home.'

Bim gave her a long look. 'When I came to this country,' he said. 'I had very little. I cleared up glasses and washed up in pubs to make ends meet. I'm just an accounts clerk who has a good eye for investment. Perhaps we shouldn't judge people by their beginnings.'

'Sorry.' Yamuna looked away. She had forgotten that Bim's wealth was hard-won. Just because she'd been able to get a job in England after a few months of trying, she'd forgotten how hard it could be. Was she being too hard on Soma? Was she letting her insecurities colour her perception of the girl?

There were footsteps and Sahan returned, towing Soma by the hand. The girl looked petrified, not triumphant. So perhaps she wasn't a gold digger. Yamuna realised with a start that she'd never actually believed that of Soma. You lived with a person for so long and you learned something about them. She'd always felt that Soma's meek subservience was because she was hiding something, but she had never thought that Soma was capable of malice. If what she had been hiding was falling in love with someone forbidden… then it all made sense.

'Sit down,' said Bim, kindly.

Soma glanced at Yamuna, then perched nervously on edge of the chair. Sahan sat on the arm of the chair, his hand on her shoulder.

'Sahan tells me that you two have been seeing each other for some time now,' said Bim, leaning forward, his attention focused on Soma.

Soma nodded.

'And you want to get married.'

She nodded again. Her eyes shifted from Bim to Yamuna. 'I'm really sorry, Madam. I don't want to leave baby Louie, but...' She turned to look up at Sahan, who smiled at her. Soma's expression changed from one of fear to something Yamuna could only describe as lovesick. It lasted only for a second or so, but it was long enough for Yamuna to feel a pang of envy. She had never felt the need to look at anyone like that. Nor had anyone looked at her the way Sahan was looking at Soma.

Soma turned back to them. 'I promise I'll be a good wife to Sahan,' she said. 'I love him. Truly.' She looked so earnest, Yamuna almost found it funny. Almost.

Yamuna looked at Bim. A frown had appeared. What had worried him? He had been all set to shower good will on this couple a minute ago. She put a hand on his arm.

Bim's gaze flicked from Sahan to Soma and back again. 'There's something else?' he said.

Soma and Sahan exchanged glances. Sahan gave her an encouraging nod. She turned imploring eyes towards Bim. 'I have a secret, I have to tell you.' She lowered her eyes.

Yamuna noticed Sahan squeeze her shoulder gently. Soma reached up and put her own hand over his and began to speak. In a quiet voice, with Sahan interjecting here and there to add details, she told her story.

At first Yamuna was outraged, but before she could process how she was feeling, Soma told them her reason for running away. All anger was washed away in the flood of sorrow that followed. She didn't need to look at Bim to know that he was affected too. The poor girl. No wonder she ran away. No wonder she took a chance to escape when she saw it, no matter the risk. Yamuna realised with sudden clarity why she'd had that feeling of discomfort about Soma. It was her subconscious telling her something was wrong. The girl looked different to the photograph she'd been sent and looked far too young to be twenty-five. Her rational mind had dismissed the thought – after all, the girl had passed two sets of passport checks, but the observation had stuck, giving her the sense of mistrust. If she had been her normal self, she would have worked that out, but being wrapped up in her own spiral of despair, she hadn't pursued it, just as she hadn't noticed all the telltale signs that Soma was suffering.

Bim had said, 'perhaps home has something she'd like to forget'. He hadn't even touched the surface of it.

'Will you help us?' said Sahan.

There was a tense silence. Yamuna stared at her fingers. Would she help them? Of course she would, but at what risk to her own family? What Soma had done was against the law. To help them was probably a crime too. This was not a decision she could make on her own.

Finally, Bim said, 'It's a big thing you've just told us. We need a bit of time to think about it.'

Sahan and Soma looked at each other. Soma bowed her head and stood up. As they reached the door, hand in hand, Yamuna said, 'Wait in the kitchen.'

When they had gone, she turned to Bim. 'His parents are going to kill me,' she said.

'They need not know about all of it,' said Bim. 'In fact, if we tell them, we'd be putting them in a very awkward position.'

'She took a huge risk telling us, she must really want to be with him… And he with her.'

'When I look at them, I see a young couple in love. I may not know a lot of about love, but I recognize passion and determination when I see it. They are both determined to make this work. If they were a company, I'd invest in them.'

Yamuna let this sink in. Bim, as always, saw the world in terms of his business sense. She tried to look at the situation objectively. If she didn't have to answer to Sahan's parents, if Soma wasn't her employee, would she see the situation differently? Probably. 'So you think we should help them?'

'Just look at them!' said Bim. 'The way they look at each other. They are in love.'

She thought so too. Just because she herself had never been in love, didn't mean she didn't recognize it in other people. She thought of the times when Soma and Sahan had been in the same room. How had she not noticed? How had she been in the same room with that much intensity of feeling and not spotted it? The answer to her own question made her ashamed. She had assumed Soma was irrelevant, a face and a pair of hands with very little personality. She had known Soma was intelligent because of how fast she picked up reading to Louie in English, and she had been more than aware of Soma being pretty, yet she hadn't seen anything between the girl and Sahan because it hadn't occurred to her that to think about Soma the real person, she'd only seen Soma the idea. This knowledge made her ashamed. And being ashamed made her angry.

This whole situation was about more than Soma, a girl who took a job and got a break. Even in the confused

293

fug of her feelings, Yamuna had to recognize that the girl hadn't had it easy. Soma had suffered so much at the hands of her stepfather and been effectively abandoned by her mother. She'd had the determination to make a new life for herself and now, with one phone call, someone, Yamuna, could take it all away from her again. No one deserved that. And everyone deserved a chance for happiness.

And Sahan. This Sahan, who hovered protectively around the girl. Who looked at Soma with such intensity. Who was willing to stand up to the parents who had always controlled him. This Sahan was almost a different person to the boy she knew. He was stronger, more solid than before. He had lost that hunted look that he'd worn throughout his time at university. He had found someone to make him happy.

'Everyone deserves a chance to be happy,' she said.

Bim smiled. A big, wide, open smile that made her smile back. 'Exactly,' he said.

Yamuna nodded. 'Okay.' She frowned. 'What she did was illegal. How can we fix it?'

'We're going to have to come up with a plan.'

Chapter Twenty-Seven

Yamuna took the stairs slowly. It had been two days since Soma and Sahan had come to talk to them and she was still digesting the implications of it all. She and Soma had been trying to carry on as normal, tiptoeing around each other carefully. Any anger at the enormity of Soma's deception had shrunk to insignificance faced with the visceral instinct to protect someone so badly harmed. Above all, she felt ashamed. Where she had been looking for reasons to dislike Soma because something felt off, Bim, with his instinct for reading people, had spotted the vulnerability in her. Granted, he had only taken notice of Soma when he had been forced to, but when he did, he had looked at her with clear eyes and sympathy. How had Yamuna missed these signs? The crying out at night. The obsession with barring the door. The sleeping with the light on. The reluctance to go out. It all made sense now.

At least her feeling that the girl was bright had held true. In the discussions that had followed, late into the night, Soma had shown a great deal of common sense, even when discussing things that clearly frightened her. She would be a good match for the less worldly-wise Sahan.

Yamuna peered into the bathroom. Soma was kneeling on the floor next the bath, where Louis was happily splashing. Soma piled bubbles on the baby's head. She was smiling, but her mouth was wobbling at the edges, as though she were fighting back tears.

The mound of bubbles slid off and Louis laughed. Soma flicked water over him, making him giggle some more.

Yamuna stepped into the bathroom. Soma looked up, fearful for a moment, until her impassive façade descended.

'Soma.' Yamuna knelt down beside her. The girl watched her. There was so much to say, but Yamuna didn't know how to start. So she said, 'I've booked you and Sahan a ticket to go to Sri Lanka in two weeks' time. We can sort this thing out.'

Soma opened her mouth and breathed in as though to speak. No words came out. She took her hand out of the bath, shaking the water off it. Yamuna pulled the towel off the rack beside her and passed it to her to dry her hands. Soma burst into tears.

'Oh. Hey. Don't cry.' At a loss, Yamuna put her hand on the girl's shoulder. 'Don't cry. It will be okay.'

'You're so kind to me,' Soma sobbed. 'So kind.'

Yamuna knew she hadn't been kind. She had been judgemental and narrow-minded and petty. This kindness was too little too late, but it was better than nothing. 'It's okay.' She repeated.

Louis, suddenly noticing Soma's tears, gave a worried squawk. His lower lip trembled. 'Oh, Louis,' said Yamuna. 'We'd better get you out of the bath.'

Soma looked at Louis. She wiped her face with the heel of her hand. 'Come baby,' she said. She stood up, expertly scooped the baby out of the bath and wrapped him in the towel. She held him close as they walked back into his room.

Yamuna noted that Soma's hair had grown to a good length now, but it was an uneven mess. That would never do. If she was going to present herself to Sahan's parents, she would need to look more polished than that. 'You know what,' she said. 'Before we go anywhere, I think I need to take you to have your hair cut.'

Soma gave her a look of surprise. 'Yes, Madam.'

'I told you, you don't have to keep calling me Madam.' She pulled Louie's pyjamas out of the drawer and passed them to Soma.

Soma took them and said, 'Thank you... Yamuna.'

The words hung in the air between them, a change in their relative positions. For a moment neither of them was sure how to deal with it. Then Louie burped and, slowly, the two women smiled at each other.

Chapter Twenty-Eight

Yamuna found a seat and pulled Louie's pushchair to rest next to her. In front of them a complicated musical fountain played an erratic tune. Louie stared at it, utterly fascinated. It was two weeks after Soma and Sahan's revelations and the Gamages were on a family day out, just the three of them. They were in the Eureka children's museum. So far, most of the things they'd seen had been aimed at older children than Louie, but this interplay of water, light and sound seemed to have captivated her son. She leaned forward to watch his face as his eyes moved from one spot to another. Every so often a bell would strike and Louie's whole body responded, applauding happily.

She still felt weighed down by the responsibility of looking after him. But knowing that the depth of feeling was there, somewhere deep inside, ready to come out if she needed it, made her feel less trapped. She wasn't broken, she was ill. Eventually, she would get better. In the meantime, she would continue to do her best with him.

Bim, who had been reading the description board, came and sat beside her. He too looked at Louie and smiled. When he looked up, he raised his eyebrows at Yamuna and smiled as though to say, 'our son. I'm so proud.'

Yamuna returned his smile. She settled back to watch the fountain herself. It wasn't that Bim had suddenly developed a romantic streak overnight, but something between them had changed. It was as though a wall of formality that had kept them apart was dissolving. They had always respected each other and had been courteous and solicitous of each other's needs. There was even a sort of friendship, maybe. But genuine affection? That was another thing that she'd assumed would arrive automatically. When her mother had said 'you'll learn to love him', she'd believed her. How naïve. They hardly knew each other. All they'd had in common was the right sort of social and cultural background and a desire to marry someone.

Even after Louie was born, they had shared a mutual understanding – a shared interest in the boy... like they were business partners.

But now, she felt something unwinding. A dormant desire to be with Bim. To get to know him. To make him happy. After a few moments, Bim moved slowly and, as though asking permission, put his arm around her. She looked up at him, surprised, but not displeased. His expression changed subtly, the smile tempered with a hint of worry. It was as though they were out on a first date. The ridiculousness of the situation made Yamuna smile. She looked back to Louie and, just as deliberately, laid her head against her husband's shoulder. They sat like that, gradually relaxing into this new familiarity.

Anyone looking at them would have thought they were a typical family unit. Yamuna looked beyond the fountain at other families: children in various states of emotion; parents with that haunted look of people who really needed more sleep; tears, laughter, boredom. Perhaps they were all fighting the same battles she was. Perhaps this really was how it was done. No magic solutions. No instant family bonding, but small victories, carefully won.

There was another chime from the fountain and Louie gave a squeal and the clapped his hands. Yamuna relaxed against the warmth of her husband. Perhaps this was as good as it got. Perhaps, she thought for the first time, this was enough.

Chapter Twenty-Nine

The sea was a dazzling, sparkling blue under the bright sun. The road shimmered in the heat haze. Soma was sitting in the back of an air conditioned taxi, sunglasses on her head. Sahan was looking out of the window, watching the houses and shops pass by. They had been back in Sri Lanka less than a day. Going back to her mother's house to find her birth certificate was the first job in a long list of things to do. On the way back, they were going to go and see Somavathi's mother. It had all seemed so sensible when they'd discussed it sitting in Yamuna's kitchen, but now, as the car turned off the trunk road into a secondary one, she wasn't so sure.

They passed the gates to the factory where she used to work. People trickled in and out of it. Lunchtime had started. Her village was only a few minutes away now. The cycle ride that had taken forever in the middle of the night, was nothing to a car.

The car slowed right down once it turned off the tarmac surface. The uneven road made it bounce and jostle the passengers. Soma looked out of the window at the familiar trees and verges and her heart pounded. There was suddenly less air in the car. A hand reached across and closed over hers. She turned her head to look at Sahan.

'It's okay,' he said, quietly.

She shook her head. 'I can't.' Her throat was closing up. The scars on her ribs prickled. 'I can't.'

'Look at me,' he said.

His eyes were like melting chocolate. A safe haven. 'All you need to do is talk to your mother and ask her for your birth certificate. That's all.'

'But what if… he's there?' He shouldn't be. That had been the whole point of coming at this time. But what if he was?

'Remember what we talked about. You aren't that person any more. You're Soma. You're not the frightened child with no one to turn to. You have me. You have Bim and Yamuna. You are not alone. He can't hurt you.' His gaze was firm. 'I won't let him hurt you. I promise.'

Her breath eased a little, but her heart still hammered. 'What if… they try to make me stay?'

'They can't,' he said, with finality. 'They can't make you do anything you don't want to. Believe that and they'll see that there is nothing they can do.'

The driver in the front slowed the car to crawl. 'Which house, miss?'

She looked over his shoulder, through the windscreen. There was the shop, where she and her mother used to go to watch teledramas in happier times, where her stepfather later pretended he spent his evenings. Her throat closed up. There was a small knot of people around the shop. They eyed the car with curiosity.

Sahan squeezed her hand.

She cleared her throat. 'Straight on. Three houses down.' Her mother should be home at this time, grabbing a few hours between one job ending and another starting. Her stepfather should be out in the lumberyard where he worked. The car stopped outside the tiny house.

'You're not that child any more,' Sahan said. 'You're my Soma.'

Which she was. She took a deep breath and pulled herself up straight. He was right. She was different. She had gone to a proper hairdresser, for the first time ever, and had her short hair styled. The face that looked back at her from the mirror wasn't Jaya, nor was she the Soma who refused to go out by herself, but a different person again. Soma lowered her sunglasses from where they were sitting atop her neat crop, opened the door and got out. She heard the car door as Sahan got out too. A small crowd of people had followed the car and now stood around, watching. She turned to face them and saw blank curiosity on their faces. They didn't recognize her. They were not expecting to see Jaya again. They didn't realise that this woman, dressed in jeans and a light cotton top, could be the same girl. They would realise eventually, she was sure, but she had a few minutes before the penny dropped.

Sahan came round to her side and touched her elbow. She nodded and strode to the house.

Alerted by the car outside, her mother came to the doorway. As she stepped into the light, the first impression Soma had was that she looked less frail. She was no longer painfully thin and she had on a blouse that Soma had not seen before.

Her mother's eyes, always distant, as though she was watching the world from far away, focused on Soma's face. 'Jaya?'

'Amma.'

The look that passed across her mother's face was not relief, as Soma had half hoped, but something akin to horror. 'No. No. Go away. You must go away.' She darted forward and pushed Soma in the chest. 'Go. Go. Before he—'

'Amma, it's okay. This is Sahan—'

Her voice dropped. 'Get away, girl. Why did you come back here? Go away. We are all better off if you're not here.'

'She needs a copy of her birth certificate,' Sahan interrupted.

She seemed to notice him for the first time. 'What?'

'Birth certificate.'

'Yes,' she said. 'Wait.' Before they could say anything else, she darted into the house. Soma turned to Sahan, gripped by sudden horror. 'We can't leave her here.' She looked over at the people watching them. 'I can't leave her with him.'

She ducked into the darkness of the house. 'Amma. Amma, come with me. I have a good life now. Come with me.'

As her eyes adjusted to the darkness, she saw her mother holding out a small envelope. 'Here. Take it. Now go.'

She took it and closed her hand over her mother's. 'Come with me.'

Her mother stepped closer and placed a hand against Soma's cheek. For an instant she looked like she had done before it all went wrong. 'No. I can't leave here. Don't worry about me,' she said. 'He doesn't hurt me. He is... since you left, he's been better. He doesn't drink like he did. He knows they're watching him.' She smiled, a ghost of the smile she had once had. 'When you left, they thought he'd killed you.' Tears filled her eyes. 'I knew you weren't dead. When I saw that you'd taken the necklace, I knew you weren't dead. I know what it feels like when a child dies. I told them.' She nodded to herself. Her hand drifted to touch her stomach. 'But it frightened him.'

'They? You mean everyone in the village?'

She nodded and patted Soma's cheek. 'I'm so sorry, my Jaya. I let you down.' She sighed. 'It all came out, after you disappeared. You tried to tell me, but I wasn't listening. I'm so sorry.'

Soma shook her head. She couldn't speak. There was so much she wanted to say and none of it would come out.

'You're a clever girl. Like your father,' her mother said. She looked over at the doorway, where Sahan was talking to someone from the village. 'Your man, is he a good man? Does he treat you well?'

'Yes.' Soma smiled. 'Yes, he does.'

'Then that's all I need.' Her mother pushed her gently towards the door. 'Now go. I don't want him to come back and see you. Things are better when you're not here.'

Her mother didn't want her there. Somehow, Soma wasn't surprised. From her bag, she pulled out a bundle of pale blue airmail sheets. 'Here.' She thrust them into her mother's hand. 'Write to me. I've put an address on them already. Write to me.'

Her mother looked at the paper. 'Yes,' she said, faintly. Soma knew she wouldn't.

She had something else. She took out a small red packet. 'I lost your chain,' she said. 'It went out into the sea. So I've got you a new one. Hide it like you hid the other one. For when you need it.'

Her mother tipped the chain onto her hand. It was simple, with slightly more gold than in the original. Finally, she smiled. 'Thank you. Now go.'

Outside, there was a small knot of people watching. Familiar faces, every one. When her father had died these were the people who had come, bringing food and kindness. The same people who sang and laughed at her mother's second wedding... and wept at the baby's funeral. They watched. They helped. But how could they help if her mother didn't want to be helped?

'Can we get anything for you, miss?' said the man from the shop. He had been talking to Sahan. Why was he calling her 'miss'?

She looked back towards Sahan, who smiled at her. 'No thank you,' she said. 'We should be going now.'

She turned her back to her mother, embraced her and whispered, 'Are you sure? You can come with me.'

Her mother pulled away and gently took Soma's face in her hands. 'This is the bed I made, I will stay here,' she said. 'Have a happy life, my girl.'

She stepped away. Sahan bowed his head to her mother and the older woman nodded to him. They walked towards the car.

As she was about to duck into the car, the shopkeeper stepped into her line of vision. 'We are looking after her now, miss,' he said. 'I don't let him drink in my shop any more. I don't think he gets it from anywhere else either.'

He was looking at her pleadingly, as though asking for forgiveness. He knew who she was. She understood why they were calling her 'miss'. With her fancy hair and upper class 'husband' she had come back as a completely different creature to the one they knew. They thought that she had somehow gained power. She felt a sudden urge to laugh. She smiled at him instead. 'Thank you.' She looked across at Sahan, who was waiting for her to get into the car. 'We appreciate it.'

As the car pulled away, she blew out her cheeks and rested her head back.

'Are you okay?' said Sahan.

She tilted her head to look at him. 'Yes,' she said, her tone full of surprise. 'Yes, I am.'

–

Somavathi's village was bigger and less remote than the one Jaya had been born in. Soma had changed her clothes when they stopped at a rest house. She had swapped her jeans for a more sedate plain cotton dress and slippers. She and Sahan left the car at the top of the road, where the last streetlight was, and walked the last few yards, guided by the torch in Sahan's hand. They had chosen to come in the evening, when people were likely to be home. It was too dark to tell how big the house was, but it looked in better repair than the one her mother lived in.

The man who answered their knock looked so much like his dead daughter that Soma nearly cried out. As it was, she merely said, 'My name is Jaya. I was on the bus that crashed. I would like to talk to you.'

The man's eyes widened. He said, 'Wait, please.'

They waited, under the unadorned light bulb in the porch, shifting position to wave away the mosquitos. She looked at Sahan. He nodded, reassuringly. They had agreed that she would do the talking. He was there just to accompany her.

When the door finally opened again, it was a woman who invited them in. She must be Somavathi's mother. 'Come,' she said, quietly. 'She's dead, isn't she?'

Her tone, half fear, half resignation, pierced Soma. It had been hard enough reading the pain in the letters that

arrived, but to see it etched on the faces of these people…
it was horrible.

'I'm sorry,' she said. 'I'm so sorry.'

The mother began to cry, big, hiccupping sobs that
shook her. The father's eyes filled with tears. He put an
arm around his wife and said, 'Sit. Tell us.'

She sat, cautiously, on a wicker chair. Sahan stood next
her, his face expressionless. Even though he said nothing,
it was hard to disguise the fact that he came from wealth
and privilege. If the couple noticed, they didn't care.

'Somavathi was sitting next to me on the bus,' Soma
began. 'When the crash happened, I was in the water
near her. I pulled her to the beach and tried to get her to
breathe again, but…' Tears filled her own eyes. She wiped
them away and realised her hands were shaking. 'She was
already gone.'

The mother let out a wail. A face peered in from one
of the adjoining rooms. There must be other children.
Somavathi's siblings. The father gestured with his hand
and the face withdrew.

'But,' he said, 'they said she was alive.'

Soma shook her head. 'I did a bad thing.' Her chest felt
tight and it was hard to breathe. Sweat prickled on her
forehead. She had to do this. 'I was running away from
people who hurt me. I found her passport and the plane
ticket in her bag and… I took it. I pretended I was her.
I'm sorry. I'm so sorry.'

The mother was sobbing loudly. A teenaged girl
emerged from the room. 'You stole my sister's name?'

'I was desperate. I know it was wrong, which is why
I'm here.'

'You took her job?' the girl continued, standing next
to her mother, glaring.

Soma nodded. She pulled out an envelope full of money. Once she had decided she was going to tell these people the truth, she had also decided that she would give them all the money left in her bank account. Since she'd only taken out a small fraction of it, there was far more than the real Somavathi would have sent home.

'I saw your letters,' she said. 'Two of them. I know she was supposed to send money home. Here. This is most of what I was paid when I was there.'

'You think you can—' The younger girl began.

The father took the envelope. 'Why?' he said. 'Why did you pretend? Why did you come here?'

'I did it because I was scared. I saw a chance to run away where I wouldn't be found and I took it. It was selfish and wrong. I know that. I can't make it right, but I am trying to make it better.'

She looked at the mother, who was crying too hard to talk. She went over to her and knelt down. 'I'm sorry,' she said again. 'If there was anything I could say to help, I would.'

The woman looked up at her through tearing eyes. 'She didn't suffer?' she said.

Soma shook her head. 'I think she was knocked out when it happened. When I saw her, she was floating. She looked… like she was asleep.'

'She was a good girl.'

She hadn't known her, but she supposed she must have been. 'Yes.' Soma looked up at the younger girl, who was crying too now. She wished there was something to say.

'I have this too.' She reached into her bag and took out Somavathi's passport. 'Here.' She handed it to the younger girl who took it, almost reverently.

She glanced over her shoulder at Sahan. He said, 'Okay. We will go now.'

'Are you a policeman?' the younger girl asked.

Sahan didn't reply. 'Come,' he said to Soma.

'Thank you for talking to me,' said Soma. 'I'm very sorry. If...'

Sahan made a noise in his throat.

'Yes, sorry. I'll go now.'

They backed away to the door. No one said anything. Soma looked back at the little family. The mother was holding the passport now. 'Thank you,' she said, suddenly. 'For telling us the truth. At least now we know.'

Soma nodded and left. Her throat felt tight. She walked behind Sahan, who had the torch, until they got to the car where the driver was waiting. She held herself together until they left the village. Only then did she break down and cry.

–

Sahan leapt out of the tuktuk the minute it stopped. He paid while Soma scrambled out. As the three-wheeler chugged off, they stood together and looked up at the big gates that shielded Sahan's family home from view of the road. The top floors of the house gleamed white in the sunlight. He had called his parents that morning and told him the purpose of his visit. They had not been happy.

'Ready?' he said, glancing at Soma.

She bit her lip and nodded. She looked terrified. That was no good. She had to look confident.

'Remember, I love you,' he said. 'You are everything.'

Her gaze met his and he saw the glow ignite. It seemed to unfurl her. She stood up a little straighter. 'Yes,' she said.

She touched her hair, as though it were a lucky talisman. 'I'm ready.'

He nodded, took her hand and knocked smartly on the gate. The gardener opened it so quickly that he must have been lurking behind it, waiting for the knock. Sahan glanced upwards and wondered who else was watching.

Head held high, he led the way in. The front door was open, but there was no one waiting for them – a deliberate sign that he was allowed in, but not being made welcome. They left their slippers by the door and stepped in. The terrazzo tiles were cool underfoot. Water tinkled in the little indoor water feature. His mother's jasmine plants were in flower. Everything was just as it had been when he'd left three years ago. The thought that this might be the last time he came here made his step falter. He glanced over at Soma, who was taking it all in wide-eyed, and thought it was worth it.

His mother was standing by the door to the veranda, her hand resting on her heart.

'Amma.' He started towards her, but stopped when his father appeared beside her. 'Thatha.'

'What is the meaning of this?' His father demanded.

His wife put a hand on his arm. 'Let's hear what the boy has to say,' she said, her tone dubious. 'Let's sit down and talk.'

'Sit down—' his father began, but a shake of his mother's head stopped him. Sahan felt absurdly grateful for her placatory tendencies.

Out on the veranda, Priyanka was lounging on a chair, flicking through a magazine with exaggerated nonchalance. She looked up and grinned before going back to the magazine. Sahan wondered what she was doing. Her apparent disinterest would only annoy their father even more.

Everyone sat down on the wicker chairs, Soma perched on the edge of hers. Both his parents were watching him, his mother wary, his father simmering. Soma glanced at him. He had to get on with it.

'This is Jaya – Jayanthi, sometimes known as Soma,' he said. They had decided to keep using Soma as a nickname. 'My fiancée.'

His father switched focus and glared at Soma. 'Who is this girl? Where did she go to school? What education has she got? Where is her family from?' He demanded, in English, as though Soma wasn't there.

Soma was staring up at his father. Her hand clenched Sahan's. Too late, he realised that an overbearing man shouting at her was the last thing Soma needed. He should never have brought her here. He moved closer to her, leaning forward to shield her.

'If you have anything to say, Thatha, say it to me,' he said. 'She did nothing to disappoint you.'

His intervention wrong-footed his father, who stared at him. Sahan took advantage of the momentary lull. 'You know the answer to all those questions. She was – is – Louie's nanny. I met her in the UK. I am going to marry her.'

'Have you taken leave of your senses, boy?' said his father. 'After all that we've done for you, this is how you repay us?'

'I didn't realise your love came with strings attached.'

His father stopped, as though slapped. Behind him, Priyanka made an impressed face.

Before he could say anything more, Soma said, in Sinhalese, 'I know I'm not the sort of girl you hoped your son would fall for, but I promise you, I will look after him.' She was looking directly at his mother. 'He is a very clever and hard-working man. He needs a wife who will support him. I can do that. I know that all you want is for him to be happy.' She glanced at him shyly and smiled, a tiny, sweet smile. 'That's all I want too.'

While his father made huffing noises, his mother was studying Soma, taking in the neat hair, the young face, the hand that was holding Sahan's like a lifeline. 'How old are you, child?'

'I'm twenty-one.' Soma's back straightened, as though challenging her to find fault with that.

'Bah. A child,' said Sahan's father. 'Children, playing stupid childish games. This is not a game, Sahan. Just think of the damage you're doing. Just think what it would do to my reputation if the press heard about this?'

It was the mention of the press that did it. Until now, Sahan had been worried about how upset his parents would be, but clearly, his father was only worried about the complexion this 'scandal' would give to his political career. All this angst worrying about hurting their feelings and they didn't care about his feelings at all.

He stood up and pulled the surprised Soma up with him. 'I'm sorry you feel I might damage your reputation,' he said, coldly. 'I came to tell you I was getting married. I'm sorry you don't feel you can be happy for me.' He tugged Soma's hand. 'Come on Soma, we're leaving.' Without waiting to hear the response, he towed her out through the living room and into the front garden. He was so angry, he could barely see. He wrenched the gate open and stepped out into the road.

'Sahan?' Soma laid her free hand on his arm. 'Are you okay?'

Someone called his name. He turned. Priyanka's head popped out through the gate. 'Sahan wait.' She slipped out.

'I just wanted to say,' she said. 'If you need someone to represent the family at your wedding, you can count me in.' She grinned at Soma. 'I don't know you, but I'm glad Sahan found someone who loves him. Someone had to, I guess.' She gave her a peck on the cheek. 'You look after him.'

'I will,' said Soma.

'And you too.' Priyanka turned to Sahan. 'I know it looked bad, but I think Amma will come round with time.' She punched Sahan lightly in the arm. 'I'd better get back in before the shit hits the fan. Keep in touch okay?' She turned and ran back inside.

They watched as the gate rolled shut. Soma pulled an umbrella out from her bag and put it up, casting a patch of shade that gave a small respite from the sun. Sahan took the umbrella, so that they were both sheltered under it. It wobbled a little and he realised his hand was trembling. 'Let's get a tuktuk from the top of the road,' he said.

They walked for a few minutes, in silence. He thought about the quiet way that Soma had said exactly the right thing to appeal to his mother. Glancing sideways at her, he was struck by how far she'd come from the timid girl with the buzz cut hair and enormous, frightened eyes. She was so much braver than he could ever be. He was lucky to have her.

She caught him looking at her and smiled. 'Don't worry,' she said. 'They'll come round.'

He really hoped she was right.

Chapter Thirty

Sahan smoothed down the bedding. He'd had to buy a brand new double duvet and covers to go on the bed that came with the flat. Fully furnished apparently meant the minimum amount of furniture, so there was nothing else in the room apart from a wardrobe and a chair. It was homely enough, though. After living in shared houses and university accommodation, even this tiny flat felt palatial. He went out into the living room, which had no sofa. The only places to sit were four dining chairs at the table. He should get a tablecloth.

He glanced back at the bedroom. He and Soma had married quietly, in a registry office – more a transaction than a wedding. It was hardly the lavish, high society wedding that his father had hoped for. His parents hadn't even come, although Priyanka had, if only for a short while. He wished things could have been different, but it was what it was and they needed time to get used to Soma's presence in his life.

He had taken his new wife out for dinner and they had walked hand in hand down the beach. That night he'd flown out so that he could move to Teesside and start his new job, leaving Soma to sort out her visa and follow. That was nearly six weeks ago now. Married life didn't start for real until she got here.

The thought of sex didn't repulse him as it once would have done. But the idea still made him nervous. Although he couldn't fully explain why. He didn't know how either of them would deal with it. A girl who had been through what Soma had was bound to be fragile. Would she even want to be touched? How would she deal with that? How would he?

All he wanted was to follow his dream of a life with the girl he loved and trust that everything would fall into place. A sudden picture of Kemasiri arose in his mind. He had been an unexpected complication. But if Kemasiri hadn't forced the situation, would Sahan have risen to the challenge? Or, for all his plans of defiance, would he have eventually given in and done what was expected of him... like he had always done before? He knew the answer. It wasn't flattering.

Kemasiri had forced him to stop and look at what he had with Soma. To really see what he stood to lose. Then Soma had confessed her secret to him and forced him to look even deeper – past the infatuation with the face and the soft voice that sang a familiar lullaby and to question what drew him to her. To question why he loved her. Or even if he loved her at all.

The girl he'd fallen in love with was quiet and kind and determined. She had learned to read and to speak English and she had done it faster than he could have. He had talked to her about myriad things and watched her soak up knowledge. He had seen the light of understanding flare in her eyes. He knew, without a doubt, that she was cleverer than he was. That given half the opportunities he'd had, she would have been a success. And strangely, instead of putting him off, it made him admire her all the more. He had grown up with girls who had never had to figure out what they had. Girls who knew what they were destined to do – be it studying to become a doctor or marking time until they could marry well. They all had a plan and were supported in their path. Yet Soma, who had nothing, less than nothing, had found a plan and made it her own. In doing so, she'd had to take on a name and another life. She had grown into that life, finding new strengths and depths of daring she didn't even realise she possessed. Soma was everything he wished he could be: daring, where he was timid, selfless where he was selfish, generous with her feelings, while he was too afraid of rejection to reach out. She was the ying to his yang. The earth to his fire. Being with her made him feel... balanced.

It would be fine. It would have to be.

Soma's train was due in an hour. Even though he had done as much as he could, he felt the need to do more. He paced into the kitchen and back out again. When his phone pinged, he pounced on it, glad of a distraction.

It was a Skype message from an ID he didn't recognize. Clicking on it, he recognized his sister Priyanka's online name. Since starting A-levels at a private college, Priyanka had set up accounts under a fictitious name, so that she could keep in touch with friends. In a nod to their father's fears, she said she refrained from posting photos. As far as he knew, his parents had no idea.

He accepted the link request. The phone immediately started playing the Skype ringtone.

'Hey you,' Priyanka said when he answered.

For a moment, he couldn't respond. He hadn't spoken to anyone from home since he'd called to tell them that he was back in England safely. When they'd cut him off, he fully expected never to hear from any of them again.

'What?' said Priyanka. 'I go to all this trouble to call you and you're not talking to me?'

'I'm just surprised, that's all. It's wonderful to speak to you, Pri.' He peered at the white tiled wall behind her. 'Where are you?'

'College,' she said. 'I'm on Anula's phone.' Her friend's hand appeared in the background and waved.

'Hi. Hi Anula.' He cleared his throat to shift the lump that had appeared there. College was one of the few places where she was away from their parents' gaze. 'How… How are you?'

'I'm okay. Although, I'm not allowed to have any fun now, since you got yourself hitched.' She rolled her eyes. 'So, apart from bored rigid, I'm good.'

'I'm sorry.' He smiled at her. She looked the same as usual, which was reassuring. For some reason he'd expected her to be angry and tear streaked. After all, she was the one at home to hear the aftermath of his actions.

She made a 'tsch' noise. 'So, how's married life?'

'I don't know yet. She's arriving today.'

'Your Soma?'

How strange it was to hear his sister say that. 'My Soma.'

She peered at him out of the screen. 'You *are* sure about this, right?'

'No. I'm sure.' With each day, he became a little more sure. 'I love her.'

She smiled. 'In that case, I'm happy for you.'

There was a pause as they both thought about the people who weren't happy.

'How are they?' he said. There was no need to say whom he meant.

For once, she didn't roll her eyes or make a joke. Her face was serious when she said, 'Amma is very upset. She keeps going on about not being able to see her grandchildren. Thatha is still roaring around the house. He thinks you've turned your back on him and everything he stands for. That you don't care about him… us.'

'That's not true. I—'

'I know, Sahan. I know. Really, deep inside Thatha probably knows too. Give him time. He'll calm down.'

'You think?' He wasn't so sure.

'I know.' She smiled again. 'Bim Aiya is a pretty cool guy. Thatha was shouting down the phone at him and Yamuna Akki the other day and Bim says, 'It's a shame you can't spin this to show that you're truly a man of the people who eschews boundaries of class and caste.' Thatha was speechless.' She grinned. 'Give him some time and you marrying beneath yourself is going to be all his idea.'

He knew she was trying to cheer him up and he was grateful. 'I am sorry, you know. I'm guessing this isn't much fun for you.'

She rolled her eyes. 'You guessed right. It's all drama, drama, drama at home. You know what the worst part is? I thought I would be the one to rebel, not you.' She looked at someone off screen. 'Listen, I'd better go. We're supposed to be in class. You take care of yourself, okay? I'll try and talk to you when I can. Email me.'

'I will. You take care too.'

But she had already cut him off.

Sahan stood in the middle of the flat, staring at the phone for a long time, feeling wretched. He missed home. Being at odds with his family hurt. But there was hope. Priyanka was right. There was a chance that things would heal over time. Bim and Yamuna were still in touch and had already invited them to come and visit when they were settled. At least he hadn't lost them. Once he and Soma were established, if they did well together, even his parents might accept Soma as a daughter-in-law. He had to hold on to that hope.

Sighing, he checked the time and put the phone back in his pocket. It was nearly time to go and pick up Soma. He pulled on his coat. There wasn't much he could do about the past. It was time to go and embrace his future.

—

The train drew into the station before she was ready for it. Soma pulled her bag off the luggage rack. In a way, she wasn't ever going to be ready, but she would plunge in anyway. Her bag was large enough to be on wheels. She smiled her thanks to the man who helped her lug it off the train and onto the platform. She had more things now than we she had first met Yamuna at the airport. Not a lot more; it all still fit in one bag, but the bag was bigger.

As the crowd thinned, she spotted Sahan hurrying down the platform, weaving between travellers. She felt a little kick of excitement. This was where it all started. Her and Sahan. She tugged her suitcase along.

Sahan gathered her up in an uncharacteristically effusive hug. Surprised, but pleased, she hugged him back. It felt strange, this warm contact. She liked it.

He took her case from her and pulled it along, talking animatedly about the flat. She let his words wash over her and watched, instead, the movement of his face, the sparkle of his eyes. He was so animated, so happy. All doubts she'd had on the way up vanished. This was the right thing to do.

'It's not huge,' said Sahan, as he unlocked the door to the flat. 'But I can comfortably afford it on my salary.'

Soma nodded. The apartment building was completely different to Yamuna's comfortable house – bare brick walls and brown lino floors that squeaked underfoot. She hoped the flat itself was less stark. As Sahan pushed open the door, she prepared herself to look at whatever lay beyond it with a favourable eye. She followed him in.

The door opened into the living room. A kitchen linked to it on one side and a bedroom on the other. It was small, but perfectly self-contained. There was a table with chairs, a low TV table, no sofa. Soma took in the large window, the empty space where more furniture could go, the little galley kitchen. She pictured herself making this place home. Happiness bubbled up, fizzing in her chest.

'It's perfect,' she said. 'Just right for us.'

Sahan beamed. She walked to the kitchen, feeling light, as though she were walking on her toes. The smell of cooking basmati wafted towards her. There was a rice cooker on the counter, steaming gently.

'I… cooked some food,' said Sahan. 'It's not much. It's only a vegetable curry and rice. I thought you might be hungry when you got here.' He slipped past her and took a Tupperware container out of the fridge. 'I made the curry last night.'

She watched, enchanted, as he fussed around, putting the curry into the microwave and pulling plates out of the cupboard. It was all so… domestic. A real life. Her real life. She looked down at her arms and wondered if this was in fact a dream. She pinched her arm. Ow.

'What are you doing?' said Sahan. He took her arm and gently rubbed the red mark that she'd made.

Soma was immediately embarrassed. How young and naïve she must look. 'I'm sorry. I just…'

'Thought you were dreaming?' He looked up, still holding her arm in his warm hand. 'I know the feeling.'

They stared at each other for a long moment. Soma felt the now familiar longing to touch him. To feel the light stubble on his cheek. To trace the softer skin of his lip. There was nothing to stop her now. She reached forward with her free hand and touched her fingertips to his face.

He drew a breath. His eyes fluttered shut for a moment, but soon flew open again. 'We… should eat,' he said and gently released her arm. Puzzled, Soma nodded.

The meal was simple, but perfectly wonderful. Admittedly, the curry wasn't very good, but it was still better than she'd hoped. She hadn't expected him to be able to cook at all. All these little things she was finding out about him. Again, there was a little thrill at the thought of being alone with him.

They washed up, side by side, talking about films they'd watched – he in big air conditioned city cinemas and she in hot, sticky rural ones. They compared notes of their childhoods. It was as though her thoughts had been unbuckled and set free after years of captivity. This was why she loved him.

It got late. Soma yawned, the journey and excitement catching up with her.

'You should go to bed,' said Sahan. He looked at her bag, still in the hallway, where he had first put it down.

She smiled and held out her hand. He examined the floor and didn't respond.

A feeling of unease stirred. 'Sahan?'

He took a deep breath and looked up. 'Soma,' he said. 'There's something I need to tell you.' He took her hand

and led her, not to the bedroom, but to the hard dining chairs. What could possibly be wrong? Had he changed his mind? Did he have some sort of deformity that he was hiding? She sat down.

He held her hand and, not looking up, he told her about Tamsin.

Soma listened, without interrupting. In her mind she saw Sahan, a younger, more innocent Sahan. She felt his shock and humiliation. She suddenly understood why he didn't try to put his arm around her. The gentle, slow blossoming pace of their relationship hadn't been because of her, but because of his fears. Without even realising it, they had seen the damage in one another and let love seep into the cracks.

His gaze was still fixed on her hand, which he was cradling gently in his own, one thumb stroking the back of her wrist. His eyelashes looked longer than ever. She took in the shape of his cheek, the long straight nose, the glossy curls. Because he was so beautiful and came from a privileged background, she'd thought there could be nothing wrong in his life. Somehow, the fact that there was, made them equal. And equal was a good place to start a new life.

She closed her hands over his. 'We both have scars,' she said, quietly.

He lifted his face, finally making eye contact. 'This must seem like a huge overreaction to a small thing,' he said. 'After what happened to you.'

'Everything is big when it happens,' she said. 'I understand.' She stood up, making him rise up with her. She took a step closer, until all that separated them was a few inches of air.

'And you still love me.' It wasn't a question. His voice was full of wonder and a tremor of happiness.

'You love me, in spite of everything.'

He reached up and placed a palm against her cheek. 'Of course I do.'

So this was what it was like to want to kiss someone. She didn't know who moved first. Perhaps they both did. His lips were dry and soft and tasted of spices. His skin was warm against hers. When they drew apart again, she felt deprived.

He held her closer and trailed his fingertips down the side of her face and down to her neck. She sighed, closed her eyes and leaned into him, wanting more. Who knew that touching someone could be like this? So gentle. So thrilling. So addictive.

His whisper came through her hair, warm against her ear. 'I haven't done this before.'

She opened her eyes so that she could draw back and look at him. His expression was so full of longing that her heart and stomach both flipped. She loved him. He loved her. This was how it was meant to be.

She raised up on her tiptoes and kissed him again. 'Don't worry,' she said. 'I haven't either.' She led the way into their new bedroom. 'We'll work it out together.'

A Letter from Jeevani

Thank you for reading *When Soma met Sahan*. I really hope you enjoyed the story!

This is a story that I knew I wanted to tell, but wasn't sure I'd ever be able to find a home for it. Soma, Yamuna and Bim came in my mind fully formed. I left them as scribbled notes in a notebook and wrote five other books (under my pen name Rhoda Baxter) before I came back to them and gave them some proper attention. I'm incredibly grateful to have the opportunity to share their story with you now. Written under my real name, too!

If you enjoyed reading *When Soma met Sahan*, please, please leave a review. It doesn't have to be long. I'm always grateful for even a few lines that say whether you liked the book or not. Quite apart from cheering up my day (thank you!), your reviews can help other readers decide whether to take a chance on a book by a relatively unknown author. They really do make the world of difference.

I wanted to write a story about postnatal depression and two women who were both united and divided by their love for the same baby. When I wrote about Yamuna, I drew from my own experience of postnatal depression. Unlike Yamuna, I had a sharp-eyed health visitor who spotted the signs and made me get help within a matter of weeks. Who knows, if it hadn't been for her intervention,

I may have ended up paranoid like Yamuna. If you have been through it – you are not alone.

I knew there needed to be something more and the missing element fell into place when I read *The Last Magdalen* by Wilkie Collins and started thinking what would happen if someone stole an identity and made a whole new life for themselves now.

I would really love to hear what you think of the story. So, apart from writing a review (hint, hint), if you want to chat to me or ask questions, I'm usually hanging around on Twitter as @jeevanicharika (or more often as @rhodabaxter). Come say hello.

If you fancy a peek behind the curtain (and a free short story), you can join my newsletter group at https: //jeevanicharika.com/.

Happy reading

Jeevani

Website: www.jeevanicharika.com

Acknowledgments

When Soma met Sahan was a book that took a long time to get from embryonic idea to a book you can actually read. In that time, we moved house from Didcot in Oxfordshire, to East Yorkshire. We found Hull to be a really friendly place, but even after the UK City of culture events, people didn't seem to know about it, so it seemed only natural to set the book there. Yamuna's house is made up, but the area in the Avenues really is full of gorgeous old townhouses.

Where was I...? Oh yes, saying thanks.

Thank you to Federica Leonardis to taking this book on and making me polish it more and more, so that it was the best book it could be. Thank you also to Keshini and Lindsey at Hera for believing in it enough to publish it! And for having a brown girl on the cover. You have no idea how happy that made me.

Thank you to Jen Hicks, who is my writing buddy and always my first reader. You're the best.

Thanks to the Romantic Novelists Association for being such a brilliantly supportive organization. Special thanks go to the ladies of the Naughty Kitchen who have provided a sympathetic ear, a shoulder to cry on, encouragement, reassurance and a lot of laughter over the years. I don't think I'd be as sane as I am (which isn't saying much, admittedly) without you.

As always, thank you to my family who put up with me rambling on about people who aren't actually real and don't complain (much) when it's the fishfingers for tea too many times. I love you. I couldn't do this without you.

Last of all, but definitely not least of all, thank you, dear reader, for reading this book and making it all worthwhile.